Quinn's mistake wasn't killing Leo Ashwood; it was bringing him back. Now in a cat and mouse game with a monster she created, Quinn learns what her powers are truly capable of.

Brought together by a vision, Cecelia and Quinn are entangled in the chase for Leo Ashwood. Cecelia, a seer who is known for sticking her nose into other's business for their better good, is now sent into a world unknown to her with no defense against the monster, her own powers, and the budding feelings for Quinn. Maggie, however, was merely at the wrong place at the wrong time and left with no other choice but to join forces. An up and coming YouTube superstar struck down by sickness, her voice is both her magical survival and death wrapped in one.

These three young, untrained witches will have to lean on each other if they want to survive. Navigating the world of humans, the new reality of witches, and the horror of magic, they might just make it... if they can keep their secrets to themselves.

BURIED

The Secrets Witches Keep

Lizzie Strong

A NineStar Press Publication

www.ninestarpress.com

Buried

Printed in the USA

ISBN: 978-1-64890-259-8

First Edition, Aprl, 2021

Also available in eBook, ISBN: 978-1-64890-258-1

CONTENT WARNING:

This book contains depictions of blood, death, and gore.

Dedicated to two people: Tyler, for without you or your endless support, I would have given up years ago. Victoria, for without you I would have never ended up here with this idea. Our countless conversations and pitches to each other inspired me above and beyond and I hope this novel is every bit what you hoped it would be when I came to you with the simple idea of "Swamp Witches.

Prologue

"Auntie... I've done... something horrible."

There was blood everywhere. Dried under my nails, in between my cold toes, caked onto my scalp to the point it itched worse than lice. With Berry's cell phone pressed to my cheek, words refused to leave my tongue. The pressure of a thousand stones lodged within my throat choked me, fear built up within me. Tears blurred my vision as I stared out across the apartment. The white marble carved, specifically to accentuate the pillars of Greek gods touching the vaulted ceiling. Their faces splattered in gore. Only a small percentage of the blood was my own. The knife dropped from my other hand.

My body trembled at the steel knife clattering to the floor. I sat on my knees, nerves and flesh numb to the chill of a winter breeze through the shattered French balcony doors. His bloody footprints trailed across crisp, white snow and over the banister of his eighteenth-story home. Snow blew in through the shattered glass and the destroyed frame.

"Quinn, sweetheart, what's going on? Where are you?" My aunt Darlin's panic fell on deaf ears as reality settled into my body. Berry Alista French still lay limp before me, eyes wide open and mouth hung ajar. Frost coated her bloody brows and cracked lips. Her blood lingered on my hands.

"I made a mistake." I swallowed the lump in my throat as exhaustion seeped steadily through my body. My magic dried up and there was nothing I could do. Berry was dead, Dead-Dead.

"Quinn... please tell me you didn't kill someone." Darlin's voice wafted through the air, a soft whisper in my ear. Sirens howled in the background. I wavered as spots filled my vision. Fresh tears licked the sides of my cheeks. My lips quivered.

"Worse." I choked as I collapsed back onto the sticky marble. My throat closed up tight, unable to speak the truth... I brought him back.

Chapter One

10-39 at 37 E street, suite 1802, back-up required.

"Quinn Gwenevieve Foster, age 16, born Idabel, Oklahoma... you sure are a long way from home." Pressure built up at the back of my head as the voice of the detective clawed at the insides of my ears. The pressure dulled but never released as I opened my eyes, which was an effort in itself. My eyelids were the weight of cement bricks.

The windows fogged in the frosty interrogation room. The only light came from the sharp halogen bulbs and the long, thin window along the top of the wall. A female officer had chained my hands to the table, which forced contact with the harsh steel, stinging my skin.

"I want a lawyer," I answered, my head hung to the right.

"Of course, and you can have one. While we wait for them, why don't we talk?"

Tears spilled down my cheeks. Exhaustion bit into my muscles, turning my bones to putty. If I did not rest soon, I would pass out. I wasted too much magic in Leo Ashwood's apartment. My aunt would not be pleased to hear how recklessly they caught me. The last time I was caught by human police, she yelled my ears raw. Out of love, out of concern and fear, it didn't matter why she was furious with me. History showed time and time again that humans were not capable of mercy to witches. Granted, the detective had not accused me of being a witch...yet.

"I want a lawyer, sir."

"It's Detective Henry Smith, Miss Foster." His face softened around the cheeks but not near his lips. The way one's face softens when they are trying to convince someone smaller and more naïve of untrue things. His lips pursed tighter. He reminded me of Officer Blevens, the officer who dragged me out of the graveyard years ago. A man who tried to lie to my face about how much trouble I was in. I was found hip-deep in what looked like an empty grave... Well, it was an empty grave by the time they got to it. The true corpse fell apart piece by piece about thirty yards north of my arrest. Darlin foamed at the mouth when Winestra called her at about two a.m. to come to the police station. Officer Blevens looked me dead in the eye that night and gave me the same face Detective Smith gave me now. 'It was just a slap on the wrist.' Liar.

"I want a lawyer." I learned my lesson from last time.

They didn't even let me shower. I stank enough to make my eyes water and gag every time I moved. They washed my hands but crusty blood lurked under my nails. My hair was a ball of grease superglued to the top of my skull and left to drape around me. I'd never felt that gross in all of my life, and I once spent six hours drenched in rainwater and coated in graveyard soil. Her gravestone illuminated behind my lids: Melissa Keen, beloved mother and daughter, born in 1981, taken too soon. She had still been fresh; it was the whole reason I dug her up. The fresher the better. If I could bring her back, then I could bring back others...

It didn't work out.

"Miss Foster—"

"I want a lawyer," I whispered for the umpteenth time. My throat, coarse from screaming and lack of water, itched from the back of my teeth down to the top of my shoulders. They offered me a glass of water in a paper cup, but it sat untouched. Darlin always said 'never drink anything offered from someone who wanted trouble' and Detective What's-his-face wanted trouble.

"And one is coming, but we can keep talking," Detective Smith repeated for the umpteenth time. He said *we*, but only he talked. I merely repeated my request every time the silence grew ^p^ptoo long. I couldn't look at him; I only stared at my disgusting reflection in the dented steel table. Handcuffs chaffed my wrists but stayed frosty against my skin. They continually pumped the room with as much A.C. as they could afford. It would not change anything. The problem with human torture was that it could never hold a flame to what I endured the night before.

I repeated myself once more. Detective Smith did not listen, but I am stubborn. He would learn nothing from me. My vision blurred. It sharply cleared for a long moment then swirled back out of focus. Energy dripped from my dirty pores and left me empty of everything. Emotionless and run ragged, I just wanted to sleep. Even my bones ached as I let my eyes flutter shut and my body swayed to the side.

A sharp, internal stab to my brain brought me back to life. I couldn't let my guard down, not here. Not while he was still loose.

"Want to tell me why you have a record for grave robbing?" Detective Smith cocked his head. I rolled my eyes before they fluttered shut again. My insides begged for sleep's sweet release but refused to fully take me away. Recovery was the hardest part. I wavered in and out of full consciousness. My aunt usually held me when exhaustion hit me that hard. Darlin would always whisper stories into my ears with her long arms around me. I could smell the soft puffs of basil and thyme on her breath as if she sat there beside me—

"Miss Foster?"

I could tell him about my record, but I wouldn't. Officer Blevens had asked me why I would spend a night in a grave, and foolishly I had answered him. He had told my aunt I had delusions and should be locked away. I learned my lesson that night, and for years to follow; reanimation was impossible. Life after death was a fool's dream. Witches weren't meant to mess with the laws of life and death. Then I brought Leo Ashwood back from the dead.

"I want... a... lawyer." Words tumbled off my lips like stones. I swayed in the seat, my bones like pudding. I would have toppled over, but the cuffs prevented me from sliding off the chair. I hit the arms of the steel chair. The cuffs held fast. Between the tension of the cuffs and the rigid chair, I was forced to sit up like a porcelain doll. Panic pumped through my chest, hot and fast. My veins raced blood to every extremity.

"You sure you don't need medical attention?" Detective Smith reached over to touch my hands again. I jerked away, and he returned to his side of the table.

A female cop moved my chair closer to the table with her foot. My stomach nearly pressed into the edge of the chilled steel. She returned to her spot in the corner, arms crossed and eyes focused on me.

"I want a lawyer," I mumbled, half alive. A short passage of time became an eternity as I wavered in and out of consciousness. Even if the detective wanted answers, I was in no position to give them. Mouth shut, even when unconscious, lips sewn shut.

"Quinn, I just want to know how—" Detective Henry finally gave up as the door swung open and a man in a tweed champagne colored suit entered the room, fury etched into his aged face.

"*That is enough!*" My gaze jumped up from the table and relief flooded my system. The man's attire screamed lawyer. I knew the type, pressed and clean, heavy scents of aftershave, hair slicked back and eyes sharp.

"My client asked for a lawyer. The questioning should have stopped the second she asked for one."

"Your client was found in a pool of blood, fingerprints all over the murder weapon, and the only survivor of a massacre—" Detective Smith stopped mid-rant as a slow yawn broke through my lips. He questioned me with his eyes, his mouth hung open ever so slightly. "Does murder bore you?"

My eyes caught the furrowed brows of the female cop. Her last name etched into a tiny sliver of silver on her chest—*Alvarez*. She pursed her lips as she stepped forward from the corner, eyes on the lawyer. The lines of a tattoo just under the collar of her uniform piqued my interest. Branches of something reached up the sides of her skin, but all I could make out was a raven in flight beneath her collar. Officer Alvarez surveyed me like a hawk as she crossed the room and hovered to the right of the table.

Her hands snatched up the cuffs. She stared me in the eyes, holding back from releasing me.

"Release her before I press harassment against your precinct," Tweed Suit Guy said. "She is a minor, and her parental figure is already on her way here. If I were you, I would rethink how you talk to me and my client." Tweed Suit Guy inched toward me, a briefcase in one hand and the other on his hip. A thick stench of rustic cabin and burnt red wood wafted off of him. It wasn't unpleasant, but the strength of his scent made my eyes water.

Detective Smith slid back from the table and scowled. My eyes settled on him; the world blurred for a moment at the sudden change in focus. There were two beauty marks upon his right cheek, one beside his upper lip and the other south of his ear. He'd missed a spot shaving. The hair on his head was thick red hair, but his facial hair was nearly blond. He met my gaze. A man who chased justice, I could see it tattooed to his flesh. I was a monster in his eyes. I was the reason for all those deaths. If only he knew that Leo Ashwood was the reason. Had Leo Ashwood just seen reason and let Berry and me go, no one would have known.

"We will talk again, Miss Foster. You are not to leave the state." Obviously, he didn't know a thing about me.

I shook my head calmly as Officer Alvarez unlocked my cuffs. She refused to look me in the eye as I stood. I hugged myself in the donated police sweatshirt and sweatpants they had given me after my own were handed over as evidence. Not that I wanted any of it back. The only thing I wanted back I had failed to get back long before they found me. Berry was gone, and her blood would cake my hands for the rest of my life.

"Miss Foster." Tweed Suit Guy stretched a hand out toward me. I shuffled around the table, my eyes locked on Detective Smith's. He refused to break eye contact. I was not as prideful. I looked away. As I passed the table, I heard Officer Alvarez finally speak under her breath.

"Creepy little witch." Although her voice was soft, the words scratched at my ears.

If only she knew the half of it. Blood fell like dandruff from under my nails as I picked them clean with my newly freed hands. The second I was safe, I'd shower and scrub off three layers of skin. Not even the swamp made my skin feel this sensitive. Every swish of the fabric against me lit up sensors all over my body. Detective Smith and Officer Alvarez stayed silent as I shuffled out of the doorway and into the loud precinct. Hours of being awake and then chained to a table seemed like nothing compared to the seconds it took to walk out of sight of the two in the room.

One gentle hand on my shoulder blades, Tweed Suit Guy led me through the hallway and toward the massive opening in the precinct. My mouth refused to unclamp as I focused on the nondescript sneakers they put on my feet. Such a shame that they dirtied such a clean pair of shoes on my toes.

"You are a lucky girl. They didn't charge you. I wonder what game they're playing," Tweed Suit Guy whispered as we walked quietly through an empty hallway. Not even murmurs filled the police station. He was keen on chit-chatting. But a Witch is never safe talking with humans. Rule number one: Never talk about Witch business with humans. I'd already broken enough rules for a lifetime.

A crackle of electricity filled my ears as I looked up through the glass ceiling. Snow covered the tips of the slanted roof. Soft plump fluff fell from the sky like feathers and slid across the glass. I smiled. I'd never seen snow before.

"Do you think the snow feels as soft as it looks?" I breathed.

"Miss Foster, your aunt—"

Before the lawyer could finish, fireworks went off behind my eyes, making the world fuzzy. Danger. My skin crawled and electricity ran up my spine. The interrogation room clicked shut behind us at the end of the hall. We rounded into the main bullpen of the precinct. Something within me snapped to action.

I grabbed his hand and pulled him forward with me. I could feel his pulse race under his skin. Exhaustion bit at my ankles, spots formed in my eyes, but I wanted to taste the freedom of winter air on my tongue. There was danger here. Shadows whispered sweet promises of relief from the pain and exhaustion if only I went outside. My lips glued shut and I focused on getting out.

Freedom. All I needed was freedom.

I burst through the doors as if I'd been shot from the police station out of a slingshot, gasping for air. Tweed

Suit Guy dropped my hand and stumbled away from me as I stepped out into the snow. The sky was a steely gray muddled with black clouds. Flakes tickled my face, and tears fell down my cheeks in fat drops. Free. I was free.

"Miss Foster?" Tweed Suit Guy choked. "What was..."

I barely heard him. The whispers from the shadows turned to roars that drowned out his gasps for air. Magic crackled across my nerves like sparks from open wires. I spun in the snow, arms out to feel the chill as it bit through the sweatshirt. Exhaustion seeped away from me and reinvigorated me entirely. Hydrated, awake, *alive!* My magic sparked at my fingertips; even my bones seemed soothed and relieved.

I smiled, truly smiled, as I stared up at the buildings around the precinct. The roads were empty of life and cars, just snow as it silently fell to the ground. I was alive! Leo Ashwood didn't kill me! The words felt so unreal, and yet, there I was, alive and smiling on the streets of New York!

Berry came to mind with a slap and my face fell. She was still very much dead and there wasn't a thing I could do. Her body laid on a slab somewhere with giant gash wounds, gutted like a fish. She was surrounded, I imagined, by at least six other people but there were no slashes to their midsections. Berry died at the end of a blade; the others in that examination room died by magic...*my* magic. It was the reason I was in that police precinct in the first place, but it was also the reason I stood ankle deep in snow and she didn't. I sucked in the hollows of my cheeks as I absorbed the world around me. The snow glared brightly against my eyes.

"I want to go home," I croaked as I turned to the Tweed Suit Guy.

Suddenly, the lawyer collapsed, his body flopping onto the frost-covered sidewalk with a sickening thud. His skin paled to a gray hue and sunken in, his eyes had rolled back in his head. His mouth hung open. Snow flurried around me like a snow globe from the disturbance of his corpse hitting the ground. My hands shivered as I reached for him. A finger grazed his cheek and I lived in silent horror as his skin sank in further. Zaps of electricity filled my veins, and I jerked my hand back. His eyes turned to puddles in his sockets and his jaw fell away from his face. Reality sank into my skin like a thousand needles pushed through my pores. I stumbled backward until my back was against a thin pole.

I touched him and sucked the life from him like a straw directly into his soul. My own bloody juice box. I pushed against the steel pole behind me. It whined as it bent. I turned toward the pole, now tilted with a sharp dent where I pushed. Strength pulsed within me as I stumbled into a different pole. With no thought or reasoning behind it, I punched the next lamppost with all my strength. My knuckles tore the metal and slid right through the other side. My jaw dropped in shock.

With a wiggle, I slipped my hand back to my side. Tears dried up on my face as I smirked. Impossible, and yet, here I was, with a massive hole through steel in front of my face and a corpse behind me. My aunt, Darlin, said that my strength came from me and only me. And yet...

I had done the impossible. I brought Leo Ashwood back to life. In all that blood, with my own magic, I brought him back to life and watched him jump out into the snow. No evidence he still lived, but I could retrace my steps. Not to mention I sucked the life from the lawyer. My magic. I felt it tingle my fingertips as I stepped around the pole.

Power coursed through my veins, and I realized I liked it.

Chapter Two

Cecelia Montreal

I woke up drenched in a cold sweat, which was unusual as it was 75 degrees outside. The bugs screamed into the sun-filled midday air and flew against my screen with abandon. Each little body that piled up outside my window only proved the potency of Emma's spell. Enchanted window screens. Who knew the next wave of inventions would include the solution to a minor problem? Actually, I did. I knew that it would be Emma's enchanted screens that would make her rich beyond her wildest dreams. Sold to the humans as a modern, high-tech screen that allowed them to save energy with open windows but keep bugs out of their house. I knew it like I knew that if Martin Walton killed those stray chickens in his yard, it would ruin his family's entire fresh egg business. Like I knew that Quinn Foster murdered a lawyer on the snowy sidewalk of New York just outside of the police station that tried to question her for other murders: because they were in my dreams.

I ripped the covers off and hung over the side of my bed. On my stomach, I jerked the drawer on the side of my bed-frame open. I grabbed a leather bound journal embellished with flaky nail polish, thanks to my rather short phase as a nail polish enthusiast, with a purple gel pen stuck in it. Shuffling back up onto my knees, I flipped it open. I needed to write down the dream before it disappeared. An unfortunate side effect of my magic was that all my dreams faded with time. Correction, most of my dreams faded with time.

I clamped my tongue between my teeth as I forced the pain to keep the dream fresh. Her name repeated in my mind over and over. A blood witch... She called herself that, I didn't doubt it for a moment. I'd never seen one before; the only other person with magic I knew of was Emma, although Emma did not give off any inkling that she was magical in person. All the dreams, all my visions up until this point didn't even touch the power Quinn held in her pinkie alone. But her face etched itself so clearly in my mind, I could draw it. If I could draw.

My visions were a movie played within my skull just for me. Yet in this one, I watched from within her head. Most nights I walked beside or along the shadows of my vision's protagonist. With Martin Walton, I walked along the edges of his house like a fly on the wall as his story unfolded. Two chickens, unusual in shape and size wandered onto his farm and he grabbed them up. As an unsure teen with little recognition for cause and effect, he snapped their necks. Then like a video tape put in fast forward, the world rushed forward until it stopped on him and his mother. They sat in the kitchen as they cried over a foreclosure notice they'd taken off the door. No chickens around the house, no sound other than the sobs of his mother as she dropped the notice onto the pile of other overdue bills.

Yet, last night, I was in Quinn's brain, as if her eyes were my own. The itchy, sticky feeling of blood dried on my skin. My mouth dried with hers, my throat cracked. I felt everything from her hot scalp to her frozen toes. And when she burst out into the snow, the buzz of excitement and the curiosity of her power surged through me. When she punched through the pole, my stomach dropped. Unlike most of my dreams, it wasn't a tape played out before my eyes; there was no future premonition, just the facts. I witnessed the murder of an innocent lawyer.

As I was just about to reach the bottom of the page, someone pounded on my bedroom door. I jumped and tossed the book into the drawer and slapped it shut. The door flew open. I rolled from my mattress onto the floor. Gretchen Montreal, my mother, stood in the doorway with her red frizzy curls up in a loose bun and permanent frown etched into her face.

"Really? It's like three in the afternoon, why are you still sleeping? Lazy girl." Gretchen brushed dust off the dresser to the left of the door with a scowl.

Silence filled the air as she rearranged the items on top to be more orderly. While my mother held the rest of the house to a tight, uncluttered standard, my room was a post tornado disaster in the small town of Idabel, Oklahoma. Mere inches outside of my door frame, the house was spotless. No dust, no item without purpose and its place, no picture frames, no decorative paintings. The only thing in the house that could be considered luxury was the piano, but that grand piano paid for the house. Gretchen Montreal even treated her bedroom like it was up for inspection—bed always made, a small collection of clothes always folded and ready to go, bathroom without a single fingerprint. She took the hair out of her hairbrush every morning and tossed it out the bathroom window.

"Mom—" I squeaked from my pile of books, old T-shirts, and a hairbrush. My room was an example of how different my mother and I were. I owned two floor rugs—one was a fuzzy rainbow I bought from the clearance bin at Walmart, the other I made from four skeins of clearance yarn from the dollar store. Both were covered in homework, projects, books and a coloring book or two. I'd installed a bookcase in one wall and filled it to the brim. Frames full of disposable camera pictures I'd taken acted as bookends, and knick-knacks and DVDs were scattered through the bookcase. My bed was entrapped by a canopy of purple curtains I'd stitched together and embellished with iron-on patches. If Gretchen Montreal spent more than five minutes in my room, her eyes would twitch.

She scowled. "Get your butt off the floor. We have guests coming."

I scrambled to stand. If only my legs were less wobbly. Everything crashed to the floor a second time.

My mother's long fingers wrapped around my arms as she hoisted me up to my feet and kicked clothing out from under my toes. For a woman no taller than five-foot-five, she had immense upper arm strength. "Do I need to repeat myself?"

"No," I chirped.

She dropped me. Once when I was seven, my mother threw an entire oak desk over her head and into the burn pile. Granted, she was livid and took it out on the wood furniture, but I could still feel the air pass around my head as she ripped the wooden chair out from under me and chucked it into the fire. That also happened to be the last time Gretchen Montreal ever dated another person. Jefferson Wiggins never asked for the furniture back. He wasn't stupid enough to piss her off twice.

"And please, take a shower. You smell like death," she grumbled as she swiped up an armful of clothing and dunked it into the basket in front of my dresser. She scooped up more armfuls of clothes and deposited them into the basket. She snatched it up and carried it to the door. Then she stopped to look at me expectantly.

"Yes, ma'am," I answered shortly, unable to even look her in the eye. She didn't like that I was five-foot-nine (and still growing) when she stopped at five-foot-five at fifteen. Then again, she smoked and refused to eat anything that wasn't deep fried or gray in color. Also, it might have to do something with my adoption, which she still hadn't brought up. Sixteen years later and we never talked about it.

"Don't make me repeat myself, Cecelia."

My mother left, but the comments under her breath vibrated through my ears. I was weird. I was strange. My throat unclenched, and I was back in control of my body. Fear sank down into the basement of my stomach as I stumbled backward into my hand-built bed frame. My mother did not have the money to buy me a real one, so I'd built it. Much like my desk, and my bookshelf, and my... everything, I'd built it myself. It was lopsided, and some spots weren't sanded well enough, and the paint job wasn't even, but it was mine. And I thought it was nice, even if my mother didn't.

I wondered if Quinn's mother was anything like mine. She thought about her aunt, back in the interrogation room. Darlin sounded like a strange first name, but who was I to talk? My mother renamed me Cecelia Montreal after her grandmother. My birth name was Feng Mian Su. Darlin sounded like a nice woman. Gretchen Montreal was not, but she was my mother... sort of.

I must reread my dream journal to burn my visions to my memory. I often take it with me, so I can remind myself of visions. The only exception was my mother. The only vision I couldn't forget was hers. January 4th, seconds after two in the afternoon. I took a small nap on the couch. Gretchen Montreal sat out on the front porch with her best friend Lilly Sellers. They both drank sweet tea and spoke in soft whispers until Lilly looked back through the front windows and smiled. *I think it was so sweet of you to adopt outside of the United States. Gives those poor unfortunate kids a home. A good, Christian home! None of that weird... eastern religion.*

Gretchen replied with an unamused snort and a roll of her eyes. *Yeah, I'm a real saint...*

I could see it as clear as day if I closed my eyes long enough. Gretchen walked down the sidewalk, sheet music in a clean folder, neatly tucked against her chest. She wore long jeans tied off with a leather strip, sheer purple button down over a gray camisole, and thick black boots that she tied off at the middle of her shins. A quarter mile from the church, Gretchen looked up and saw a woman on the front steps. She seemed passed out, curled around a bundle of something. Gretchen almost whirled around, but she stopped herself. She about-faced and marched down the street, wary of the unconscious woman until she walked upon the steps of the church and came to the horrible realization that the woman wasn't asleep. Gretchen sighed as she knelt down at the top step, two fingers to the woman's throat. Stone cold even in the morning light, lips purple, eyes crusted shut. Then a bundle of blankets moved in the dead woman's arms.

Gretchen put down her music and peeled the blanket back. A baby's head, my head, appeared out of the blankets. I whined and wiggled in the stiff arms of my dead mother. Gretchen's hands slithered into my mother's arms and snaked me back out gently. She wrapped the soft purple blanket with golden embellishment around me tightly and pulled me into her embrace. That was the first and only time I saw my name. Sewn into the blanket, *Feng Mian Su* glistened in the sunrise. Gretchen stood up, baby clutched to her chest and music under her arm and stepped inside the church and shut the door on my dead mother.

Gretchen Montreal was no saint, but she was not without her moments of mercy and kindness. In a short moment, she saw a baby in the arms of a dead woman and took her in. I never asked if she told the police. I never questioned why she wanted a child—I didn't want to seem ungrateful. Despite all her harsh edges and sharp tongue, Gretchen was a good mother. She fed me healthy food despite eating trash herself. When I wanted to learn to cook at eight, she took me to classes at the community center. When I wanted to build my bed frame, she brought home wood for me. When I said I loved books, she always gave me at least three books at Christmas and two on my birthday. When she stumbled upon a baby, she took care of it like she took care of everything—on her own and with her bare hands.

And that's exactly why I forgave her every time. When she was mean and short tempered, when she called me strange and lazy, no matter what, I forgave her because she could have left me there, but she didn't.

The only dream I couldn't forget and the only dream I didn't write down. Just in case my mother might stumble upon my vision journal, I never wanted her to know that I knew...other than the fact I was clearly, physically, not her daughter. Surprisingly, no one other than me ever questioned it. As if I was the only one who could see that I was a tree giant stood beside a dwarf with no beard.

"Are you *daydreaming* again!" my mother shouted.

"No!" I squawked as I launched toward the bathroom. My mother sighed with relief at the slam of the door. Embarrassment burned my cheeks and fingertips as I tried my best not to fiddle with my nightclothes. I stank. But I took a shower the night before? My limbs froze in the middle of my bathroom as I raised an arm to my nose. Dried blood and graveyard soil filled my nose. My throat tightened as I jerked my arm to my side. Magic. Must be magic. There was no reason for me to stink the exact same stench of Quinn the Blood Witch—a new development I did not like. It took me over six years to finally accept my visions. No instruction manual, no guidance, no explanation and that scared me.

I flipped the tap on, but my body turned to cement. Pressure built at the back of my head and my vision swirled at the edges. For only a second the water ran red. Viscous blood dribbled out of the faucet, coagulated and forced out of the pipes in globs. I blinked and it disappeared. But it had been there! I saw it! Panic choked me as I stumbled back into the wall of my bathroom. A sob broke through my lips and my hands flew to my mouth. Tears of shock trickled down my cheeks. Vomit threatened to project out violently from my insides.

I'd never seen real blood in that quantity... As if the pipes were full of it, as if I were covered in it. I blinked away tears. My bathroom returned to normal—soft white tile, beige walls with swirls of chocolate; a piano design in warm honeys and browns on the trim; a mirror framed in driftwood; and a shower curtain of coffee beans with tap shoes. This was my bathroom. The bathroom I painted with my mother only two years ago when we both stood in it with tear-stained cheeks and admitted that we hated the old color. There was no blood. The disgust and fear remained in my system. Steam filled the room finally.

I pulled the curtain open and stepped in. The pressure at the back of my head eased; it sat at the base of my skull. My heart turned to sludge in my chest. An intrusive image of the blood in my faucet made my heart kick within the sludge erratically. Shampoo in hand, I clenched my eyes shut and scrubbed my scalp harder than necessary. Tingles ran the length of my back as I grew dizzy. My body swayed in the hot water, and the tingles rolled over my scalp. Pressure built up slowly until it took over and nearly dragged me to the floor.

When I opened my eyes, a squeak of surprise left my mouth. I wasn't in my bathroom. I stared at the pink tile in a frosted glass shower, which contrasted with a mint green wall in a misty room.

A back was pressed into mine, slick and soft, and a head leaned against my scalp. "I wondered who walked into my mind."

Hands slithered across my throat to my jawline. My skin turned stiff and cold. Every touch filled my nervous system like fireworks. Soft fingers tickled my face, sliding across my cheeks and my ears. "I'm... I'm... this..."

Long wet hair slipped down my shoulders and stuck to my collar bone as the person dove their fingers in my hair. Shock glued my feet to the slick pink tile, my mouth clamped shut. The fingers slowly peeled away, and I twisted at my hips. Quinn Foster stood in her shower, long chestnut hair soaked against her pale skin. One green eye, one blue, a gash across the bridge of her nose. I memorized her face. Then the dream returned to the back of my head and I realized... I remembered it. Like it was a memory, a novel I'd devoured.

"Quinn," I gasped. My body whirred to life. I stumbled back and bumped into the wall.

The pressure in my head released instantly and I fell limp. Steam filled the bathroom, but it was my own brown bathroom. Coffee beans and wood framed mirrors and no murderous teenagers standing just behind me. My heart raced its way beneath my tonsils. I could have chewed on my organs if I moved my jaw an inch. I searched for her in every inch of my bathroom, but Quinn was gone. The tingles and dizziness faded, and I was alone... and there was soap in my eyes. I hissed as I dipped my face into the water and grabbed through the curtain for a towel. After I nearly drowned, I squished my face into it. Reality set in and a cold chill ran down my spine.

"That... really... just happened." I snatched up a bar of soap and viciously scrubbed my body in horror. I blinked into the same space as the girl who murdered an innocent lawyer. She saw me! "Oh my god she could have killed me what if she had—" My words tumbled out in a rush.

"Cecelia!" my mother yelled. "What are you yapping about?!"

I flipped off the faucet and stood naked in the shower, my skin prickled with goosebumps. My muscles refused to move as I repeated the thirty second ordeal over and over in my head. I hugged my towel. Quinn the blood witch in my shower. Blood dribbled out of my faucet, and Quinn Foster smiled at me. My heart pounded against the roof of my mouth and I gagged on it. Finally, my mouth opened, and one word came out. "Sorry!"

The clunk of our washing machine filled the air and finally switched on after I finished my shower. A small mercy my mother gave me, as a shower with the washer on would mean a shower in frozen water with zero water pressure. I wrapped the towel around my body and numbly stepped out onto the bathroom mat.

"Hurry up! I picked out some clothes for you." My mother's voice was just on the other side of the door.

For a moment, I let myself drift. It was daytime. I was not asleep. Normal Saturday, not a vision. Mother had worked through piano lesson appointments, at least four today before she came to check on me. I would clean up; we would make food for the neighbors who were bound to show up. Gretchen would entertain them for two hours before she used me as an excuse to make them leave— 'Cecelia needs to do homework before church tomorrow.' Then we would sit in peace and quiet in the living room for an hour, me with a book, her with the newspaper or a crossword. A normal day, not a nightmare with murderous teenage witches.

No time to reminisce over my shower with death. There were guests coming! "Coming!"

"Could you whip up that scrumptious chickpea thing you make with the garlic and crackers again?"

Gretchen's voice floated through the steam, soft and reminding exactly why I loved her. Even when she was grouchy and mean, when she was bitter and rude, I was the only person she loved. A shut-in, left only to communicate with her daughter, piano students and their parents, and nosy neighbors, Gretchen Montreal was not a nice lady... but she was my mom.

I smiled as I grabbed my hair towel and wrapped it around my scalp tightly. "Of course!"

Chapter Three

Maggie Walton

Ding! Another text from Kitty. *Ding!* I sighed and dropped my phone into my mother's purse. "She's wigging out," I croaked.

"You know our Kitty, if even a hair is out of place, she turns into a molting chicken," my mother teased as she scooped her purse up onto her arm and turned the van off. I swallowed the fire in my throat as I swung to face the door. Another muffled ding filled the air, and I sighed again.

"Have you told her you're here?"

"Yeah! And that's the problem." I coughed through my words. The van door creaked open as I swung my legs out into the hot afternoon air. "She's threatening to drive me to Houston to see her mom's throat doctor, Mcmoneypants!"

I regretted the last statement, not for the metaphorical burn but for the physical burn. My throat clenched down tight and sent me into a fit of coughs. I balled up my fists, and my rib cage rattled like nails in a glass jar. My mother appeared in front of me and whisked me onto my feet.

As my mother shut the van door behind me, I heard the tell-tale squeal of teenage girls who watched me. Despite the lack of makeup on my face and my hair up in a messy bun, my fans still recognized me. Today was not a particularly good day for them to see me, but it wasn't the worst. With my face washed, clean jeans, and a tie-dye loose tank-top, the blond hair and MW logo on the back of my tank gave me away. Damn marketing ploys. Thankfully my father was already inside to check me in, or else he'd rush me past them. My mother loved my fans. My father did not.

I whirled around with a wide grin on my face as two girls, probably twelve at the most, danced on their tiptoes. A mom with 'I'm so sorry' etched into her soft face stood behind them as the girls scrambled across the clinic parking lot. The two girls stopped an arm's length from me, hands out as if they wanted to hug me but were waiting for permission. "Oh! Mah! Gosh! You're Maggie Walton!" one of them exclaimed.

The girls looked so similar they could be twins, braces glistened with new bands in the morning sun. They beamed as they met my gaze. It was adorable. I couldn't help it—I broke. "Can I hug you?"

My squeak was diminished by their unison squeals, "Yes! Oh mah gosh yes!"

What was the harm? Besides... I could use a bear hug. Their embrace was tight, slightly sweaty, but comfortable. I tried not to cough over them as my lungs bubbled. My vocal cords restricted in my throat tight enough to snap. Tears trickled over my cheeks as they pulled back. "Y'all made my day,"

One girl let out a string of gibberish, but I was able to make out a request to sign their shirts. I nodded. The back of my knuckles lifted to dab my eyes dry as my mother whipped out one of the sharpies in her purse. Ever since the lost marker fiasco in Houston last October, my mother made sure she always had three of varying colors. I sent my mother an apologetic look as I uncapped the marker.

The girls spun like a stiff wind and shoved their short brown hair from their shoulders. Both of them wore white gym shirts; they had obviously whisked out of school for check-up appointments. That made it better, in my opinion, as my signature wouldn't ruin any of their nice clothes. It wouldn't mean much in a few years. I made my signature as large and decorative as possible.

"There, now you can tell everyone you snuck out to get a signature instead." I covered my mouth as I wheezed. I regretted the words immediately.

"Are you all right?" The taller sister whirled around, and her face fell immediately.

"Oh yeah!" I coughed. "Just an upper respiratory infection," I lied.

"Is that why you haven't uploaded this week?" the second asked.

I winced but played it off with a nod and another cough to add to my dramatics. "Yeah, I didn't think anyone would notice." I swallowed hard over the lump in my throat.

"What?! You're one of the best! We watch you every Friday night! Mom bought us your hoodie for Christmas."

"That's amazing." I winced again. My mother stepped in and put an arm around my shoulders.

"Sorry, girls, I hate to cut this short, but Maggie's gotta get antibiotics, or else she won't be uploadin' for a few more weeks."

Both of their faces paled instantly. I grimaced at them apologetically before I pulled out my phone.

"Let's just get a photo, real quick, I don't have-ta-talk-fer-that," I wheezed out in one breath.

They hopped to my side like bunny rabbits. My mother sighed but took the phone. I ripped my scrunchie out and ruffled my hair before I struck the goofiest pose I could muster without death by suffocation from my lungs. The girls joined in, both with fingers in their mouths to make their smiles huge and wide bug eyes. After a small click from both parents, I smiled and patted the shoulders of both girls.

I wish I hadn't lied to them. I wish it was an infection. I wish some antibiotics and a few bowls of my mother's hot soup would fix it. My mother whisked me away from the girls and shoved me toward the doors. She bent near my shoulder with a sigh. "You could have told them the truth."

"Should I tell them I'm losing my voice?" I wheezed.

"No..." she whispered. "You're gonna be fine, Magpie. You're just stuck with a chest bug or some weird infection they've never seen. You know how special you are. Watch, Dr. Higgins is going to tell us it's some weird, super rare infection you got from touring all those weird cities, and we're going to be fine. You're going to be fine."

My mother's warmth barely breached my insides as the tickle of a cough took over my chest.

"I don't wanna upset any of them... I don't... We don't even..." I coughed hard. My mother bent over in the doorway and blocked me from view of those behind as I hacked up a lung into my hands. I pulled back to stand. My body trembled. Blood speckled my palms. I clenched them shut and let my mother whisk me into the back office.

For several weeks, I've been nauseous, I've fainted and dropped to the ground. Then when I try to talk, it becomes painful and my throat is rubbed raw. No amount of honey or tea or ginger or any other herb could fix it. Until about two weeks ago, I thought it was a horrible flu. Then I coughed up blood in my bed. My mother came into my room to tell me we might want to see a doctor about my cold when she saw me lying in a puddle of my own blood as it dribbled down my chin.

Jenny West, the office receptionist, stood by the opened door and eyed me the whole time. An eternity passed as I sat in the frozen tundra of Dr. Higgin's office. Then I blinked, and Thomas Higgins sat on the seat opposite me with a pale face.

My eyes left the wall of doctoral posters to look back to Dr. Higgins as he shuffled the stool directly before me. After a long time of not knowing, the doctor's office called this morning. They wanted us to come in. I knew it was bad when I saw Jenny look at me and forcefully hide her sad frown. Jenny was a pretty girl, but when she tried to hide the grief in her face it twisted up to the point where it was painful to look at.

"The results are..." the doctor began, but he trailed off. He pulled his glasses off his face and rubbed the bridge of his nose. Tears he tried to hide swiped by his thumbs, he licked his lips nervously. I saw Dr. Higgins every time I felt ill. He was my family doctor... he was *everyone's* family doctor. He was the only man I trusted even more than my parents. He took out the ingrown hair in my brother's armpit and then turned around and treated the spider bite on my butt when I was eight, all in the same day. The best thing about Dr. Higgins was his honesty. If you asked a question, even about stuff my parents deemed too adult for me, he would give me an honest, logical answer.

My lips trembled as he shook his head and put the file down. "What is it?"

"Maggie, your parents should really be in here when I tell you this." He sighed as he stood up and knocked on the back of the door.

My stomach bottomed out. Jenny West poked her head in, whispered something to Higgins and then stared at me. There were tears all over her face, and they doubled when she locked eyes with me. My heart shattered. I knew the answer before Dr. Higgins even told me.

I was sick. My hands slowly lifted to my throat and my insides clawed along my vocal chords. I thought it was strep. It couldn't be worse than anything I'd faced before. Public school and unwashed drinking fountains had nothing on my immune system. Until they tested me for strep and it wasn't. Time passed with a horrific pain in my throat. I couldn't even record a new song for my channel. The last time I opened my mouth to sing, my voice broke on stream. My voice grew worse by the day and fear became my new best friend. Scared wasn't descriptive enough... I didn't even tell my friends and made my parents swear they wouldn't either. Not till we knew what it was.

"Mom... Dad?" I croaked as the door opened again.

My mom dove into the room and scooped me up into her arms. Her sweater smelled of goat, as if she brought the farm with her. I choked on the familiar scent of home, of safety, as I spared a look over her shoulder. Glassy eyed, stony faced, my father lingered in the door frame. He held back tears as he peered at me with regret and pain.

My lips quivered. "What's going on?"

"It's cancer. Glottic, as far as we can tell. It's run the length of your throat, and there's no way to know what stage it is from our equipment here. Tulsa sent back a report asking you to be transferred, Maggie... there's no way we can treat you here, we don't have that kind of equipment. I'm- I'm so sorry, Maggie."

The air sucked out of the room. My bones turned to water as I melted into my mother's grasp. My toes buzzed with how numb they were.

Dr. Higgins swallowed hard, and tears welled in his eyes. He concentrated on the papers that quivered in his hands. My heart didn't break till he whispered, "I'm so sorry, Maggie, I'm so sorry."

I choked as air refused to pump in and out of my lungs. "Are... are... are you sure?" I squeaked. Tears poured down my face. A traitorous hiccup left my lips as my mother sank down onto the hospital bed next to me.

"Yes." Dr. Higgins locked eyes with me and I shattered into a million pieces. The silence in the room turned to a massive roar in my ears. My mother sniffled into my shoulder as reality sank into my skin. Acid ate skin off my arms and legs. Left bare to the bone, only a skeleton of Maggie sat on the hospital bed. "Look, Maggie, I know this is hard to come to terms with—"

"I don't smoke." I gasped for air. The white walls swirled with the soft mint of the counters and chairs in the room. My eyes watered as a knot of vomit and nerves built up behind my tongue. My organs choked me. With a cough, my body trembled. It rattled through me and the hope in the room died. I covered my mouth and I coughed harder than I had all day. Liquid sprayed into my hands, but I was too scared to look. Instead, I stuffed my wet palms into my lap and kept my eyes clenched shut. A napkin was swiped across my lower lip, my mother's soft touch dabbed any residue away.

"But your parents do. Maggie, everyone in this town smokes, even your classmates. Your brother, Martin, smokes—"

I couldn't hold it back any more. Another cough mixed with a sob wrecked my posture as I collapsed in half. A howl of pain filled the room. Wrapped around my knees, I refused to look up.

"Maggie?" my mother whimpered.

My mother pulled back. Everything pent up within me burst out of my chest. I let out scream after scream of horror and anger. A ringing sound filled my ears as I coughed then screamed, then coughed and then screamed. Over and over a reminder that I was sick. Everything I'd worked for! My vocal cords were my ticket to a good life! Over two hundred thousand subscribers to my music channel ran out of my bedroom. When I streamed music lessons and critique for hourly pay, I paid for a beat-up truck. My views paid for the house additions when my mom got pregnant with Frankie and we needed a new room. Cancer? My voice was our salvation and it was dying. I was dying. I shivered as I nuzzled my tear-stained cheeks into my knees. My screams stopped externally, but they filled my brain.

"Maggie... please, it could be early stage. We don't know. If it's early stage, you could have the tumor's destroyed without surgery, using chemo. It would be like it never happened." Dr. Higgins reached out but stopped inches short of my shoulder. Hope glowed in his smile, but I couldn't feel it.

I peered up from my lap, tears trailed my face. "And what happens if it's not?" I uttered.

Dr. Higgin's mouth fell open. I didn't need an answer as my heart sunk into the caverns of my feet. "Maggie, it's not that simple."

"What will happen to my voice?" I tried not to collapse again as my mother wrapped her arms around me tightly. Panic swelled up in my chest as words began to pour out of my mouth. A foreign force slid up my back like a snake. It slithered along my spine as I shot off the hospital bed and out of her arms. It filled me to the brim with a toxicity that stained my words. "What will happen to me? Dr. Higgins, what will happen to me? Am I going to die? What happens if they can't fix it! Will they rip out my vocal cords? How will that help me!? I was born to sing, Dr. Higgins, they can't just take my voice!"

"Maggie, please, you have to calm down," he pleaded as he reached out for my hands. His hands often held mine as I received shots; they held mine softly when I asked about my grandmother's illness. He never took, only gave, and he gave me the chance to take his hands. His hands out to me, he offered his calm and soothing grasp to bring me back. Yet I stepped back, my fury broiled my insides.

"They can't take my voice! That would take away my life! This would kill me! Don't you understand!? Don't you? A world without me would kill you? Or would you even care!" Something came out when the words left my lips. That force that slithered up my spine came out of my mouth. I froze in fear as the pressure took flight from my tongue and landed in Dr. Higgins's face. Blood dribbled down my lips as I gawked at him wide eyed.

My scalp tingled as I realized what I'd done a second too late. In all my fear, I'd never imagined my magic would seep into my words. It only worked when I sang. A magical voice, the sound of angels, blessed vocal chords... all of those were the compliments I held dear. When I sang, I was free. All day I was crammed in a cage until I created something with my voice. It was magic and I could fly. As I grew older, I realized my voice did more than carry across a room. At some point I realized I was magic. When I sang in the choir, I moved entire theatres full of people to tears. Then once I sang to little Frankie and he turned out like a light the next second. I experimented but mostly, it only fuelled my love to sing and create music. Never once had my spoken voice done anything to anyone.

Until now. Dr. Higgins's eyes glazed over and stared into the beyond. My heart pounded in my ears as I slapped my hands over my mouth. I wanted to take it back. He straightened up to his feet and bent his head to the left in slow motion. His jaw fell open as his eyes gazed through me in silence.

"Dr. Higgins?" My father stepped forward. He instantly jerked backward as Dr. Higgins gripped his pen with deadly force and drove it into his throat. "Nurse!" he shouted.

Screams filled the room as Dr. Higgins ripped the pen out of his throat and ran it back through over and over. I was unable to move as I watched my family doctor stab himself with a BIC pen repeatedly.

The nurse shoved me out of the way, but she was helpless to stop him. No one could. Not after I'd sung my siren song. Blood splattered over my face as Dr. Higgins was dragged out of the office, limp and dead. It happened in a matter of seconds, but it dragged on for minutes inside my head. My heart plummeted into my stomach and dissolved. My eyes drifted to the wall behind the hospital bed. The blood sprayed across the walls. The vision replayed over in my mind, a broken record repeating in a nightmarish loop.

"I didn't... I didn't mean..." I muttered as my mother launched to protect my vision from the bloody display before me. It didn't matter. My eyelids held onto the mental image of him, flat against the floor, his blood pooled around him. "Mom, I didn't mean—"

"Sweetheart, you didn't. He did it all on his own. You were upset," my mother whispered softly in my ear.

But she didn't know. Neither of them knew. Out of three children and maybe twenty first cousins alone, I was the only one with this power. A secret I would take to the grave now that my magic killed the only good man in town. Thomas Higgins did not deserve to die, and I'd bewitched him to take his own life...viciously.

I was a monster.

Chapter Four

Quinn the Grave Robber

How in hell fire did that girl weasel her way into my shower? I brewed over the idea that I let my guard down. Someone, whom I'd never met in my darkest dreams, broke through my magic and into my eyes. She saw me! Then she squeaked, as if she knew me. "She must have sought me out," I grumbled into another chunk of bread.

"What was that?" Darlin chuckled as she ducked into view. I snapped back to reality with a blink and smiled at her softly. My aunt tried every moment since she took my hand at the train station to figure out what happened. For a long eight hours, I feigned exhaustion and she bought it. I passed out in her arms and woke up in my bed. She babied me, cuddled up next to me and read stories while I dozed in and out of sleep. Magic pulsed through my veins, but I had spent more than thirty hours awake. Physically I was exhausted after the first zing of magic.

Then I beat around the bush like my life depended on it. Darlin was many things—unfortunately, patient was one of them. Given the chance, she would wait months for me to confess. The truth devoured my intestine with little concern for my sanity. As I mulled over my thoughts, she walked back to the flour-covered counter. I perched myself at the kitchen table as she kneaded dough with her hands in rhythmic motions. My bread dropped into the soup and a yawn broke through my lips. "Just something that happened in the shower."

My aunt did not turn her head—she didn't have to. Her spell book stared right at me. Its eyes peered straight through me and shifted with each twist of my body. She would watch me for the rest of my life at this point. Two times I snuck out, two times I was busted by the police. My luck for teenage rebellion had an extremely low success rate. For weeks after the grave robbery, she berated me and ran me through the ringer. Chores on top of chores for hours on top of my studies. Winestra, my tutor, was told under no circumstance to go easy on me. Then she burnt my left eyebrow half off. Winestra swore to take it a smidgen easier on me. Now I'd snuck out of view twice, disguised myself specifically to her, then came back drenched in blood... I doubt she'd let me off easy. Grounded was not a term we used in this house. Restricted was.

"It wasn't like I fell or anything." I sheepishly laughed.

"I know you didn't, because I would have heard the roar of elephants as you took out every bottle and loofah and hairbrush and lotion and bath bomb—"

"I get it, I have a lot of stuff in my shower," I grumbled.

"Point is, I would have heard you crash," my aunt teased and winked in my direction. "What happened in the shower?"

"Um... I think I saw someone," I muttered between strategic bites of bread drenched in stew. Inch by inch, my aunt faced me completely, her doughy hands resting on her hips.

"Quinn, you and I both know you'll have to be a smidgen more specific in this house. Your great-great grandmother haunts this house and so does your uncle Teddy. Plus, there's the poltergeist in my closet and the haunting spirit in the jar of the library." She cocked a brow.

I sunk down into the chair as I mulled over my options. If I told the truth, she might give me answers or wring my neck harder. If I lied, she might think I was overreacting for a normal activity and call my bluff.

My aunt, with the patience of a god in troubled times, cocked a hip out and eyed me. "Quinn."

"Auntie, have you ever met a witch that could like, you know... connect with your brain?" I piped up as I stirred sourdough bread into the beef stew. The smell of broth filled my nose and steam tickled my cheeks. My Aunt Darlin made the best stew—beef so tender it fell off the bone, vegetables the size of my thumb, a broth so herby and garlicky it fixed all ailments. She always made it when someone was sick or when I was exhausted. I wasn't, but I pretended I was because she would be suspicious if I wasn't.

My aunt sighed and shook her head, her hands moved back toward the dough. "Well, on occasions Seers have been known to extend their magic— Wait, does this have anything to do with New York?" Darlin whipped around so fast it made my head spin.

I laughed nervously as I slumped further down the chair for dramatic effect. She rushed from the kitchen counter to my side. She put the back of her hand to my forehead and checked my face thoroughly before she stepped back. Raw dough stuck to her fingers, and now my forehead, as she held them up in front of her.

I rolled my head back against the chair to look up at her with innocent eyes. Which was a mistake because she cocked a brow and stepped closer. "What happened in New York? You call me from some mystery phone, using the emergency line, in hysterics, which is very unlike you, you're taken in by the police. Then when I come to get you, that damn weasel of a lawyer just up and leaves you at the train station alone? Why would you run off in the middle of the night like that, Quinn? I was worried sick! No note! Nothing!"

I shrugged as innocently as possible. Darlin Foster was the smartest person in my life, which was a problem. Always so sharp and quick to see past lies. Her suspicions didn't help me when I tried to clean up the mess I made. Part of my mess being how fast I called my aunt in a time of crisis and how I believed that was the only option. If Darlin ever found out what I'd created, she'd never let me out of the house again. Worse than restriction, I would be banished from the light of day. She'd curse me to my room and refuse to let up on the spell, a fate worse than death.

My aunt was a spellslinger. She cast spells with words and incantations, sometimes she needed ingredients if the spell called for it. Sometimes I had dreams her spell book followed me around just to keep an eye on me, which was a joke Darlin made all the time as her book had five eyes on the front. One was a glass eye enchanted by her grandmother, one was a crystal carved to look like an eye, one was the eye of a snake. Two were real eyes taken from the face of a seer who'd been executed for murder, and all were bound in a thick leather cover with a spell burnt into the back cover. That spell kept them all active and fresh, they blinked and shifted as if to watch. Everything they saw, Darlin saw.

Some mothers had eyes in the back of their head, my aunt had five magic eyes watching for *everything*, so I almost never got away with *anything*. Until now. I wished I hadn't.

"I was freaked out. I thought I killed someone," I lied through my teeth as I tossed my arms out. My aunt's face drained of color, and her lips fell open. Huge mistake. I reeled my emotions in as best as possible, my hands up weakly in defense. "But he was fine, and I'm fine! It was a huge misunderstanding!"

My aunt turned from me gradually, her book's eyes still focused on me. I glanced at the book propped up on the clean side of the kitchen counter. All eyes bore into me with suspicion. She didn't believe me, but she didn't have proof I'd lied. So she kept her mouth shut and so did I. A small game I was confident I would lose in the end. I slouched forward and dipped more bread into my stew.

Darlin went back to mixing dough, her long fingers kneaded it into place. Half the counter was covered in flour and kneaded dough balls under tea towels to rise. One of the few things Darlin and I did the human way was cooking. Magic cooking could never deliver the complexity of human cooking. Plus, I think my aunt liked the mini escape from reality that happened when she dove headfirst into a recipe.

Everyone else in the coven gossiped about how Darlin never cooked before. Then, when my mom died, Darlin cooked a lot. She was always in the kitchen, and I stood right next to her. The kitchen was our place. My stomach twisted up as I stuffed my cheeks with sloppy bread. The kitchen used to be my mother's favorite place—a small, drunken fact whispered over candles on the anniversary of her death. Darlin never repeated herself. Her shoulders squared up as if she came up with another question. I cut her off.

"I'll tell you about New York," I sputtered, "If you tell me about Mom." It was a challenge I was confident I could win.

Darlin's back went rigid. The eyes on her book shifted to her, but then the two seer eyes snapped back to me. A dead silence filled the kitchen as she shook her head. It should make my stomach untangle to know she gave in. My stomach tightened harder as I realized I only knew hearsay. I flopped back in the wooden chair. My aunt was patient, even in a storm cloud, poised, witty and sharp, intelligent, and damaged. She would never speak of my mother; her death haunted her. Thyme and garlic filled the air as Darlin moved to the sink to wash her hands.

She covered up the stench of secrets with herbs.

My mother haunted my aunt and abandoned me to a dark abyss. How do I miss someone I've never met? I was terribly silent and miserable often. Late at night, huddled in my bed with the shreds of my mother I collected over the years. I hoarded her; I dug desperately for anything on her—the veil she wore to her wedding, the picture of my aunt and my mother in front of the house, the last bottle of perfume she brewed on her own, and a small cookbook—a piece of history I stole from the kitchen long ago. My aunt avoided its presence at every turn. Darlin locked her away in a drawer. She didn't even notice, or she never mentioned it. This kitchen became the one place in the house I felt connected to her past and disconnected from her soul.

"I'm sorry," I murmured.

"I know you want to know her, but it's best to leave the dead in their graves," my aunt whispered an ominous warning over the rack of bread left to rest.

Our kitchen wasn't large, but it was the biggest room in the house. Our house was built on stilts in the middle of the swamp, circled around a willow tree like a tutu on a child. The kitchen was a long bar on the inside of the house that ended with a fridge we'd rummaged out of the junkyard and parts we found in the swamp. The fire pit in the middle of the kitchen encased by a semi-circle dinner table made of bricks and stones. This house was built by my great-grandfather for his wife, Serephine Foster, who was the first witch in our household. Matthew Foster was helplessly in love with her and built them a home in the swamp to be closer to her magic.

A home my mother was supposed to inherit.

Instead, Darlin and I lived in it alone, in the middle of the swamp, in the middle of nowhere, where the closest road was three miles away. Don't get me started on how far away school is from my house. The location of the school wasn't the reason I was home-schooled... it's because I am a witch. And as history would show, witches do not do well in public spaces.

"What about this connection with your brain?" Darlin changed the conversation like a smooth salesperson on a bad review. Her hands wrapped up in a towel as she twisted to look at me.

"It... I felt like there was something watching me, for just a moment. Then, in the shower, I saw her. Like she was physically there, but then she disappeared," I explained, unsure of how to even do so. One moment I existed in my shower and tried to scrub the shock and blood off of my body. In the blink of an eye, the sharp pressure at the back of my skull a body appeared behind mine. I smelt her blood before I felt her presence. A horrifying new discovery in my magic. After my lawyer snack, all sorts of magic unlocked for me—things I'd only read about in journals my aunt kept on witches.

Most journals she held were vast and displayed many examples: pictures, maps, entries from multiple people. Darlin had started this collection young and was called the librarian for a reason, but that didn't help when it came to Blood witches. That knowledge was thin and very vague. Blood scent, a gift vaguely hinted at, etched into the tiny journal with only one sentence: *Witches may be able to distinguish others by their blood, much like a hound.* That was it and it infuriated me. Darlin knew more information than she left in the library. She never answered me when I asked why.

"That is unusual. Most seers can only connect mentally." Darlin furrowed her brow. "Was it someone we know? Maybe you mixed magic with a seer we know?"

"Nope. New girl, maybe sixteen. She looked scared to see me. Like she'd never done that before."

Darlin and I pursed our lips, arms crossed as we shifted our eyes from each other to her book. The snake eye blinked slowly and opened to a full black eye. For a long moment, it seemed to spin. I called it Darlin's loading screen, as the snake was her eye that looked for information. She used that eye when she wanted to read over documents to keep in memory, or any piece of information that might be useful to the coven. Our coven, the Family, was a loose collection of powerful witches in Oklahoma; my aunt is an elder. Like my mother, I would inherit my position into the coven when I turned eighteen. That is, if they never found out I brought Leo Ashwood back from the dead and turned him into a monster.

"Whatcha' got?" I asked as the eye stopped its spin and blinked back into position.

Darlin sighed and shook her head. "There aren't a lot of sixteen year old seers that we don't know of. She can't be with the Family or even a family..." Darlin huffed as she put her hands to her hips. "I can't even see her."

"Ha, get it, see the seer?" I snickered. Darlin shot me a cocked brow that only made me laugh harder. I pushed back from the table. My feet gingerly tested the floor and made a show of cracking my joints to cement my illusion of exhaustion. "She was really tall."

"That tells me nothing, Quinn," Darlin chuckled. "You're five foot three—everyone is tall to you."

"Hey!" I quipped. The flash of warmth and humor in Darlin's eyes warmed me. Our family traits were the only thing she talked about in regards to my mother, which were things I'd seen in photographs. I was the spitting image, a living memory; everyone always spoke about how similar we looked: five foot three, long chestnut hair, left eye green and right eye blue. Darlin, blessed with her father's genetics, stood five foot six with short dirty blond hair, left eye green and right eye blue. Amendir, another elder in our coven, always said the way to spot a Foster: their eyes. One eye green, one eye blue. Darlin reminded me that mine were the color of fresh grass and the sea in the morning light. Beauty and brains, even if she flinched when she saw me. Late at night, after a long day, I could see it in her face. She would mistake me for her sister, and it would take her breath away. She would hug me and kiss my head, but she wouldn't look me in the eyes.

Even now, the sadness shimmered under the happy in her eyes as she memorized my face. Darlin walked from the counter to the table. She enveloped me in a hug that I welcomed. I wrapped my arms around her tightly and stuffed my face into her collar bone. Baked bread and basil filled my nose, her hair held hints of mint from her hand stirred shampoo.

"You scared me, you know," Darlin croaked into my scalp as she nuzzled her nose against my hair.

"I scared me too," I whimpered as I dug my fingers into her.

"What happened? Just tell me why you were arrested?" She pulled back just an inch to look down at my face.

"I, uh, did the teenager thing where I let peer pressure talk me into breaking into some person's house," I lied. My scalp tingled as she pouted and ran her hands through my hair. It had come to my attention at the train station that the tweed suit lawyer, whose name I never learned, had not told my aunt what I was charged with.

He didn't tell her anything but to come directly to New York to talk. On the train I learned that she almost didn't come; she believed it was a prank by one of the young witches in the family. Then she used her book to look for me and found she couldn't see me.

Darlin cupped my face with her hands. "Honey."

"I know, I know, it was stupid, but the girl said that he stole something from her. Turns out she just wanted to rob him. Then he called the cops, and I couldn't escape. You know, mortals and their camera phones!" I lied and lied and lied. Well, half lied, and half lied, then completely lied. Leo Ashwood never called the cops. It was a stranger who saw him jump out of his 26th story window and run off along the street below who called the cops. That much I figured out from Detective Smith and Officer Alvarez, though mostly Detective Smith. Alvarez never said a word to me. I wondered how long it would take Detective Smith to realize I no longer existed in New York, or how long it would take them to find the lawyer's body, which I had returned for and dragged away in the snow. Thankfully, the snow fall piled up fast and left him preserved after I knocked some sense back into myself.

"And so what did we learn?"

"That mortals are stupid and cops are stupid and I should never leave this house again." I smirked only to flinch as Darlin planted a smack to the back of my head. "Hey! Ow!"

"Don't get smart with me, Quinn." Despite her serious tone of voice, Darlin kissed my head again and hugged me tight. "I love you, Quinn Foster, please don't forget that. I will always be on your side."

And my heart sank into my feet. I believed her, but I knew better than to do so. Darlin could never find out what I'd done. I made Leo Ashwood into a monster. I defied all common sense and brought him back from the dead. I would take that secret to the grave.

Chapter Five

Cecelia the Freak Show

"And they said the bodies were all ripped to shreds, like a bear the size of a Mack Truck ate 'em," Jess said. "I'm not sure what that means, because like, Antlers isn't that far away from us. Like I could spit and I'd hit a deer and Izzy Goats-a-lot Henrick. I heard she got an award at a goat show or whatever, some like, diamond blooded goat. I didn't know goats could be blue bloods, but you learn something every day I guess... Back to the point, they said it was an animal attack but I doubt that, what kind of animal attacks a person in their own backyard in the middle of town. Especially in a town full of hillbillies and farmers who shoot at shadows—hey! Are you listening?"

I blinked as Jess waved a hand in front of my face. My legs jumped but my torso tensed as I glanced over my shoulder. "Sorry, what about Antlers?"

Jessica Grace Harris had loose curls of auburn hair jammed into a ponytail and an attitude built out of sheer muscle stuffed into a teenage body. I grimaced sheepishly as she wiggled a brow at me with a snicker. "I was telling you about the murders."

"Are they murders if an animal did it?" I quipped.

"That's what I was talking about, there's no way it was an animal. Maybe some science jacked grizzly bear, if he were shot up with Captain America juice and slapped by the Hulk, maybe." She scoffed then nudged my elbow. I stumbled forward in the lunch line from the force. "There have been a few murders in the news all over the place; I bet they're all connected."

"Remind me again, who is the oracle?" I teased with a wide grin. Twisting at the hips, I examined Jess swaying behind me. She wiggled her eyebrows as she nibbled upon her thumbnail again. My hands smacked hers away and she smacked mine with her opposite one. I shoved her weakly, and she shoved me forward in line. Her palms planted firmly on my shoulder blades, she waddled us both through the line. My mind wandered back. The world was a blurred cloud as I floated back in time to my bathroom. Quinn's face behind my eyelids, she haunted my dreams and made reality hazy. Saturday, I witnessed someone die. Yet, in no time, it was noon on a Monday.

What was expected to be an uneventful weekend turned into a fast pace rollercoaster that ended with school as reality rammed into me. Quinn made me feel like a damsel tied to train tracks that were on fire with an out-of-control train half a foot from me and a bomb strapped to my chest. A terrible, quick succession of things had stacked on top of the anxiety and fear that fueled my sleepless nights—half blurry dreams, half of Quinn's face as she hovered over my corpse.

Then I was at school, backpack digging into my shoulder as the bell rang overhead. There was something missing but I couldn't recall what it was. Teenagers bustled around me, teachers droned on in circles, and I woke up in the lunchroom. A hard jab to my shoulder blade brought me out of my fuzzy daydream. I caught eyes with Kitty as blue eyes bore through my soul. There was death in her face, her long manicured nails clawed down the front of her history textbook that propped up her bag of veggie straws.

I clenched up rigid as a corpse. Her baby blues narrowed on me. Textbooks clutched to my chest, I broke eye contact with her and shuffled down the line toward the 'food' offered in school. Water, that's all I wanted, a bottle of water and maybe a cookie. Their 'pizza' was trash but their cookies were bought from a local bakery and worth the two dollars.

"Earth to Ce?" Jess said.

"Sorry, Jess," I muttered. Despite my day as one large blur, it went relatively smooth—no murderous witch in my shower, no nosy town gossip complaints that my hummus was too 'spicy', just me and the slow burn of the school day. Until I saw Kitty Justin and I realized that today would end in flames. My mother was going to rip me a new one when I got home. How could I be so careless to forget? Her face rang bells in my skull but I scrambled for what they were for. If Kitty didn't kill me, Gretchen would.

"Cranky Panky, ten o'clock," Jess whispered to my back. A spark of electricity zapped my fingertips. Danger. I jerked my head up in time to receive a cartoonishly hard slap to my cheeks that spun me from the line and knocked me to the ground. Jess tossed her books to the ground.

"Whoa! What the—" I choked on my own voice.

"You think this is funny, Montreal? What's he want with a freak like you, huh? What did you tell him? Some freaky bull-crap, huh? Answer me freak!" Kitty's screech rang in my ears and bounced off the walls of my skull. I spun in my own skin. If I were honest, the nicknames were not her best. I've been called worse... by her.

I rubbed my cheek with my free hand while I tried to get up with the other, but Kitty shoved me mercilessly to the ground again. She knelt over me, grabbed me at my shoulders and shook me. For some reason, I froze—jaw clenched shut like iron gates, my eyes sewn shut, my muscles locked down. I let her slam me into the ground again and again. Thankfully, it only lasted thirty seconds until Jess recovered from shock and Aragorn tossed Kitty across the lunchroom. Except, instead of a graceful Gimli landing, Kitty crashed into a table and rolled across the floor audibly like a nazgûl. All fluttering fabric and screeches, a cloaked rider of the shadows from Lord of the Rings whose screams could break even the thickest goblets of wine.

Jess Harris was good at two things: tossing dwarves and shooting squirrels off her porch. She said my biggest talent was putting my nose right where it didn't belong. I was labeled a freak early on, and it never left. Gretchen claimed my height as the culprit, but I always believed it might be something else. Until Jess took one look at me in fifth grade and told me to my face, 'You! We're going to be best friends,' and I never left. Jess, realistically the only person who talked to me outside of civil conversation, adopted me that day. Sure, this was the South, and everyone is nice outwardly and civil to their neighbor. But there is a difference between civility and friendship. Jess and Gretchen were my only friends—sad really but true.

"All right, hold up!"

I opened my eyes and unlocked my arms from around my head to see Vice Principal Justin and Lance McCalister hovered over me. I beamed sheepishly up at them. Lance put out a hand to help me up, but Vice Principal Justin stared at me. With his deep-set brown eyes, thin skin over a sharp bone structure, Vice Principal Justin looked like the grim reaper with warm cheeks. He scowled hard as Lance dusted off my shoulders. Vice Principal Justin crossed his arms. A stiff black pinstripe suit with silver buttons along the arms and front, he made sure everyone could see the perfect sheen on them. A power play, one I was accustomed to in this school.

"What is going on?" Vice Principal Justin cocked a thin brow. The background noise of the lunchroom vacuumed out and left the air thick around me. It hurt to inhale as he peered down at me with his sharp grimace. There was no sign of stubble, no piece of hair out of place, slick from his salt and pepper strands to his shoes that never made a sound.

"Kitty lost her marbles and slapped the bejesus out of Cecelia!" Jess snapped just to my left. Lance let go of me with a sympathetic look. I winced at him as he tucked a lock of hair behind my ear. Lance McCalister was the entire reason Kitty attacked me, and yet, I wanted to apologize. He had shaggy dirty blond hair, a crooked nose from a fist fight in third grade, and glowing skin. For the captain of the senior soccer team, son of the mayor, and all around favorite boy in town, Lance was incredibly kind to me.

Which is exactly why I came to him the morning after my dream last week. My last vision overshadowed by the murder that lurked at the back of my mind. Kitty's slap was a reality check. The consequence for forgetting that I snitched on Kitty to her boyfriend.

"I see, and that will be addressed. My question is, why would Kitty do anything like that?" Vice Principal Justin growled. The Vice Principal loomed over me, his toes an inch from mine. He brushed Lance out of the way, the skin on his face sagged. My mouth dropped open as I whirled to look at Kitty behind me. She stood up with a pout, tears streaming down her cheeks. I was speechless. I turned back around only to see Vice Principal Justin with an unimpressed look on his face.

"It doesn't matter why she done it. I saw her slap Cecelia." Lance sighed as he shot a dark look to Kitty. Kindness and civil classwork memories were shredded before my face as I witnessed the dirtiest look on Lance's face. This was not the Lance I knew. The room turned to ice around me. My spine straightened as the death stare from Kitty's baby blue eyes bore into me.

"Will be addressed?" Jess sneered, "You mean slap on the wrist."

"This school is a no-tolerance school," Vice Principal Justin quipped as his hands tugged his suit flat against his chest. No-tolerance? A joke. All no-tolerance taught people like Jess and Kitty was that you might as well swing, because you're both getting expelled.

"Until the attacker is your niece!" Jess stepped forward, lips curled up in a snarl.

"Watch your tongue, young lady." His gaze cut into Jess as I tugged her back from him.

"Well, maybe some people shouldn't provoke other people? Gets them in trouble," the Vice Principal scoffed under his breath, soft enough that even I barely heard it. My face paled as our eyes locked—no one else even heard it. With two years of little quips like that, I could write a book of his tiny incisions into my confidence. Kitty Justin's parents paid for the football field and soccer field. Kitty was untouchable—students were afraid of her uncle's power, and adults seemed to agree with her on everything. And I'd royally pissed her off.

For as long as I could remember, I'd tried not to even come upon Kitty's radar. From kindergarten to sophomore year, I'd succeeded in practically staying under all radars. A freak who knew stuff, sure. But other than needless teasing and a few hair tugs when we were ten, they left me alone. Since I was five foot nine, most girls didn't want to chance it and most guys were intimidated. Well, except for Jess, she was my Gimli: five foot four, a mess of red wavy curls, freckles and biceps for days. Unafraid of my elf status, ready to fight the world at my side. Feisty and witty, she was my favorite person in the world.

"That seems a bit unfair. I was the victim here," I blurted out with a whine. Wrong answer. I regretted it immediately.

"No tolerance does not allow for a victim—"

"She did it! Cecelia is a V-I-C-T-I-M! We have witnesses, you even saw it! You found her smacking Cecelia into the ground!" Jess barked. She flung her hands out to her side, and our books tumbled to the ground. I jumped in my skin as they set off fireworks in my ear drums. Panic and shock fought for control of my system. Deja vu sunk into my blood, like a viper's venom blurring my vision and vibrating in my veins.

"Even if I believed such a thing, it does not matter. No tolerance is no tolerance!" Vice Principal Justin interjected with a fiery glare pointed Jess's way. "It only leads me to ask why such an event occurred?"

"It's... my fault." Lance sighed and I clamped my mouth shut. The whole lunchroom turned into a haunted melody of low whispers and hushed conversations. A hush ran over the ground as Kitty's classic click of heels headed my way. "Cecelia told me that Kitty cheated on me and I broke it off with her."

"What!" Kitty screeched. Honest confusion contorted her features. She launched away from the small collection of onlookers and stormed my way. I wondered if there was a way to swallow my head. If I could just fit my lower lip over my face and just... disappear! That'd be great. Her expression shifted, in an instant as she lumbered in my direction, no longer confused but furious. "That's why you broke up with me? I thought you broke up with me for her!"

"I suddenly don't want any water or cookies," I muttered. My hand slapped at Jess beside me. She bent down and scooped up our books.

"Agreed. I'm out, come on," Jess grumbled as she hooked arms with me. A ding went off, a familiar tone of a Facebook notification. Realization snapped the deja vu venom out of my blood. Chills ran up my spine and my hair stood on edge. Dings went off all over the lunchroom and my heart stopped. Flashes filled my eyelids and I looked to Jess with my lips parted. Her face twisted up and her right eye twitched.

"Not so fast—" Vice Principal Justin was interrupted by mass laughter. The whole lunchroom burst into mad laughter and my heart sunk. My dream came back in a painful flash. I'd been in such a rush this morning, I hadn't written it down. Now it haunted me as I mouthed *vision* to Jess with a horrified expression. She relaxed her face with a sigh before she pulled out her cell phone. Everyone in the lunchroom held up their phones to one another and I knew what was on it. A viral video shared to the school's Facebook page... of Kitty kissing a boy that wasn't Lance.

"What is the meaning of this!?" Vice Principal Justin roared. I pulled out my own phone to find myself tagged in a post like most everyone. I cleared the notification because I already knew what was on it. I'd seen the video first person point of view as if I was the camera phone; disgust and unease filled my stomach when I woke up. The sounds of wet lips as they smacked together would haunt me for the rest of my life. Which was gradually shortened by the second as everyone turned to look at Kitty.

"You—" I spun to look back to Kitty, my eyebrows practically in my hairline. Her phone clattered out of her hand to the floor. Horror and shame etched into her wide eyes. She shot toward me, face twisted up near her lips and nose.

"I didn't do it!" I squeaked. Jess jerked my body away from Kitty as she lunged at me, her finger in my face.

"You're the only one who knew!" Kitty snarled, every facial muscle contracted. Her teeth bared at me as her hands shook in my face. Jess yanked me back a step in the same breath she stepped forward. If Kitty wasn't careful, it would be Jess who was suspended and not me. Jess had been suspended before, and she was not afraid to do it again.

"You're forgetting one other person." Lance jumped between Kitty and me. He pulled out his phone to show the video of Kitty and Johnny 'Bucktooth' Smith making out in the back of his truck. I gagged at the sound as the video played live before me. Jess rolled her eyes. "It was Johnny who videotaped it. And when Cecelia told me last Monday that you were cheating on me, I asked him about it. He said it was true. I told him I didn't believe him... Then he showed me, and I posted it to the page, so here's my proof. Looks like the eggs on my face, Kitty. But you'll always be the cheater."

Suddenly, I didn't feel bad for Lance. In that instance, it was Kitty I pitied.

My heart sank as Jess pulled me out of the explosion that happened within seconds. Kitty broke down into tears and begged Lance to forgive her. Lance told her to get away from him. I didn't like Kitty, nor did I particularly hate her, but it wasn't my best work. I'd tried for so long to use my visions for good. I told Lance about Kitty, but he didn't want to believe me. It was for the best, but at least he knew. But this morning, I should have told her. I should have stopped the video. I let myself wrap my mind up in Quinn and the magic, I forgot about the people I actually knew.

After Quinn broke into my dreams and mind, I lost control. "Jess, how bad is my bruise?"

"Not as bad as the table mark Kitty's about to have on her spine. I tossed her like a sack of potatoes." Jess grinned widely as we ducked around pillars and out of the lunchroom.

"I should have told her..." I sighed before we both fell silent. We snuck into the music hallway and stopped a foot short of the band room. We were a good half-hour early. Often, we sat in the hallway and ate lunch if it was quiet. Today, the whole world cranked the volume to max.

Quinn's dream happened Friday night, and I saw her in the shower Saturday morning. My days were in a whirl. I held onto Jess who had the right mind to pick up all our books and tug us out of the situation. My back found the long tan colored brick of the hallway and sank down to the ground. My hands fell onto the top of my head with a sigh.

I knew the video would destroy Kitty! Just like I knew she would become the butt end of a cruel line of jokes all day because of the video. Visions are never fully clear but I knew a few important details. Firstly, Kitty was a very passionate kisser. Secondly, Kayleigh Sanders would show Destini Cleary at the lunch table. Thirdly the video would spread like wildfire even after it was taken down. Lastly, at the end of the day Mary Anne would face her mother in the parking lot. Her mother would yell and embarrass Kitty more, who would then cry the whole ride home. What good is this gift if I can't stop things like that?

"Did you know that was going to happen like that? What else did you see?" Jess asked. She knelt, slid down beside me. She dropped my books into the space between us as she pulled out her lunch box and plopped it into her lap.

"Yeah, I saw it, not the part where she slapped me but the part where everyone laughed...but I forgot about it because I didn't hear my alarm this morning and slept in. I didn't write it down," I muttered. My fingers laced together over my head until she yanked them down and dropped half a peanut-butter and jelly sandwich into them. With my eyes forward, I held the sandwich up to my mouth and munched it slowly. Jess wolfed hers down before she threw back a huge swig of water. She passed it over and I took a small sip.

"You're a bad oracle," Jess chuckled.

"I know," I whimpered between bites of sandwich. Jess reached over and shoved me forward in order to get into my backpack. She rummaged around until she found my lunch sack and pulled it out. I shoved the rest of the sandwich in my mouth as she cracked my chewy bar in half.

"I was kidding. Damn, did Kitty smack you that hard?" she teased as she handed me my half. I shrugged with a frown. "Whoa there, Sad Face McGee, why the long face?"

"I hurt Kitty."

"Kitty hurt herself, and you!"

Vice Principal Justin would *definitely* call Gretchen and tell her I'd instigated a fight in school. That would lead to my mother standing at the front door when I got home. I would have to tell her what happened, minus the visions, and then she would call me weird and tell me not to get in fights with 'useless rich people.' I would apologize and she would make some remark about how she couldn't afford a lawyer to bail me out of jail.

"I'm a bad daughter," I whispered under my breath. The chewy bar tasted like sand in my mouth as I munched it despite the taste. My insides churned. Jess swiveled to look at me once more.

"Whoa! Back up, where's that coming from?" Jess cocked her head to the right. Long red curls fell from her shoulders to her side. They were loose enough to be waves but curled enough to bounce. I often wished that I had her hair, as my hair was long and thick. Then she would brush her hair in the morning and loudly proclaim she wanted my hair. I tucked a loose strand of my own hair behind my ear.

"I just, you know…" I trailed off and shrugged again.

"You two get into a fight again?" She jostled my knee with a light tap.

"Kinda. But mostly we will get into a fight when I get home, and I deserve it." I muttered. My shoulders slumped. "It's hard enough without me getting into fights in school."

"Well, you did tell Lance about Kitty then you didn't tell her about the video so…" I snapped my head up to look at Jess with worry. She smiled at me softly as she put a hand to my shoulder. "I'm proud you told Lance; it was the right thing to do."

"Was it?" I flinched.

"Sure he's heartbroken now, and sure Kitty's pissed, but in the long run, it's better. Sometimes, the right thing doesn't make everyone happy like it did with Emma or chicken walton. The truth's a bitch for a reason. Though, you really should have told Kitty about the video. That's on you. Well, mostly on Lance, and the next time we're in chemistry, I'm sticking something in his hair for posting it. But, yeah." We sat in silence as we munched along; the murmur of band kids as they talked in the room drifted in and out.

"So… Um… You know how I said Friday I had a nightmare?" I confessed.

"Yeah?" Jess looked up from her pack of gummy bears. She popped a green one into my open mouth before she dumped four orange and clear ones into her own. "Yew-newver-saed-whut-it-was."

I blinked as the words processed in my brain. "I wasn't sure how to explain. But I don't think there really is a way to explain, so I'm just going to say it."

"Well, then spit it out, Ce. What happened?" Jess swiveled as she popped a new green bear into my mouth. I chewed slowly as the words mewled in my head.

"I saw someone get murdered," I confessed.

"What!" she barked. She coughed, clearing her throat as she nearly projected food into my face in surprise.

"But the killer... She was a witch."

Jess stayed dead silent, eyes wide as she looked over me.

I let the words settle in the air before I sighed. "Um, well then, I need to tell you about Quinn." I pouted.

"Who is Quinn? How? What?" Jess cocked a brow.

"I'm not sure but, I think she's in trouble. Or maybe...she is the trouble."

Chapter Six

Maggie the Superstar

"Magpie, you want a BLT for lunch? I'm frying up some bacon now." My mother called from the kitchen into the living room. My eyes bore into my phone screen. Kitty hadn't texted me back. Frankie sat in my lap, passed out cold from a long day of mission MMSA: Make Maggie Smile Again. He whispered it into my ear as I walked through the goat barn with him for the third time to find the 'garden fairy' he said I must see. My mother tasked him with a simple mission: use his pudgy toddler face to make me smile with whatever antics he could manage. Frankie was nothing if not a well accomplished bullshitter. House guests? Frankie could make them laugh the second they walked in the door with a perfected nose bubble and monologue about frogs. Martin's college age friends come home for a warm home cooked meal? Frankie would greet them individually with their new super hero names and what their powers were, along with home-made capes out of towels that matched their gift.

If I was our savior in my parents' time of financial need, Frankie was god's gift to my heart strings. I hugged my pudgy brother close to my chest and shook my head. A ping stole my attention from my brother to my phone. It was Instagram; nothing important.

"You sure? It's the good stuff." My mom pried as she rounded the wall that separated the kitchen from the living room.

I nodded softly as I buried my face into Frankie's hair.

"Magpie—" she began.

"Mom, don't," I begged as my eyes closed softly. The sigh that fell off her lips made my heart ache physically.

"I just want to hear you say you're going to fight it," she murmured.

Tears welled up behind my clenched eyelids. Frankie stirred in my lap and I slid him onto the couch. My legs, weak to the anger and pain that gnawed on my nerve endings, wobbled and wheeled me back toward my room.

"Maggie," my mom said again.

"Mom! Please!" I whined.

"Talk to me."

"What is there to talk about? I have cancer! It's not a nightmare. I'm as good as dead," I croaked, my voice husky as it crackled toward the end and died in my throat. My heart fluttered in a painful way. Air turned to a vacuum in my lungs as I forced my feet to walk away from her. I opened my eyes to avoid Reginald the cat by the tip of his tail.

"Maggie, I don't like the way you're talking. Please, if you won't talk to me, call Kitty or Lance or anyone. You have to talk to someone," she pleaded.

I ignored her and marched to my room. Shoulders squared and eyes downcast, I bumped past the door into my room.

"She's ghosting me, and he wouldn't understand." It stung that Kitty hadn't replied to my good morning text. But, if I were honest, if I called Kitty, she would drop everything to come over and hug me till we were both in tears. I couldn't ask her to do that... not after the day I had. I would just dump on her and ruin her happiness.

I was a horrible friend. I was at the doctor's office and couldn't even tell her why. She asked multiple times, but I iced her out. She must be upset, probably betrayed, as she iced me back. Granted, if we stacked our problems next to one another, mine would out stack hers. But I didn't want to bother her; she was already upset. She gave the tell-tale sign of her in full sulk mode: one vaguely depressive Facebook post about betrayal, no communication except one skull emoji on snapchat, and no posts to any other social media. Something we shared was our dislike of meltdowns on social media. I shut myself away and let myself hurt in the dark.

I unlocked my phone and found my timeline opened to my memories. Last year I was on a chorus field trip to Oklahoma City for some festival. We sang on a stage on wheels and traveled a square block. Photos filled with my memories of my classmates and me in selfies and tagged pictures of me in the middle of my solo. My heart sank.

No more solos, no music field trips, and no singing. My voice was a part of the past. The bed melted around me as I sank deep into the fluff. Even after I closed the app and slid my phone under my pillow, the pain stung deep within my chest. Then I saw Dr. Higgins and I stuffed my pillow into my mouth to stifle a sob.

Dr. Higgins hid behind my eyelids, and his blood coated my fingers in the dark. Why did I have to live out my pain, why was I still here? Dr. Higgins deserved to die as an old man in bed, surrounded by his loved ones in his family home not stabbed to death. They called it an accident in the paper, said it was reckless suicide, and no one could understand it. A good man taken too soon. If I hadn't forced his hands, he might have lived twenty more years. I rubbed my palms against my eyes as endless tears streamed down my cheeks and soaked into my pillow. All I wanted was to sleep and wake up three days ago, cancer free.

I begged my mind to shut off and take me to sleep. My thoughts continued to be merciless and unforgiving. My body was drained of energy but never gave into slumber. My heart, a bloody mess that crumbled, still ached. His blood stained my hands. Magic tickled the backside of my throat worse than any cough. I drowned the tickles with misery and locked up my voice. My parents talked for me and I existed as a dark cloud behind them.

The way his eyes glazed over replayed in my head. Sprawled out on my bed, I tried to blink him away. I reached across my bed to the bedside table and grabbed my cheap arcade-won Nerf gun. My hand raised up into the air over me, nerf gun in hand. I aimed steadily at the ceiling and hit the trigger. A Nerf dart soared through the air and stuck to the poster above my bed. Dead center on my face printed out on a merch edition poster.

All of my ceiling was covered from corner to corner with posters. Most were music tours I'd been to, from rock bands to the Trans-Siberian Orchestra whom I'd seen three years in a row. Thanks to the support from my viewers, I went and reviewed the show. I even made a cover of a song or two from the events on my channel. Thanks to them I did a lot of things. My heart clenched down as my phone went off again for the umpteenth time in an hour. I declined the call and put my phone on silent. My manager tried fourteen times to call me, thirteen text messages, twelve emails, but I ignored them all. I cut everyone off.

I couldn't face them, let alone my family. My mother bought an AirGenius at Walmart yesterday, but it didn't matter. All the air purification and nonsense holistic remedies couldn't remove the cancer from my body. Because of all that happened, everything tasted like salt. Especially after this morning. The whole reason for Frankie's mission that left him passed out in my lap earlier. We spent three hours in a massive hospital. They stamped two words on my skin: stage three. Doctors were beyond impressed I talked let alone sang. What was there to say? Magic saved my vocal chords. When I sang my whole body healed. I sang all the time. And it wasn't until recently, when I'd taken a break, the effects sank in.

So stupid. I never should have stopped!

I wanted to release an album of originals, so I stopped for a whole month. Then I turned sick, and it prolonged the silence. My eyes fell to my bedside table covered in folders and papers scrawled with words and doodles on music sheets filled to the brim with instrumental ideas. Cover images, mock up photo shoots, all of it ready to record. My hands snapped into action and rammed all of it off the table and onto the floor.

All this music and all these lyrics, and my death sentence hung over my head. They wanted to run more tests, to put me under the knife... they wanted... I wanted...

Tears fell down my cheeks again as I choked on my own air. I flopped over on my bed and sobbed into my pillows. My fingers clawed at the cover as the scratch crawled up in my throat again. I wanted to wail, to scream, to throw a fit. Then Dr. Higgins filled my head and I pulled myself back.

I could never let myself go again. My phone buzzed against the bed and I tossed it out from under the pillow onto the floor. Maybe my mom was right—I needed to talk to someone, but I wasn't ready to hear them say anything back.

There was a way for me to talk, where I could cry and get it all out, and no one could talk back. No pitied glances, no sad faces, nothing but my cry out into the void. I got back up onto my knees, took my laptop off my bedside table, and flipped it open. Panic filled my veins. There was only one thing I wanted to do, and I couldn't. If I opened my mouth, I would do more damage than good. What if I made my mother beat her head into a table by just talking? What if I made Frankie break his own teeth? What was stopping me?

Which led me to pull out a marker and a notebook discarded beside my bed. Usually, I would clean up and dress specifically for a video. It didn't matter now. I flipped open my web-camera and hit record. I had a camera on a stand in my closet, with light boxes and a microphone. I gazed directly at the web camera.

I have cancer on my vocal cords.

It was the only thing I thought to write as I held up the notebook paper. I saw my reflection on the computer and instantly broke down into tears. My face twisted up, my body trembled, my lips broken open and chapped. I dropped the notebook. It was too heavy to pick back up. My reflection broke the last straw of hope within my soul. The camera was witness to every sob, recording every tear that streamed down my face. I couldn't stop. The marker felt like a cement brick in my fingers as I flipped the pages of the notebook.

I can't sing. I can't talk.

I lifted the page in front of my face, unsure if it was focused or not. It didn't matter. I dropped the notebook again. My face buried in my hands, I crumpled down in front of my laptop. Everything shook as I flipped the page again. The world blurred around my tears as I cried onto the next and final page. I held up the last page.

Goodbye.

I slapped at my laptop until the video stopped recording. It took me a solid ten minutes to stop shaking long enough to look up. My reflection in the web camera only filled me with regret for my decision. If I posted it, they might hate me. If I didn't post it and I died, they would wonder what happened. Did strangers deserve to know? I'd made a connection with them, but I didn't tell them everything. I didn't tell them the reason all of them were so enthralled with me was because of my magic. My magic that couldn't stop my cancer now. Magic that couldn't help me anymore. What good was power if it couldn't help me!?

I uploaded it. The webpage opened and I let it go live. Then I crawled out of bed. If my voice disappeared, if my magic abandoned me, if there was no me, then I would at least get out of this house! No more 'Magpie, please talk to me!' or 'You're gonna make it', just for one night! I pulled on a pair of jeans and put on a plaid button down over my tank-top. After putting my hair in a ponytail, I stuffed my wallet in my pocket and bolted out of my room.

The house was silent as the grave, with Martin at work and Mom outside with Frankie on the porch. My dad was asleep on the couch, left as a poor 'Maggie' guard. They didn't want me to leave without one of them. But I didn't *want* to be trapped in my depressing room with my phone and my laptop blowing up. Instead, I desperately needed to be out there. Somewhere out of town, somewhere else, and with people who didn't know me.

I tossed myself into the truck and flew down the driveway without a look to the rear view. My mother would realize at some point that it was me that left and not Martin coming home. She would call me and find I didn't pick up. Maybe she'd check my room and see the video up and browser open. It didn't matter.

Engine revved, I barreled down the gravel road and hit the turn a smidgen too fast. My truck lurched and creaked but flopped its tires down around the curve like a champ. I grinned from ear to ear as I threw it into the next gear and slammed down on the gas pedal. The one good thing about backwater country roads—hardly any cops. And when there were, I knew because I was friends with most of their kids. Friends who were only surface level. When the news sunk in, I wanted to tell no one. Not Lance, not Kayleigh, not even Jeff—I had my phone in my hand all day and not once did I feel the urge to message them. Except Kitty—I wanted to tell her everything. Kitty would offer to come over, to be with me and drop the rest of the world behind thick glass. Kayleigh might cry with me, Jeff would pat me on the back and offer words of condolence...but that's not what I wanted.

I flew through two stop signs and hardly tapped my breaks for a yellow light before I rocketed out of town and onto the main highway, my windows cracked all the way down, the radio cranked all the way up, my arms spread out into the breeze. Fresh grass and hints of water on trimmed branches filled the air. If I sniffed hard enough, I could smell the farm animals on all sides. Soft moos mixed with the warbled sound of my radio. The world only a road ahead of me and grass on the sides. My back pressed into the seat, my legs and arms stretched out before me. I felt numb deep within my soul but a glimmer of hope hovered just beyond the horizon. I just had to outrun my problems.

Then I slammed on my breaks as a monstrous, humanoid moose barreled out into the street. My truck stopped mere inches of the— "Holy smokes."

If it was a person, it was no longer a human. It looked like a human built as if they were stuffed and stretched from the center, with skin the color of dried blood and veins pushed through the skin. Large black eyes whipped my direction and it twisted to me fully. Hands the size of my tires grabbed the front of my truck and crunched the edges of the frame.

I don't like rollercoasters. Even with science to back up the fact they won't crash down in a fiery-explosion-Michael-Bay way, I don't trust them. So when the monster hoisted my truck up off the ground and held me vertical with it, I lost it. I'm not ashamed... I peed myself. Then I screamed. My loud scream blasted my windshield into a million tiny pieces filling my ears. I couldn't stop. The beast howled out a gaping maw and tossed me away. I screeched harder and louder as the beast clamped its meaty hands over shredded ears. My truck bounced like a rubber ball as it rolled backward and skittered to a stop. For a second, my heart pounded from within my skull, my stomach rolled in my toes. Vomit threatened my throat only to be squelched by my shrieks of terror.

Panic pumped through my body that turned quickly into rage. I bared my teeth. Magic slashed through my throat, pain radiated between my vocal cords and my screech echoed. The beast thrashed, beating its head with its hands.

My voice cut out and the world went silent. I gasped for air, my hands clawed at my throat. Blood trickled across my tongue and down my lower lip. Blood splattered across my steering wheel as I coughed for air. The beast held still for a long moment before it took off into the trees. Spots filled my eyes as I gagged on blood. My vision spotted as air in my lung drowned under gallons of blood, and terror returned to my system. Was this how I died? My head smacked down into my steering wheel and I was gone to the world.

Chapter Seven

Quinn Hunts for Her Mr. Hyde

Three dead in three days. The news rumbled over the streets. Gossip filled every nook and cranny of the marketplace. A monster of a man or a beast the size of a truck, every witness statement as realistic as sightings of Bigfoot. Soft whispers, newspapers, all of the information bounced from wall to wall of this town. Police were confused how three people were murdered in their own homes. Walls smashed like a thousand sledge hammers fueled by spiteful men people ripped out of their beds in the night, nothing but pieces of them to prove their death. I didn't believe it at first until a blurry picture on the front page of the newspaper in my hand confirmed my fears. Another person missing, but I knew better. Leo Ashwood devoured them. His hunger grew to new levels and scared me. My monster was hungry, and he turned into an excellent hunter... and he currently lurked in my backyard.

He followed me home. Magic truly was impossible and amazing, but also horrifying because my personal monster followed me across half the country. No explanation for how he did so, but then my personal nightmare made front page news.

"Quinn? Are you all right?" Darlin teased as she rounded my right side. Her eyes followed mine to the stack of newspapers in a small booth just across the farmer's market from both of us.

I jumped in my skin. One of the many chores she bore me with was groceries. I followed and held the bags for her while she stocked our cabinets. We did not *need* the groceries, but she knew I abhorred the chore. Fresh vegetables out of carts with nosey women and their homemade hemp clothing. Their natural perfume filled my nostrils with mint leaves and sweat. I gagged at the mere mention of grocery shopping, which is exactly why she forced me to come with.

Darlin sighed as she placed my newspaper back on the stand. "Ah! Amendir and I spoke on that issue earlier."

Rule number one: never talk about witch business in front of humans.

"And do you have any idea what seems to be the problem?" I pried my aunt.

She dove under the cover of another tent. The sun beat down over head and turned the asphalt of the large parking lot into a tar pit. My sneakers stuck to the black top as I followed her into the next hand-made tent. Patched pieces of tarp and thick upholstery fabric on top of poles from old canopy tents. Freshly cut pineapple filled my nose. Thankfully, acidic fruit overpowered everyone else in the tent: A man stained in dirt and soil including his beard, the couple behind the wooden cart full of fruit, my aunt and I, one teenage person crouched next to the wooden cart with a camera over a smashed fruit upon the ground.

"No idea, but it seems like a curious case, like it's cursed or something."

Curse. They believed Leo Ashwood was a curse on some poor soul. The plan might be to hunt him down and try to reverse the curse—trap and fix, like a rabid animal stuck in a raccoon trap. I rounded my aunt's right side and stared at the fruit she ran her fingers over. "The kind we tread lightly with or... should I be worried?" She snapped her head to me with a worried expression.

I played off my curiosity with a worried look of my own.

"Oh, lovely, there is nothing to worry about. Not while the smartest person in the family-scratch that, in the world, is working on it." She winked.

"Smart enough to see a teenager's mistake and let her off the hook early?" I beamed with a smile across my whole face. The two behind the cart let out soft chuckles as Darlin shook her head. "Can't blame a girl for trying."

"You can when she sneaks out without permission," Darlin retorted with a cocked brow. I hung my head as the vendors chuckled more behind their curtain of displayed goods. Darlin picked up a few apples and handed them to the closest of the two behind the cart. The rustle of a bag and the click of a scale filled the silence of the booth—a moment of pure peace before he tainted it. A shiver ran up my spine and every hair stood on edge. My blood sent a sharp pressure to the back of my shoulders. I pivoted on my toes, my eyes followed the wall of the tent back out to the marketplace. Across the street, through the crowd, I caught his scent.

My nose tingled with a flavor unlike anything else—raw sewage, spoiled milk, rotten flesh left in a hot moist environment, all mixed into a spray bottle and spritzed over the dump became a sour taste on my tongue. Putrid death left my knees weak. I stumbled toward the entrance as my eyes searched for him.

"Quinn?"

I choked on his presence. Darlin examined me from over my shoulder.

"Sorry..." I whimpered, "I caught a whiff of something awful."

"I bet it was that book seller three booths down. I could smell him from the edge of town." She bent close to my ear to whisper to me. I laughed softly with a quick nod. My aunt caught my arm and whisked me out of the tent and down another tent. Every shift, every movement in my peripheral made my muscles tense and my nostril's flare. His stench slithered in and out of my nose. I hesitated outside of the next booth. It was him, I knew it was him. There was nothing else out there to explain *that* scent. My face twisted up as I searched for him.

Then my eyes caught hold of my nightmare. Leo Ashwood followed me all the way to Oklahoma. My paranoia was confirmed. Fear brewed new acid in my stomach as he lumbered out of the shadows.

He lingered just down the road in between buildings. A monster cast into the shadows—my monster. Blood magic was not a kind practice. Leo Ashwood stood at least seven feet tall, his shoulders expanded further away from his original bones. Long white hair left from his past life fell around his engorged face. His skin, dark shades of purple and gray around pus yellows and greens, burst open around his muscles and veins. His hands were the size of car tires and uneven, like he suffered from internal bleeding on a massive scale. Bruises covered his meaty hands and feet, scraps of clothing hung around him like tattered curtains of an open window in a hurricane. My mouth hung open as he slunk out of sight at the honk of a horn.

"You son of a—"

"What?"

Panic filled my veins as I whipped back to Darlin. She paid for a bag of vegetables and moved toward the next cart. She spared a glance at my direction in confusion. My lips glued together as she hovered over the stand. More fruit under a simple canopy cover, an older lady in hot pink offered a slice of exotic fruit. "Auntie?"

"Huh?" She peeked up at me. "I know, I know, it's boring but this is part of your punishment, Quinn. You need to learn the weight of your mistakes. Plus, we need more starfruit in our lives, don't you think?"

"Sure! Of course, but maybe I should carry all these bags with me to the library! Prisoners are still allowed decent literature," I lied through my teeth as I pointed to the building down the street.

"Oh! Yes! Good idea. Pick me up a copy of the new mystery novel by what's his face. You know the one with the punch buggies on the front!" Darlin beamed, a false smile upon her lips.

I smiled back and backed up nervously. That was too easy. I watched her suspicions switch from me toward the building behind me. No! Don't look! As I whirled away from her, a hand clamped down on my shoulder. Leo

Ashwood ducked away from the side of a building too slowly.

"I know, I know, Dean House-something's novels..." I trailed off, but she didn't buy it. Darlin turned me inch by inch till I faced her again. Her eyes narrowed, not on me, but at the spot where Leo Ashwood lingered just moments before. She stepped past me, her hand still clamped down on my shoulder.

"Never mind the book, love. Take the groceries home," she whispered softly.

"Auntie, what's wrong?" I swiveled to try to catch a look at her face. She merely turned to me and put the bags she carried into my arms. I wobbled under the weight of all the food, but my feet refused to be moved. If I spared a look for Leo Ashwood, she might suspect me again. I had to play innocent. My head cocked to the side as I examined her face in worry.

Darlin stared at me dead in the eyes, her fingers dug into my shoulders. "Go home and I want you to promise me you'll sit near the book. Do not open the door for anyone." Her voice was grave. She saw him.

A harsh chill ran up my spine as I stumbled back from her. "Auntie, you're scaring me."

"Good." She stepped back. "A healthy dose of fear is needed in times like these. Now, get."

I lurched after her. Darlin spun from me and marched down the road from the market. The asphalt pinched at the bottom of my sneakers. My aunt seemed to float over the ground, unfazed, toward the edge of the buildings. The empty part of town was in view, run over with underbrush and empty buildings with open doors. It was mostly full of wild animals and vagrants, raided often and sprayed clean by the city's maintenance. He picked a good hiding spot, which worried me more. If he picked it, then it meant he concocted a trap through. Leo Ashwood had thoughts! More than a hungry monster going from meal to meal, he thought. Hunt at night, hide from sight, taunt and tease me away from my aunt, he was no rabid animal... and that was a problem! The bags grew heavier with every step as I tried my hardest to follow her.

Magic turned me sluggish as I dragged myself across the road and into the alleyway between two buildings. My aunt hovered at the edge into the empty side. I caught her eye as she whispered a spell in my direction. The bags dragged me closer to the ground. I slumped against the side of a building with wide eyes. "Hey! Rude! I want to help—"

"Rengrassa A la Kas—"

With a snap of her fingers, in the shadows of the alleyway, I disappeared out of town and landed onto the front porch of our house. I set down the groceries with a soft hand before I whirled to the banister and kicked it as hard as I could. Rage heated my cheeks as I kicked two other beams, my fists clenched tight. "Come on!" I shouted. "This is hardly fair!"

But she couldn't hear me. No one but the willow could hear me. A huff of frustration broke through my lips as I punched one of the many pillars on the porch. Nothing, not even the kick of wind or croak of frogs to answer me. I sighed for far longer than necessary, then I took up the groceries and stomped inside. The book swiveled on the kitchen counter to see me. Gently, I dropped the bags on the table and stuck my tongue out to the book. It merely blinked. I unloaded fruits and vegetables, loafs of strange bread and odd meats into the cabinets and fridge. The book followed me the whole time.

"Look! This is cruel and unusual punishment!" I huffed as I slammed the fridge door shut in front of me. The book settled down upon the counter, eyes hyperfocused on me. She was worried. Darlin used the book to keep a literal few eyes on me, which only meant she thought of me. "You're distracted with me here, and you there! I can help! Please! Auntie! You never let me use my magic out there like you! I just want to show you what I'm capable of!"

The book blinked.

I stomped my foot and tossed my arms out to the side. "What good is magic if I can't use it?!"

Nothing. The book swiveled to stare at me harder.

"I know you can hear me! The book can hear me!" I slapped my hands back to my sides as I marched toward the table. It took only a minute to fold the bags back up and stuff them into the box of other bags we hid under the table.

If I left now, she would see me. My aunt Darlin would drop out of the sky like a dragon and beat me silly if I tried to defy her, especially after New York, considering my escape plan took months to perfect. She'd know I left and she would find me. I dropped my hands to my hips as I faced the book. The snake eye blinked and the crystal eye shifted to look out the window. I followed its gaze and rolled my eyes. "I wish you would trust me to take care of myself!"

I stormed up to the first shutters in the kitchen and took a hold of them. The slam of them as they collided with the frame felt good. My muscles relaxed despite my temper tantrum. A smile crept onto my lips. Then my face plummeted as the putrid scent crawled up into my nose and sheer panic filled my veins. Just a whiff, but suddenly my nose stung. I slithered up to the second set of shutters and hesitated. Hair on the back of my neck stood up. The willow covered up the house from the sky, but if someone walked the swamp, they'd still see it. Kind of hard not to. I gently shut the second set. As I moved to the third set, my nose flinched, and my face scrunched. A scent so acidic, like a rotten lime stuffed up my nose. I shoved my back to the wall and edged closer to the window.

Leo Ashwood lurked shin deep in the swamp water like the slender man of swamp monsters. Our eyes met and I knew that no amount of closed shutters would solve my problem. My monster followed me! He was capable enough to track me. Despite magic, despite my aunt's spells, he'd tracked me back to my home and got me alone. He trapped me.

I'd never brought anyone back to life...And my first attempt I brought back fucking Houdini.

My eyes snapped to the book and wished I fought harder to stay with my aunt. All the eyes narrowed in on me as I sank steadily to the ground. My knees stung as I crawled deathly slow across the floor. The natural sounds of the swamp hushed around the house. I held my breath as I slithered across the floor, eyes dead set on the book. Her shield spell was inside, used to guard someone from bodily harm. If I could get to the book and recite it with a drop of my own blood, I could enhance it. Hope filled my fingertips as I reached up to the counter toward the book, until the front door burst open and I launched face first into the cabinets. The book flew into my arms, and I hugged it tightly. My legs wobbled but held firm as I scrambled to my feet.

I bolted down the left side of the house toward the back porch. Thunder filled my ears as Leo Ashwood chased after me. A howl that could scare off elephants in a full charge filled the house. The floor cracked and whined as his feet broke through some of the weaker floorboards.

A yelp of fear broke through my lips as a meaty hand connected with the right side of my body. Everything stopped in time for a moment. Then I forcibly broke through the hallway window. Freefall sent my body into shock. My house was now several feet above me, my monster looming in the broken window. Swamp moss and water slapped my back and I sunk into the earth. The book clung to my chest. I kicked my feet through the murky water. My death descended upon me like a black cloud on a sunny day.

Leo Ashwood flung his huge form out the window. His massive splash threw me across the water only to be yanked back by a large hand. I screamed. My fingers slipped, and the book flew behind me as Leo Ashwood launched me in the opposite direction.

The memory of his apartment flashed before my eyes. There on the marble floor, knife in hand, tears poured down my cheeks. Leo loomed over me then with rage in his eyes, only to catch his reflection in the knife as I held it up. A monster, he looked the same inside and out now. Snot trickled down from my nose as I trembled, knife held up to him. I tried not to break down before my death. Then he tossed himself out the window and left me in a puddle of blood and surrounded by bodies.

I could not afford to freeze again. As I skittered across the ground, my back collided with one of the pillars of the house. Something in me snapped, just like it had back there... before I lost all sense, before I murdered him in cold blood and tried to bring Berry back. An abyss crawled over my senses and logic. I saw red. Bloody hands clapped together and the world stopped. Magic tickled my flesh as bones and bodies shot to the top of the swamp.

Leo whipped to face me, his mouth unhinged in a tree shaking roar. All his luxurious hair had been ripped out of his scalp and his eyes bulged, too big for their sockets; he no longer looked like the recluse millionaire he once was. He was a monster. He was my mess. He was my problem to deal with!

I raised my hands over my head. Bones of creatures snapped together, meat and flesh from corpses filled the joints and in the blink of an eye, a new monster stood before me—a vassal, larger than anything I'd ever mashed together. Thralls were a simple creatures meant for one task. Half mismatched bones, half rotten flesh and swamp moss, my newest creation lumbered a foot taller than Leo with the jaw of an alligator and the hands of a man. My newest monster lunged across the water toward Leo and tossed him into the air and through a handful of thin trees. With its prey in sight, my newest creation lunged with the curl of my fists.

Leo stumbled and his meaty hands broke through the trees he attempted to leverage himself against. My beast slashed him across his torso and freed a long stretch of flesh from his body. Blackened lungs wiggled between molded rib bones. Leo's hands slapped to his chest. He flung himself from me, away from the willow tree, and away from my beast. The latter grabbed a hold of his arms and twirled him in the air. Leo kicked out and broke chipped, rotten bones off my creation. Two halves of a beast lunged at him wildly. The roar from Leo's lips shook the swamp as he jerked further from me.

I kept my hands steady, my magic lit up my insides in a blissful way. A wicked smile crawled upon my lips as Leo screeched loudly enough to shake the thin trees. He burst across the swamp, his legs stuck in secret pockets of mud and deep water. I leapt over logs and slid down muddy banks, and my creations lunged after him. Like two dogs after a bleeding meat truck, they swiped and bit at him as new body parts appeared and snapped together. Awe and fascination struck me at my beast's transformation. Antlers, thin and sharp, sprouted from the jaw as it hunched down on all four legs. The skeletal form expanded sharply and muscles squeezed around the frame. Swamp moss and water dribbled down its new spine as serpent-like heads snapped at Leo from within my creation's chest. I was unstoppable... Until the surge of power turned off.

I deflated like a balloon as exhaustion crept up my spine. My body sank into the swamp. Horror filled my face as Leo came to a complete halt. Both skeleton thralls fell off of him and splashed down into the swamp. Knees deep in moss and water, I sat alone and without magic. My arms ached, my magic ran out, and I was left to face my monster.

Leo Ashwood whirled to face me and tossed both arms out beside him. I recoiled, my arms up in defense. No ace up my sleeve. The exhaustion I bandaged over with the life of the Tweed Suit Guy was just that, a Band-Aid.

He left me empty handed. Run! My hands dug into the earth and I tossed myself to my feet.

He let out a roar as I whirled on my toes. I pumped my arms and I raced in any direction away from him. The water trembled beneath his feet. The ground turned to quicksand under me. If my aunt found me, I would be just another body lingering below the water of the swamp.

At least she'd never know it was me who created the monster.

Chapter Eight

Cecelia Tries to Save the Day

What have I done... What have I made... What can I do...

Again? How! How is it always her I see the clearest of all? Foreign, alien panic filled my veins. My lungs collapsed and sheer terror dug its icy fingers into my body. My dreams meant something. The visions, the connection, it had to mean I was meant for something! Quinn was going to die! I was the only one who knew where she was! Fight the terror!

I shot up off of Jess's couch and straight to my feet. Jess barked out a snort of confusion as she rose to life in the recliner. The Netflix screen judged us with its 'are you still watching' message. We'd skipped through multiple episodes in our sleep of some anime she clicked on to fill the air. Dreams mashed together with the vision and my brain was bogged down with words. Quinn, her face clear as day behind my eyes. Pinched in fear, she cried out into the night. Clarity ran a shiver down my spine and cleansed my skull of sleepiness. I rubbed my face but the panic that fueled my veins was real. It wasn't mine, but it was real. Quinn! She was in danger.

"The monster!" My body flopped onto the floor and up onto my feet. I attempted to run toward the front door. Then my knee connected with the coffee table and I clattered to the floor. Jess let out a sleepy chuckle. I clawed my way back up onto my hands and feet, then stood upright. "I meant to do that."

"Liar," Jess snickered. "Go back to sleep. We have a test tomorrow."

"I can't," I whispered softly, as to let Jess's father slumber, who was a kind man who let me sleep over whenever I wanted as long as he got his sleep. My jacket fell into my hand as I slapped around on the couch for it. In my rubber ducky pajamas, sneakers haphazardly tossed on my feet, I found the keys to my car. Jess sat up fully.

"Whoa, where you going?" she croaked as she rubbed her face in circles.

I winced as she moved from her reclined position in her chair. "I told you—the monster," I whispered as I blindly searched for my phone and wallet. I found both tucked beside the couch next to my bookbag. I stuffed my phone and wallet into the pockets of my jacket and left my bag on the ground.

"What?" Jess blinked rapidly.

I raced around the couch, my hands in my hair to tame it. A scrunchy pinched and pulled my hair but there was no time to brush it. "I'll explain at school tomorrow. Just... don't freak out." I hesitated at the front door. Jess stared at me as I held onto the doorknob. Silence filled the air between us as I locked eyes with her. My hands trembled. Halfway off the recliner, Jess dug her fingers into the arm of the chair.

"Can you promise me that you'll be at school tomorrow?" she growled, her eyes alive with concern and frustration. I shook my head. "Ce!"

"Stay here! Please!" I squeaked as I ripped the door open, and I tossed myself out her door and into the night air. The dream was fresh behind my eyes. This was it, the time my visions got me killed. Panic forced me to drop my keys once as I scrambled toward the car. Jess knocked things over from inside her house as the porch lights flipped on.

Despite the fact it was forty-five degrees in January, I was on fire. My skin prickled as I raced across her driveway. My car door creaked as I shoved myself inside. The front door opened and flooded the driveway with light. Frosty air forced me to pull my jacket on inside my tiny Toyota Corolla. I cranked the vehicle on despite the sound of gravel crunching under Jess's boots. I spared her an apologetic look then threw the car into motion.

My wheels spun gravel out behind me as I shot up the rocky driveway. I blasted the heater as a replacement for the air my lungs refused to produce. Cold air sliced my skin. My throat and cheeks were still red hot as the rest of me shivered. Jess stood in my rear view, eyes on the red lights of my breaks illuminating the small home behind me. If this vision killed me, it would never hurt her. I wouldn't let it! Quinn's pain-filled face haunted me as I steadied my hands on the steering wheel.

Quinn was in the middle of an even tinier town to the west of me, almost all the way to Hugo, which was a miracle in itself because she was on foot. She ran out of the tree line into the center of town. Barefoot, covered in mud and leaves, she gasped for air before she collapsed on the street. Car lights crawled over her and fear sunk into my stomach. Except, the car's lights cut off and suddenly the night was illuminated by a fire as the car crashed nose first into the street. A monster the size of my house loomed over Quinn in the fire light.

The name Leo Ashwood repeated in my head as I pushed the gas pedal down. Leo Ashwood would break her neck and throw her into the car fire, the vision told me, along with her. It would make at least four deaths in total in one night. Horror crept up my spine and tightened my jaw. I watched Quinn die. What was worse, I witnessed her die through her eyes. Large hands grabbed her neck and throttled her like a chicken. My right hand left the comforts of my sleeve and the steering wheel to rub my throat. In the dream, I watched in shock as I flew through the air and into the fire. Organs clenched tight as the image replayed over in my head. This vision had not happened yet.

I was meant to save Quinn. Why my visions showed her to me in the first place, why I connected with her... it had to mean I was meant to save her. If it didn't mean to save her, then why did my magic turn from mundane to extreme? I only saw chicken farms, stubbed toes, and magic screens up until this moment. Why her?

"Why me?" I whined as I whirled around a corner too fast. The car lurched but stayed upright with all wheels on the ground. The soft murmur of the radio fried my nerves. After I flicked it off, panic and reality settled into my bones. "I'm about to drive twenty or more minutes in the middle of the night just to...what? Scream at her not to die?"

I hit the gas pedal harder. The truth was I couldn't do much, but not doing anything would be worse. My Corolla roared as I soared through stop signs and caution lights. In a tiny town any time after sunset there would be no one but deer on the roads. The chirp from my phone made me jerk and the car swiveled in and out of the lane. I clumsily shoved it into my bra strap as I accepted it and hit the screen for the speaker phone.

"I gotta know, what is going on?" Jess begged as she inhaled slowly. Cigarettes. The reverberated chirp of crickets and frogs meant the back porch. I could picture Jess sitting there, wrapped up in a jacket, two cigarettes in her lap with a lighter she stashed in the floorboard of the porch. She called it her 'thinking' spot. Jess sighed, and I imagined the smoke as it billowed out of her nose.

"Why are you smoking at three a.m.?" I laughed, the heat finally built up in the engine to warm my numb finger tips. The world around me was pitch black, not even street lights. Only a good thirty feet was visible ahead of me due to the flatness of the road. Nothing was but roads and trees for miles. The deer tended to stay closer to the hilly end of the road. As the thought popped into my head I quietly knocked on my steering wheel, just in case.

"Why are you driving like a lunatic at three a.m.?" Jess countered as she let out a low, slow breath.

"Quinn, she's in trouble." I sighed as I forced myself to slow down. An actual stop light flooded my eyes as I came to the edge of town. Red illuminated the street and showed a pack of bats and birds huddled on its wires and poles for warmth. This stop light sat before the train tracks, the last stop for over thirty miles. There was only one road with no speed limit sign as the only connection from one town to the other. The only light came from the stop light as it kicked to green. I shot across the road. My heart thundered in my throat. My jaw tight, I nearly choked on tension.

"The same Quinn who murdered a guy by touching him?" The confusion and grumble in her voice made me question myself more. It was hard to do, but Jess had perfected the 'that sounds like a dumb idea' tone and used it on me often.

"Yup!" I squeaked.

"You know how asinine this sounds, right?" Jess sighed. There was a sizzle on the other end of the phone, then a thud. She would have put the cigarette into the cup of rainwater on the back porch and kicked out her feet against the banister. We sat there practically every time I spent the night as we ate dinner—a rickety porch her mother built with her bare hands to make their tiny house feel more like a home. When we sat there, I felt like Jess and I were still young, munching on bland spaghetti as her mother built another table or desk for some rich New York mogul who wanted a hand-crafted piece for a cabin they bought to only use three days a year. Jess and I also spread her mother's ashes under the same porch.

"He's going to kill her, Jess. Or that thing is going to kill her. I don't think he's a person anymore. I can't tell what he is, but he's...he's a monster," I blabbered. My fingers tightened around the steering wheel as I searched the road for any signs of wildlife. I wanted to turn around, but then again, I wanted to stomp my gas pedal to the floor and fly through the night. An urge of unknown proportions rolled around in my tight stomach and fueled me forward.

"So you're going to what?" She cut through me with a single sentence. My mouth hung open for a long moment.

I licked my lips nervously, "I haven't figured that out yet."

"Ce, you see the future, you're not some battle mage," she huffed.

My heart sank for some reason. She was right. I didn't have magic, not like some of the people in my dreams. Emma could enchant mundane items, she made things! Her magic crafted objects into magical instruments. What did I do? Spy on people in my sleep? Quinn had magic, actual, legitimate magic. And I was useless...

What have I done! Her words resurfaced in my mind and I steeled my nerves. It didn't matter! I had to try!

"I have to try," I murmured as I gripped the steering wheel. Tears threatened my eyes as I forced my shoulders to stay flat against the chair.

"Okay, well, then make me a promise." The wood creaked as Jess moved across the deck, and wind blew into the receiver of the phone. "I don't care if you save Quinn, I don't know her, but I know you, and you have to promise me you will come home. If you can't stop the future, then come home immediately. Ce, you better promise me you'll come home."

"I promise."

I might have lied.

In the silence, I hung up the phone and tucked it into the cup holder. My heart fought me the whole way down the road. The night sky darkened despite the stars as the dream replayed in my head. She battled her way out the brush, exhausted and low on magic. That is where I can help her. If I got her back the energy or even got her out before he found her, she might stand a chance.

The town came upon me swiftly and there was no time to figure it out. Bright lights blinded me; buildings sprung out of the ground. It grew from a small sparse collection of buildings and homes to an actual town. Then I hit the brakes as a hospital came into view. Out front in the parking lot the car from my vision idled, lights on, ready to move. Two adults and a teenager clambered into the vehicle and I slowed my car down. They swiftly flipped on their turn signal lights and the car crawled from the parking lot. They would run into the monster first. That's when the worst idea came to mind and my anxiety spiked in my veins.

I cut off my lights and made my seat belt extra tight. The minivan crept along the exit to the hospital and as they left the safety of the curb, I floored it. My Corolla hit thirty miles per hour before I smacked the rear end of their minivan and spun them to face me. The airbag in my Corolla half deployed out of the steering wheel before it deflated and the whole car screamed with bells.

"Well, it's best that I found out you don't work on my terms," I snarled as I cut off the engine and threw off my seat belt.

My anxiety returned like a boulder on my chest as a large man in a cowboy hat and leather boots stepped out of the driver's side of the minivan. In the shadows of his hat and the space between street lights, I couldn't see his face or inside the van. But they were safe and stopped. Then he raised a finger toward me. Oh yeah...I flung open the door and did my best: I ran.

I bolted between the vehicles and booked it across the street. My arms pumped at my sides as I realized the only thing in my hands were my keys, my wallet, and phone were in the car. As if it would make a difference—they would call the police and take down my plate. Gretchen would ground me and I would take a driver's course over the weekend at the courthouse, then I could forget that I purposely drove into someone's car. If only I could explain.

"Hey! Wait!" Someone shouted from behind me.

And my body lurched. My feet halted and my heart nearly stopped, my mind suddenly out of sync with my limbs. Frozen in place, my chest turned into a techno concert full of tap dancers. Tears formed in my eyes as someone chased after me. Steadily, my body loosened. A hand nearly grazed my back before I flung myself further. If I spared a look back, I would only lose my nerve. I ran with the knowledge that something stopped me in my tracks and that something ran after me. It was like magic.

"Stop!" My legs stopped and I crumbled to the ground. Ungracefully, my cheeks spread asphalt into my pores. My fingers clenched along the rocks as I flipped over.

On my back, I glanced up to a blonde teenager who wheezed for air. Her hands to her knees, she coughed and gasped for air as she hovered over me. Then her eyes opened. "You!"

"Oh shoot." I clawed my way backward. I knew her. Oh no! She knew me!

"You?" She cocked a brow.

"You!" I laughed nervously. Maggie Walton, the single most popular girl in all of town and YouTube star... also the sister of Martin, whom I stopped from the death of two chickens that labelled me as 'that weird girl' in school for all days... stared down at me in confusion and fury.

"What the hell was that?" she growled.

"Um, well, that's kinda—it's complicated—"

"You slammed into us!" she barked before her hands flew to her mouth. Maggie coughed hard and her whole body jerked. I blinked rapidly as bloody fingers peeled away from her mouth and a dark liquid dribbled down her lips toward her chin.

"Ma-Ma-Ma-Maggie?" I stuttered in shock as my eyes flew open wide. She swallowed, her hands clenched.

"Don't you dare—"

Time's up. The hairs on my arms and back of my neck turned into steel spears on my flesh. The ground rumbled and my heart sank into my stomach. Maggie and I locked eyes. The lights flickered before they cut off completely as a massive body flew into view. It landed a foot behind Maggie from the sky, a meteor launched from off the top of a nearby building. The monster was the size of a house, made of pieces of a human, eyes that glowed like jack-o-lanterns in the dark of the street.

"There... you... are..."

"It speaks!" I cried out.

"I'm not crazy!" Maggie screeched seconds before the beast launched forward. It was more surreal than my dream. Skin red and purple and grey, its flesh burst at the seams with blood and pus. Its eyes were twice the natural size and a body expanded thrice what should be humanly possible. The veins on its chunky hands popped under the skin as it clenched its fists. Only a small clump of hair on the lower back side of the skull, like the rest fell out or was forced out of his skin.

"Leo Ashwood." The words fell from my lips as the monster took hold of the lamp post nearest us. Maggie stumbled back; her knees wobbled. I clambered to my feet in slow, calculated movements. Leo Ashwood ripped the lamp post out of the ground like it was a common garden weed.

"You know this thing!" Maggie whirled to look at me.

"Not exactly." I grimaced. Something in me screamed, much like a pot whistle inside my head. Without a second thought, I yanked Maggie's hand and yanked her toward me. The lamppost flew past our faces within inches of our noses. The ground trembled as Leo Ashwood ripped another weed lamp post and swung it at us. We dropped to the ground with short lived screams. Panic filled my stomach as I scrambled backward. Maggie clawed her hand into mine before she flipped on her hands and knees. We struggled to our feet before we burst across the road.

"How do you know its name?" Maggie howled. There was a crack that filled the air. I felt a flick to the back of my skull, and my spine shivered as a chill ran up the flesh on my arms. Something clicked in me as I yanked my hand from hers and shoved us both to the ground. The lamppost flew over our heads and crashed before us. Maggie's eyes were saucers in her skull as I stared at the lamppost. "How did you do that?"

A scream filled the air for only a second. Guttural and sharp, it ran tingles up my body.

"I... um..." I swallowed before I clambered back up to my feet. My head snapped to peer behind me like an idiot and fear bit into my stomach. Maggie clambered to her feet, and her hand yanked mine to her side in fear. The monster lumbered only a few inches from us with a new lamp post and an arm. "Where did he get that?"

"Seer... tiny... seer..."

Blood dribbled out of the arm in tiny spurts. The arm steamed at the joints as the air grew colder by proximity. Tears trickled down my cheeks as I peered up into the face of Leo Ashwood. Lips spread open more on the right than on the left to expose a skeleton not attached to the muscles and skin. Rot infested his mouth from his teeth to his jaw.

Maggie whimpered to my left. I swallowed hard on vomit that threatened my stature. Another foot back, there lay a body. It wasn't Quinn, it wasn't the cowboy, it wasn't anyone I knew. An innocent person who stepped out at the wrong time.

"Scream... siren..."

I snapped to life, my eyes fell on Maggie. Tears streamed down her face as she clenched down on my hand. Her lips quivered as she stumbled back a step. I squeezed her hand back as we stepped back together. This was it... how I died. My throat tightened as I swallowed and stared right into the monster's lit-up eyes.

"Leo Ashwood!" The street went quiet as the monster's yellow beams moved from Maggie and I to something behind us. I slowly turned in place to the voice from behind us. Quinn stood in the flesh two feet down from me. Not a shower illusion, not a dream, a real Quinn with blood lust in her eyes and a box cutter in her hand. A crooked smirk crawled on her lips as her eyes fell from the monster down to me. She winked at me. "Ah! The seer in my dreams, good to finally meet you in person!"

Chapter Nine

Maggie Walton Just Wants a Nap.

"Who. The. Fuck. Is. *That*?" I ground out between my teeth, on my hands and knees as Birdo Baggins and I crawled through yet another bush. Cecelia Montreal or Birdo Baggins as Kitty labelled her in middle school. The weird girl who burst into our yard one day to tell Martin not to kill these two chickens. I thought it was because they were her chickens, but after she saved my neck from two death swings by the monster, I started to think maybe she knew something I didn't. I needed to ask her what would have happened if he did.

"Her name is Quinn," Birdo- Cecelia whispered as she huddled next to me. The ground rumbled again as the monster lunged and tumbled into another building. As if my night couldn't get any weirder, a girl broke out of the trees and went toe to toe with Frankenstein's monster. I snapped my head to look at Cecelia.

First, I woke up in the hospital, not sure how that happened, with my parents in pieces. They sobbed as they explained to me how they found me. They were sorry they made me feel this way, what was I thinking, and so many other things. I wasn't even able to speak, let alone explain I didn't drive my car into a post on purpose or anything. Had I been frantic and depressed all day? Sure! Had I been weirdly dark and broody? Definitely! But my car crash was not my fault! And thanks to a detective who swore up and down it had to have been a hit and run, I was free to leave the hospital with my parents. Then, within two minutes in the van, my parents tried to grill me for my outburst. Thankfully, or unfortunately, we were rear ended by a car in the dark!

"How do you know all of this?" I hissed.

"I... um..." She clammed up again and I rolled my eyes. Leave it to the Birdo to freeze up. I planted my hands to the ground and steeled myself to move until I saw it again. The monster flew over the bush and into another building behind us. My body froze and suddenly, I hated Cecelia a lot less. Bones made of cement, skin made of marble, I trembled inside that bush. "Maggie?"

I shivered as I lowered myself back to the ground. Foliage covered my sight of the world around me. Cecelia reached out and took one of my hands. My neck muscles loosened just enough to turn and I saw the fear in her eyes. "I drove into it yesterday."

"What?" Cecelia craned her neck to peer behind us. She jerked both of us to the right suddenly. I rolled us out of the bush and into a new one seconds before a foot the size of my keyboard smashed through the brush.

"I ran my truck into it, then it threw me in the air and... that's all I remember of yesterday."

Cecelia stared at me in concern. For a second, the wheels turned in her head. She was going to ask, I could see it etched in her scrunched brows and pursed lips. A nosey, goody two-shoes since middle school, Cecelia wanted to pry. Her lips quivered before she let out a sigh. "I, um, saw this happening."

"You what?" I hissed. "You knew this would happen?"

"Kinda. Sort of. Not necessarily this. But I saw the monster, and he killed... oh no." Her eyes shot open in panic. "In my vision, it was your car."

"What? You're speaking gibberish, Birdo." I shook my head. Her eyebrows knitted and my mouth hung open. Frustration didn't cover what burned inside me as I sank lower to the ground next to her. "Sorry."

"It's all right, I'm used to it," she muttered before she peered up through the foliage. My mouth opened to speak again but she left me speechless. A hand grabbed me around the waist and hoisted me up into the air like a crane. Cecelia let out a scream as my throat closed up entirely. All I could hear was the doctor.

No singing, no screaming, talk very low, learn sign language. If I screamed, my vocal cords might burst again, like they did in the truck. My magic barely held them together as it was. If I screamed, it would escalate things. Back when Cecelia hit the car, I wasn't thinking. I demanded she stop and wait, and her body halted, unable to deny my request. My magic grew stronger as the cancer destroyed my body, and I could do nothing about it. I should let the monster eat me, just get it over with. Yet, panic flowed through me as the beast twisted me to look him in the face. That wicked grin, the gross pus that seeped out as his mouth opened, I couldn't help it. I screamed.

The beast howled in pain as it dropped me to the ground. I wouldn't stop; magic thrummed within me. My feet hit the ground and I stood sturdy. A blood curdling scream turned into a soprano C and I felt... fine. Relief spread through my body and I cracked bones left stiff for days again. Butterflies filled my stomach as I spread my arms out and held out the note. The monster clawed at its ears and face clumsily; its fingers peeled away layers of flesh that crumbled to the ground. All the beauty and soothing relief stopped completely in an instant. I gagged and the note died in a horrible pitch at the back of my throat.

Blood splashed the inside of my throat before I coughed it up onto the ground. My knees buckled.

"A siren?" Everything blurred as a body stepped into my vision. I blinked hard to focus on the swamp girl. She stood in front of me, her eyes wide and mouth hung open. "I've only heard stories..."

"Quinn! Look out!" Her hands snatched me by the bicep and jerked the both of us to the left. The monster lunged at us in the blink of an eye and flung itself at us repeatedly. My hands clung to the girl in desperation. Limbs turned to pudding and spots colored my sight, but I found her face in the blur. Her left eye blue, right eye green, and they both glistened like shattered colored glass behind candles. She grinned down at me. Then I stared at the large gash across her nose.

"It's been a while since I've seen a siren...alive, that is." She chuckled seconds before we landed on the ground. She grunted as we ran into something stiff. A cough shook my internal organs and blood sprayed out my mouth. My blood splashed over her face. I sank through her hands to the rubble beneath us. My head tumbled back against a rock and the pain dulled as it felt like my soul separated from my body. I floated over my body as I peered up to her face, spots steadily filled my vision till only swamp girl existed in my vision.

She cocked her head to the side and bent over me. The spots broke away as her hands cupped my cheek. Horror jerked my soul back into my body and pain lit up my body... the blood soaked into her skin. A wide grin grew across her lips as she looked over my face. "Your blood, it's tainted!"

"Gee, thanks." I swallowed the cough until the tickle at the back of my throat grew too intense, then I coughed hard.

She put her hand in front of my mouth and let out a low chuckle. I eyed her, my mouth unhinged as she wiped the blood off the bottom of my lip with her pointer finger. She poked her finger into her mouth and sucked it clean. "What the—"

"Quinn!" Cecelia squealed from the other side of the road.

She jerked her head up in time to shove a hand out before the monster. Her palm pressed back against his fist and my stomach plummeted. I sank lower down into the rubble as she spread her stance and fought back. A swing from her right hand landed square on the monster's cheek. It flew away from us like she'd hit it with a carnival hammer. The monster clattered to the ground, some '90s cartoon villain slain by a poorly dressed hero. An evil laugh broke her lips as she looked down at me.

"What did you do?" I sputtered as the spots grew in my vision again. My hand jerked out to take her hand again. She hoisted me up onto my feet and the spot faded from my vision. "How are you doing this?"

"You don't know what you are, do you?" Her voice was soft, a cold press to the roaring fire within my throat, and her eyes burned through my skull.

A hot blush ran across my face and my bones gathered back up into my body. "I sing and it...does stuff. Sometimes when I just speak," I muttered as my eyes shot to Cecelia. She broke into a run across the road toward us. "What are you two?"

"You're a witch, much like her and me." Quinn nodded at Cecelia with a wide, toothy grin. I could breathe! I inhaled hungrily as she held onto me without a second thought. Relief spread through my vocal chords. The world filled my nostrils again. Quinn stunk like a swamp. She wore a t-shirt so faded and soaked I couldn't see anything on it other than the blood, and a pair of ripped, drenched jeans that stuck to her like they were painted on. Quinn let out a low chuckle, "Hi, Seer."

"Uh-oh, hey, so... yeah." Cecelia shut down before my eyes as a huge blush flooded her pale face. Her brown eyes shot to the ground; her fingers fiddled with her pajama top. I realized suddenly that she wore ducky pajamas to this fight she had foreseen.

I let out a snort as I pointed at her attire. "Nice pajamas."

"Look, I didn't have time to change," she whined.

"So, then my theory is right—you saw this in a vision?" Quinn sighed as she turned from both of us to stare in the direction the monster fell. "And he's gone. Great."

"Yeah! Great! That's a good thing," I huffed.

"Not great," she shot back as she snapped back my direction. "You heard him speak—he's learning. He's not just a walking corpse, he's still Ashwood, but worse. He's a consuming, hunting, thinking—"

"Monster strength and cannibal Leo Ashwood," Cecelia butted in with a grimace on her face.

Quinn furrowed her brows as she looked to Cecelia with concern. Her nose scrunched and accentuated the gash across it, her lips pursed into a thin line. "How do you know his name?" Quinn snapped, her body lurched toward Cecelia.

Cecelia stumbled back a step with her hands up. "Because you know it... Look, I'm not completely sure on the whole matter, but we should probably leave now." Cecelia wheeled around to see the road around us. I searched the buildings as noise kicked up. What was once a silent street was now full of whispers and lights as they flickered on. We stood in the yard of someone's home as their porch light snapped on.

"What for?" Quinn cocked a brow. I shot her a confused look.

"This town isn't exactly deserted. He ate someone, someone's bound to call—" My voice fell to the wayside.

Sirens flooded the air and the three of us booked it down the road. Cecelia headed the pack of us as Quinn held me up as best she could. We ran for the cars. Well, Quinn ran, I did my best. My parents watched in shock as we barreled towards them. Well...I hobbled, and Quinn barreled after Cecelia.

"What is going on!" my father boomed as Cecelia dove into the driver's seat just to snatch up two items. She fumbled to pull something out of her wallet when Quinn and I caught up with her. I expected Quinn to stop, but she didn't.

"I'm so sorry, Mr. and Mrs. Walton—" Quinn linked arms with Cecelia and continued our run straight past my parents. I lurched toward them, my hand out. My mother stood in utter shock as I locked eyes with her. My father jumped toward me but stumbled inches short as Quinn shot out of reach of both of them. Police cars filled the horizon and ambulances left the hospital in packs. My heart turned to a packet of fireworks trapped in my chest, all on fire.

"There's no time, come on," Quinn barked, a crazed look in her shattered glass eyes.

I made an attempt to look back at my parents, but the world blurred. In Quinn's arms, my death was pushed aside. I should have stopped and demanded to go home with my parents but then I found the blood on my clothes. The monster grabbed me with his blood covered fingers, and it was all over my sweatpants and jacket my parents brought to the hospital. There was no way I could stick around and answer questions from the cops.

Yeah, his blood is on me, but like suspiciously in a handprint form? I could feel the handcuffs already as Quinn lifted both Cecelia and me from the main road and into the treeline. Swiftly, she tossed me over one shoulder and wheeled Cecelia to run beside her. I watched from Quinn's back as the town lit up in police lights and sirens filled the air. All of it disappeared behind trees. The night swallowed up the world and left me on the shoulder of a witch I didn't know, with a witch I did know. I was a witch.

I was a witch...

"Stop!" I barked and Quinn and Cecelia froze. With a shove to her shoulders, I stumbled away from Quinn. I wavered side to side until she grabbed my hand and I steadied on the grass. "What is going on? What was that thing? Where are we running? Why do you make the cancer stop?"

"Cancer? You have cancer?" Cecelia squeaked.

I refused to look her in the eyes as the pain and pity radiated off her in waves. A scowl etched onto my face.

"Cancer—is that what taints your blood? It ravages your blood like nothing I've ever felt before!" Quinn beamed as she squeezed my hand.

I grimaced; my body recoiled but I held a firm grip on her.

"Could you not?" I swallowed hard before I blinked, my eyebrows knitted. Quinn cocked her head to the side, shoulders slumped in confusion.

"How did I not know you had cancer?" Cecelia whispered as she examined my face. She stepped behind Quinn to look directly at me, thus denying me the chance to ignore her. I shot her a dirty glare and then moved in Quinn's direction.

"Not what?" Quinn shrugged with a cocked brow. "Can I not what?"

"Be creepy?" I snapped, my lips pursed into a thin line.

"I wasn't." She recoiled with a grimace. Slowly she looked away from both of us, as if to scan the forest. Her back straightened and her nostrils flared in a way that sent my hairs on edge. Quinn searched the area, eyes lit up in the dark. Then she relaxed and shook her head. "False alarm, he barreled through here, the scent of his blood is old and fading."

"See, that, that right there is creepy," I barked before I glared at Cecelia. Her ducky pajamas were covered in dirt and grass stains, her zipper hoodie ripped and burnt in two or three places. What surprised me the most was how messy her hair was. In school Cecelia was clean and well groomed. "What did you get me involved in?"

"Me?" She clutched her chest. "You chased me, remember?"

"Yeah! Only after you hit our van and bolted from the scene of the crime!" A hand clamped over my mouth and I wheeled backward. Quinn pulled her hand away before she put her finger to her lips.

"Leo Ashwood isn't here, but the police are. Maybe we could finish this conversation at a safer location." She hushed me and nudged both Cecelia and me with her hand. I stomped beside her as she led us by the arm across the mossy ground. Thick forest turned to soft ground and mushy grass. The foliage darkened and the trees spread out as we traipsed through the swamp. Paths of fuzzy forest creatures turned to sloppy footsteps and fallen tree husks. My eyes followed the ground; I was unable to let go of Quinn's hand, but I did not want to lean on her. Step by step, I focused on just the journey. Cecelia spoke maybe three words, most of them grunts and curse words as we blindly followed Quinn through the pitch-black swamp lands.

Exhaustion seeped into my bones and I transformed into a lump of body parts. I blinked away sleep as she pulled us over rocks and through the trees. My body leaned into hers, my legs unable to hold me up fully. Quinn switched to slide an arm around my midsection as my head fell against her shoulders with a hard thud. We stopped for a moment as I wavered in and out. Quinn looked as worse for wear as sweat poured down her face. She switched to have Cecelia on the other side of me. One arm over Quinn's shoulder, one over Cecelia's, a sack of wet, moldy potatoes.

"How do you even know where to go?" Cecelia whispered, the silence finally broken.

"I have spent my whole life in the forest and swamps, just like you drive the roads. But... I don't use gas." Quinn sent a smile Cecelia's way. A blush lit up Cecelia's face even in the dark. "Though, I admit I got turned around a bit while he chased me. If I knew I was this close to town, I would have never led him straight here."

"Why was it chasing you anyway?" I grumbled, one eye open. She set me down as she patted a log and put a hand out to Cecelia.

Quinn went silent as she helped Cecelia over a dark log, then turned to aid me. Her eyes fell to the ground as she hoisted me up. "He's mad I killed him."

"Uh, excuse me?" I choked as she sat me back down.

"What?" Cecelia wheeled back toward us both.

"It's kind of a long story, okay?" Quinn cut through both of us and continued to trudge on. Cecelia scooped up my side again, and Quinn tossed my arm over her shoulder. I dragged my feet across the ground, my sneakers full to the brim of sludge. I wanted to pull back, but I knew the outcome. If I let go or pushed Quinn away, I would fall unconscious, but this time, it would be worse than before. She was the only thing that worked and so I let her drag my half alive body. But Cecelia, I wasn't sure why she followed us. I looked to the right, directly at her and found her eyes on me.

"Maggie, when did—"

"Can we not talk about it?" I scowled.

"Yeah, sure, no problem." She looked away.

"Maybe we should just not talk until we get there," Quinn suggested with a sigh.

"Where is there?" Cecelia looked past us. Quinn situated me higher up on her shoulders and brought both Cecelia and I closer to her torso. My shoulders ached with the height difference. Cecelia was at least five foot nine, compared to my five foot five stature which towered over Quinn who maybe pushed five foot three. My head flopped to the side as both Cecelia and I looked to Quinn.

"The swamp. My house, my aunt will know what to do," she muttered nearly under her breath.

Chapter Ten

Quinn Foster Lies Again

"Quinn! Skies above, you're okay!" The sunrise broke over the swamp water as I carried the siren's half dead body across the threshold. The seer trudged along with me, sluggish but her steps were the equivalent of one of mine. Darlin lingered at the edge of the porch with her book clutched to her chest. The evidence that my aunt spent most of the night tearing the swamp apart to find me filled my vision: Pieces of beasts used as eyes to scout for me covered the ground, and small animals feasted on their magically created corpses. My nostrils filled with the scent of thick magic in the air. Serias and Amendir lingered at the door, their eyes on me and the two with me. I suddenly wished I hadn't thought to bring them here. The coven obviously already knew about the monster, or else they wouldn't be here. Serias the collector and Amendir the teacher, the only other elders, other than Darlin, of a family of witches. A coven I was expected to join when I turned of age. "Who are your guests?"

I grinned up tiredly at Darlin as she clambered down the porch steps to the soggy land below us. "Well, this is..."

"Cecelia." The seer spoke up with a tired smile of her own.

"She's the seer I told you about." I laughed as my eyes nearly forgot to open again. They forced themselves open and I wavered in my steps. "And this is our new siren friend... um... I..."

"That's Maggie," Cecelia added before she broke in half, hands on her knees. Her body gave way. Mine would do the same if the toxic blood of Maggie's didn't pump my body with poisonous energy. My muscles were exhausted, and my eyes tried to shut completely, but my magic buzzed, like a thousand bees under my fingernails, ready to fight at any moment.

"Is she dead?" Serias snickered as she moved to the banister of the porch. Her bangs shifted to expose the third eye tattoo on her forehead. In the light, the silver lines of the eye seemed to move to stare at me directly. Her hair fell in choppy black and purple waves around her only to enhance the look of all the other tattoos up her exposed arms—all swirled depictions of visions, some she talked about, most she didn't.

"Not right now, but she might be soon." I swallowed hard.

"Why?" Amendir cocked her head. Long black locks fell around her as her hair clip, a white lotus, tumbled down through the broken hole of the porch and fell toward the water. Amendir's face pinched before she snapped her fingers. The clip stopped short of the water and flung itself back up through the hole and into her hair. Amendir was the only person other than Cecelia that I considered tall. She was five foot nine, with hair that fell to her hips, and deep tan skin accented by the pearl clothing that draped from her lithe frame.

"Maggie has cancer," Cecelia whispered as if she were punched in the gut. I spared a glance in her direction; she kept her eyes on her toes as she panted for air.

"Oh, that's a nasty affliction," Darlin sighed, her eyes never leaving me. I smiled up at her, and the worry etched deeper into her face. Relief, her emotions radiated off her skin in waves as she reached out toward me. Her long fingers wrapped around my cheeks and eased the weight of my skull off my neck. I melted into her touch; tears welled in my eyes. She swallowed audibly and let out a low sigh. "When you are both rested, we can see to the cure. The family will find a temporary fix for now."

"What?" Cecelia straightened to her full height.

I wheezed as I tried my hardest to step forward. My legs wobbled and Darlin lurched out to catch me. The basil scent on her clothes wafted around me before I smelled her blood— strong, explosive, like pop rocks in my mouth that turned sour as I nearly dropped Maggie. She groaned but stayed in my arms. Cecelia dragged herself up the stairs as Darlin hoisted Maggie up into her arms. I crawled up the stairs on my hands and feet until I collapsed upon the porch.

"Poor little Quinn—did the big bad monster tire you out?" Serias teased as she hovered over me. I flopped onto my back only to flip my middle finger in her direction. "Aww, really sweetheart, you shouldn't use such cutesy words on me."

I rolled my eyes. "Says the seer who didn't even see the monster coming."

"No one did," she scoffed.

"I did," Cecelia grumbled over her shoulder.

Serias's face fell pale. I grinned to myself as Serias stood tall and put her palms to her leather covered hips. Her mouth hung an inch ajar before she clamped it shut and stared back down to me. It was Amendir who scooped up my arms and dragged me through the house. She carried me like a blanket, weightless in her hands as she dropped me upon the pile of blankets and pillows in the foyer. My head sunk into them.

"Where's Maggie?" I swallowed the sleep for only a moment.

Darlin stepped into view with a soft smile on her lips. "I put her in a healing circle, it will allow her to stay well while you rest up. She will only drain you in your sleep." Darlin knelt in front of me. Her hands were soft and cold against the fires that existed beneath the skin of my cheeks.

I furrowed my brow as she peered over my face lovingly. "Auntie," I murmured. "What drain?"

The words garbled in my mouth as I fought the sleep. I wanted to know what she meant but I couldn't find the energy. Exhaustion sunk into my flesh hard and dragged me further into the pillows. Tears trickled down her face and splashed my cheeks. My body lay numb except to her tears and her hands. I inhaled sharply as pain ran up my insides like a cramp up my entire muscle system.

"Quinn?"

"It hurts," I croaked as my body lurched painfully away from the pillows.

"That's your magic—you've used too much."

"No it's not—"

"Quinn, I'm sorry I never explained your gifts enough, I'm sorry there is nothing I can do but make you sleep it off. I'll explain the leech magic another day, when you can focus and hear me. I promise." And then her tears welled up again, and her voice wavered as she cupped my cheeks.

My eyes clamped closed as she rubbed her thumbs against my cheeks in soothing circles. Pain erupted through my body, miniature explosions jerked my body across the pillows. Darlin held me down as she opened my mouth again. "*Dornumnum...*"

Sleep zapped my system of everything, and my muscles relaxed. "I'm so sorry, sweetheart. I thought if I sent you home, you'd be safe," she whispered as her hands soothed my cheeks, a kiss placed to my forehead.

Sleep took hold of my body and dragged me down into the abyss. The last thing I saw was her face as guilt slithered its way into my mind. My aunt had no idea the monster hunted for me, not because of animalistic need. This was no misuse of magic, no accident in a potion lab— this was my mistake. I tried to fix it, but I needed more power.

Maggie's poisoned blood swam through my brain as I lay in that dark abyss. It floated around me like fairy lights, dancing around my body and lighting up the darkness. My dreams didn't exist here, only my mind floated in the darkness. The blood dissolved around me; the darkness devoured everything.

I shouldn't have been able to bring Leo Ashwood back, but I did. Thralls were easy, as they weren't people—

they were a collection of dead things that did as I commanded. Leo thought his own thoughts, he even learned to speak again. He hunted and realized the danger of my strength with Maggie in my hands, and he made the decision to run. Somehow, I killed a disgusting billionaire witch in his home and brought him back twice as bad. If he relearned his magic, it was over. Whatever his magic was, it was not something I wanted to find out. He needed to die and stay dead this time.

My body jerked and my mind snapped awake. Eyes open wide, I looked to the person who shook me vigorously. "What?"

Cecelia hovered over me, her hands lingered inches from my shoulders. "You were screaming."

"No, I wasn't." I furrowed my brow. My elbows pushed up against the pillows as the light of the day faded behind the treeline. A whole day wasted passed out, and the exhaustion took its toll on my body. I surveyed around the both of us and found the living room empty. Gently, I turned back to her with a cocked brow. Her face fell as she looked around. If I screamed, my aunt would have dropped from the ceiling. The scent of roasted beef and vegetables floated around the circular home; the murmur of talk within the kitchen perked both of our ears.

"It must have been a nightmare." She recoiled backward into the pillows. Her movements allowed me to look her over properly. The shower had been so quick, I never saw much of her. But here, in my home, I couldn't help but stare. Her face was soft with no blemishes or scars, brown eyes like melted chocolate over pretzels, a thin nose and round face. Her fingers wrapped around her shins as she hugged her legs close to her chest.

"Well, thank you for waking me, either way," I chuckled as I let myself back down. My arms stretched out above me a wonderful crack filled the air. Relief spread all the way to my toes as I wiggled them in front of me. Warmth in my bones woke my extremities as I pushed up onto my feet. No pain, no explosions, no toxic blood—I slept it all out of my system. A smile crept on my lips as I glanced through the doorway for any sign of my aunt. They were sitting at the table, the only thing visible was the book, sat up in the doorway, eyes peeled on me. I made a small, curt wave to it before I turned to Cecelia.

"You're welcome?" She flinched. I cocked a brow at her and took a step toward her. She shuffled backward into the pillows from me.

"Are you all right? You seem nervous?" I spread my arms out and bent at the waist to both sides.

"Do I? I hadn't noticed," she stammered, unable to look me in the eyes. Cecelia peered up at me suddenly, her eyes searched my face. "How are you all right with all of this?"

I sighed, hands to my hips. "What part of 'this' are you not 'all right' with?" I used my fingers as quotes, a smirk on my lips. It fell as she stared me down with a worried frown. Her lower lip quivered and tears welled up in her eyes. I dropped to my knees instantly and folded my hands before my waist. "Whoa, whoa."

"We could have died, Quinn," she whimpered as a tear trickled down her right cheek. Then, all at once, the tears rolled down her face, and she broke into a sob. Her hands clutched her pajamas and she buried her face into her knees. She jerked away from my touch before, but I couldn't just let her cry. She was scared! She had every right to be scared.

I hesitated. What could I do? "There's no need for that." I sighed. My right hand reached out to rub her arm. Inches from her bicep, my hand jerked back as she flung herself from my touch. I recoiled with a furrowed brow.

She looked up from her knees. There was fear in her eyes. Fear directed at me. I tumbled back from my heels to my butt, deflated.

"Don't touch me," she snarled, her lip curled aggressively.

I huffed, my face scrunched. "Sorry for trying to comfort you." I scoffed and folded my arms under my chest.

"I saw what you did to Tweed Suit Guy—"

No! Oh no!

"Listen here—" I snatched up her wrist and pulled her close. There was a scream that died deep in her throat as I clamped a hand over her mouth. Her blood smelt like lilac and my stomach clenched. Fireworks exploded in my ears and my heart skipped a beat. I lurched in pain as the compression of my heart radiated through every nerve in my body.

I let go of her and shoved myself away from her. "What was that?" I snapped, my eyes darting from my hands to her face.

Fear pooled in her eyes. "What are you talking about?" she cried in a hushed tone as she pedaled backward on the floor.

"You... Your blood..." My mouth hung open as the thick scent of lilac filled my mouth and ran my tongue dry.

Her blood didn't smell like blood. I swallowed hard. Our eyes connected. "Just, don't talk about him. He was an accident. My aunt doesn't know."

"Do you even know what you did?" she spat under her breath.

I opened my mouth then promptly closed it. With a few swift blinks, I sat back and stared at her in confusion. "Of course, I know what—"

"Do. You. Know. *How*. You. Did. It?" she said with her teeth ground together.

My face fell as her head shook. The leech magic, as Darlin put it. There was nothing in her works that described anything about leech magic. A spell to summon leeches, a potion made with leeches, a healing technique with leeches, but nothing to the effect of what I did. I sighed, my hands ran up to my neck and rubbed the back of it. "I don't."

"Then how are you sure you won't do it to me?"

I blinked, my eyes shot up to meet hers. "I wouldn't."

"How could you be sure?" She straightened up among the pillows.

"I am in control of my magic," I lied through a scowl. She stared me down, no signs of belief in her face. "I am!"

Cecelia stayed silent as I was unable to disconnect from her stare. The tears stopped, but her lip quivered harder and her hands shook around her knees. Out of everyone I thought would be scared of me, it wasn't her. What had I done to her? It stung, and I didn't like it. Finally, my eyes dropped to the floor and I sighed. The murmur of the kitchen filled the air between us as I fiddled with the ribbons of jeans around my ankles. She was afraid of me—it repeated over and over in my skull as I twisted strings of denim into knots around my legs.

"Did it ever occur to you that you could have died?" Cecelia broke the silence.

My eyes shot up from my ruined pants to her. Brown eyes stared me down, eyebrows knitted on her face. "It occurs to me often, actually." The air twisted tight in my lungs. My memory flashed back to that apartment, on the bloody floor. Leo Ashwood loomed over me with the ceremonial dagger in his right hand, the tip of the blade at my throat. Helplessness flooded my system, just enough to wake me up to reality. I snapped my eyes up to Cecelia, my jaw clenched tight. "I refuse to be killed by Leo Ashwood."

"Why is he like that?" Cecelia asked, her nose scrunched.

My shoulders grew tense as I spared a look to the doorway. The book was gone, thankfully returned to my aunt's arms probably. I debated a lie, one that wouldn't upset her. But the truth knocked on the back side of my teeth till I was unable to do anything but spit it out. I slid close to her and pulled my knees to my chest. She stayed still this time and allowed me to approach her inch by inch. I leaned in, my teeth bit into the meat of my cheeks. Then I released them and sighed.

"Bringing someone back from the dead is much harder than imagined. The soul may return but the body... it still died, and—er, well," I trailed off, my eyes shifted from her then to the door.

Cecelia slid closer by two inches and stopped with her arms folded just between our two sets of feet. "So that comment about you already killing him?"

My eyes shot back to her. I pursed my lips. If I lied, she might know I lied. She was a seer; she could discover the truth without my saying so. She already existed in my head, somehow, and I couldn't risk her anger. An angry seer was worse than a drunk doctor with a scalpel and open access to the brain. "I was in New York, a short time ago as you know, and Leo Ashwood was there—"

"Did. You. Kill. Him?" Cecelia ground out between her teeth.

I searched her face as she locked eyes with me. My mouth fell open, unable to do much else. "Yes," I confessed, barely even a whisper, as the air left my chest. "Only after he tried to slit my throat."

"What!?" She dropped her voice to a breath, I almost didn't hear it. Cecelia slid herself forward till she was an inch from her toes to mine. Her hands fell into her lap. "Why bring him back then?"

"I didn't say I—"

"I can read context clues, Quinn," she interjected with a sharp look.

"I..." My mouth fell open for a moment. Fear nibbled at my toes. In a blink, I sat in that pool of blood. I shivered as my hands dug through the carnage toward Berry. She lay, neck snapped and eyes rolled back, cold in my grasp. Her death, all of those deaths were on my hands. I lost control! I blinked away the image but the feeling chilled my bones. "I wasn't trying to bring *him* back."

Cecelia studied my face for a long moment. "Quinn—"

Berry's face blinded me as Cecelia choked on words. Blood covered her face, the ceremony knife ripped through her like butter. It was the first time, as a blood witch, I ever felt uncomfortable around death.

"Food's done, come on, sweetheart. Bring your new friend, the roast is carved."

My eyes snapped up to the open frame that led to the kitchen, my aunt stood just below the drooped curtain that hung from it. I nodded and pushed up to my feet again. My stomach growled in acknowledgment. When Darlin turned from us, I glanced to Cecelia with a fierce stare. "None of this leaves this room."

Cecelia said nothing as she clambered to her feet. Blankets and pillows flopped away from her as she stepped off the pile and onto the floor next to me. "I just want to go home. I promised my friend I'd come home."

"Well, that's going to be kind of hard," I scoffed as I walked around her. She eyed me as I sent her a smirk. "The only way you're getting out is with the help of me or my aunt, and I guarantee we both have questions for you."

"So you're holding me hostage?" Cecelia scowled, arms crossed and nose pinched at the bridge. She made it hard to take her seriously in rubber ducky pajamas. They were adorable; I couldn't help the wicked glee in my eyes as I examined her pinched face. It only scrunched harder, her hands clenched tightly.

"Consider it protective custody?" I shrugged as I twirled away from her.

She wasn't pleased, and her frowning scowl deepened. Her face showed the cogs as they turned in her head.

I stepped toward the doorway, my shoulders squared and the pillows behind me. A long moment of silence passed between us. The door was a good option but the walk back to civilization was not. There were no roads, no signs, and the swamp was a maze of dips into a murky water or squishy moss.

"I have a phone, you know." She whipped it out from the pocket of her bright pajamas.

"Oh no! Human technology! Whatever shall I do," I teased, my hands out in front of me in a dramatic display.

A look of horror fell on her face. "There's no service here," she whispered, her anger deflated to dreaded realization.

"There's only one device that works in this house, and only my aunt and I know where it is. Come on, my aunt is the best cook in the world." I winked as I backed into the kitchen.

Chapter Eleven

Cecelia Sees Leo Ashwood Again

They trapped me here. I was Thorin, trapped in the forest, unable to find a way out. No clever Bilbo to save me here. If I wanted to go home, I would have to be my own Bilbo.

Warmth radiated around me as I stalked into the kitchen after Quinn. The wood floors creaked beneath my feet, but they didn't bow. I passed doorways carved in thick oak; a spiderweb dangled from the high archway. Their ceiling was at least seven feet tall. In Jess's home, I ducked through most doorways.

Quinn stopped at a warped circular table; chairs made of ashwood enclosed it. There was a design carved into the top of the wood, painted gold, then sealed with a thick layer of gloss. It was slick to the touch, not sticky or gummy. Gretchen would hate it here. There were odd end items strewn around the corners, nothing organized. A long, sloppy shelf of books lined the top of the kitchen all the way around. Papers were stuffed in between books, and peculiar kitchen utensils had been shoved between what looked like scrolls. Despite the house being my temporary prison, it radiated warmth and comfort.

"So, Cecelia, was it?" Quinn's aunt smiled at me as I slipped into the kitchen after Quinn.

I sheepishly beamed back, my hands hugged around my torso. Was Gretchen looking for me yet? Was Jess?

"Yeah." The air restricted to the bottom of my lungs, weighed down by thick stones. I shuffled past her toward the table. Quinn set a plate on the table in front of the chair I attached myself to. She cocked a brow at me. My eyes fell to the plate of food that steamed up and filled my nose with garlic and basil.

Jess was definitely pissed! No text messages, no calls, no smoke signals, plus my car probably sat at impound awaiting my eventual arrival. Guilt stabbed into my skin and prickled down my arms.

A soft hand applied pressure to my right shoulder and snapped me to life. I jerked away and looked up into a silvery eye tattooed on a stranger's forehead. She put her hand up apologetically as she slid a cup toward me. I took it gingerly and cupped it close. Its frosty exterior cooled my skin that sat at the temperature of the surface of the sun. My face was hot from sleep and embarrassment, and my eyes stalked the stranger around the table. Purple and black hair in short strands fluffed around a heart shaped face; her real eyes watched me with interest.

"That's Serias." Quinn's whisper sent shivers down from my shoulders to the dip of my back. Quinn set a fork down next to my plate. "She's a seer as well—one of the best."

I furrowed my brow as I twisted to look up at Quinn. She settled down into the chair next to me, tossing back a long swig of her drink. It took my brain far longer than necessary to form words. A seer? That's what the monster called me. Magic filled the air, nearly tangible with how it settled on my skin like glitter. "Is everyone here a witch?"

"Why, yes, we all are." Another woman appeared from my blind spot. I watched in complete awe as a queen floated through the kitchen toward the table. "Darlin, where did we find such confused children?"

"We didn't. Quinn found her," Darlin chuckled as she sat down beside Serias.

The royal took up a small wine glass and put it to her lips. She stopped and set it back down as her eyes locked with mine. She wore traditional cream robes over a simple pearl gown, accented with lotus shaped earrings and hair pin. Amber eyes glowed as they locked with mine.

"How peculiar," she whispered after a long moment and took a sip of her wine.

"That's Amendir. She's a spellslinger, like my aunt," Quinn whispered to me. I sat absolutely silent.

Dinner lasted for ages as the right side of the table sat quietly. Quinn munched gracefully and kept her eyes on the others who spoke. Words evaded my every effort. Serias and Amendir, the two newest witches to my list of witches I've never known, talked with Darlin the whole time. They discussed the monster and possibilities of where it came from. Darlin existed as a whole page of her own in the notebook within my head—five foot two, chestnut hair tousled in beach waves, left eye blue and right eye light green, the genetics of mismatched eyes ran strong in Quinn's family.

I wanted to ask about her parents, but I didn't. I wanted to ask about the monster, but I didn't. I wanted to ask a thousand questions, but I poked food in my mouth and kept my lips sealed between mouthfuls. Nothing could make me comfortable enough to talk when I could see Maggie through an open doorway.

Outside of the kitchen in an open room, Maggie lay at the center of a mixture of symbols. Candles floated around her in a circle, spinning in lazy circles as if suspended in water. She glowed a sallow color under the candles, her blonde hair splayed around her.

"You both have been very quiet," Darlin said.

I choked on a carrot chunk as Darlin reached around the table to touch my bicep. With a cough and a smack to my collar bone, I dislodged the vegetable. Darlin eyed me with concern.

I grimaced. "Um, still processing," I chuckled nervously. My hair fell down into my face as my fingers moved up into my hair to undo the knot. I focused on fixing it up and out of my face, cheeks hot as fire. Everyone stared directly at me as my fingers fumbled under their gaze.

"Then let us turn the conversation to you, Seer." Serias asked, her eyes focused on me like lasers. Serias was wrapped in a thick leather jacket. She wore black lipstick and had two lip piercings. She scared me. The soft cream color of Amendir's ensemble had given me the impression she held a soft demeanor, but I realized that was wrong. Both witches stared at me with the intensity of the sun. Serias was Balrog scary, Amendir was Thrandil with a grudge scary.

I smiled sheepishly, my fingers trapped in my hair for a long moment. Finally, I swallowed and put my hands to the edge of the table. "It's Cecelia." I pushed my chair back an inch so that Maggie was blocked from my view by Darlin and Amendir. Serias crossed her wrists on the table and lay her palms flat on the table. "And I'm kind of a boring read."

"Are you calling yourself an open book?" Quinn teased with a smirk. I shot her a dark glare that only made her lips curl up more. "Because you're harder to read than you think."

"Quinn is right. You have been zip-lipped this whole time. I hardly know who you are, and yet you are the reason our Quinn is alive today. So, tell us, Cecelia, who does your family belong to? Is your mother also a Seer?" Darlin piped up with a brilliant smile. It made her face soften and pulled at the edges of her eyes.

I glanced between Darlin and Serias, unsure who would cause me more harm. Serias still examined me from edge to edge, as if she studied a textbook and not a teenage girl out of her depth. Everyone's gaze bore into me and I drowned in my own unspoken words. I didn't want to open my mouth.

"I don't know." I confessed with a wheeze, my chest squeezed tight. "I'm adopted."

"Unusual, but not completely uncommon. There are still a fair share of witches not raised in familiar homes." Amendir sighed and shook her head softly. Pearl colored lotuses decorated her ears and a small stud upon her left nostril. I examined each of them; Gretchen's influence repeated within my mind. Attention to detail, remember names and times, report everything. Like how all of them seemed out of place in the homely kitchen. Until Amendir shifted to sit back in the chair, one arm cocked on Serias' chair and one hand around her glass of wine she threw back with vigor. I realized then it wasn't the three women who seemed out of place—it was me.

"Familiar homes?" I forced out of my lips. I glanced toward Quinn for answers but she focused on a point within the hallway. My body's must have brought her to look toward Maggie. She stared with hawk focus on the hallway; her stony expression explained nothing. My eyes shifted back to the adults.

"A special term for homes full of witches," Amendir said. "Quinn was raised in a familiar home, as was I. But Serias, like you, was adopted and raised by humans for much of her childhood. Many witches slip through the cracks till they are found. We have a program in our coven alone for finding and aiding uncared for witches, like yourself, though, most of that comes from magic sensing and not monster hunting." Amendir chuckled softly as she spared a look to Serias. Serias's navy eyes softened at her before they returned to me. The silvery tattoo of an eye stared at me from her forehead, a chill ran down my spine.

"Well, I've always been an overachiever." I laughed nervously as I brushed my hair back behind my shoulder blades. Serias leaned back in her seat, her expression softened again as a smile graced her thin lips. "I, um, my...my mother is Gretchen Montreal—"

At the mention of my mother, Quinn and Darlin lit up.

"That awful church pianist?" Darlin scoffed.

"I like her, she always says her mind at the market." Quinn snickered as she nudged my arm with her elbow.

"My mother is very honest." I shrugged as I edged away from her and hugged myself.

"And a perpetual grump," Amendir interjected, her brow raised perfectly on the right side. "But she is a grand pianist; she has mastered her craft."

My cheeks warmed. No surprise that Gretchen Montreal was well known, even in the swamp. My mother played in many churches over the state of Oklahoma and Texas; she even played the Christmas special for a mega church in Austin last year. An angel on the keys, but also a perpetual grump. "Thank you."

"What about you, Cecelia? Do you have a fondness for music?" Darlin cocked her head to the side.

I licked my lips nervously. Show and tell was never my favorite activity at school. My throat tightened as I shifted back and forth in the seat subtly. "Absolutely not. I play the flute in the school band because it is required to do some kind of music, but I have no talent for it," I blurted out before my lips clamped shut and a harsh blush ran over my cheeks.

"That seems a bit harsh." Quinn pulled my attention to her swiftly. Her head cocked to the side as her eyes scanned my features. "Don't you think?"

"Not particularly. It's true. Gretchen has all the talent, and I..." I trailed off as the words glued themselves to my tongue. Strange tingles ran up my arms as I tried to speak. "I... I have..."

"Magic," Quinn finished.

"Precisely." I swallowed hard.

"Cecelia, walk with me." Serias rose from the table and rounded the kitchen.

I hesitated. My eyes snapped back to Quinn who nodded after Serias, a soft smile on her lips. I sloppily rushed to my feet.

Serias walked swiftly out onto the porch and down along the length of the house. I found it hard to follow after as my feet transformed into cement blocks determined to sink me to the bottom of the swamp below. Stale water and cold air filled my nose as the stars lit up the damp leaves of the willow. Serias reached out to touch a thin branch as I stopped an arm's length from her.

The house was bathed in the soft light from candles; the flame from one candle on the top the porch danced in my eyes. Trees broke through stagnant water and touched the sky before me. Branches and leaves tickled the horizon, dancing in a light breeze of the night. The path we took last night was obscured from the front of the porch. The house wrapped around a massive willow tree; the tree's long dainty branches draped over everything and blocked any view of the house from above. If you didn't know where it was, I could see why no one ever found Quinn or Darlin before. They truly trapped me here until they took me home.

"This must seem so strange for you." Serias's soft voice broke my concentration.

I twisted toward her as she leaned against the frame of the porch. "Surreal would be the word. I... I...It's..." I stumbled over my words, unable to keep my thoughts straight. Panic filled my heart as I tried to swallow over the lump in my throat. My eyes focused on Serias and followed the length of her outstretched arm. Upon her hand were hints of tattoos all over her skin. A thick leather jacket covered her arms up to her wrist, but swirls of ink and images poked out from under her clothes. A small flower bloomed at the base of her neck in between where the jacket covered and where her hair fell. "I'm scared and curious and I want to know more but—"

"But you almost died last night," Serias whispered. She pivoted to me with a soft expression. My stomach plummeted into my toes as tears welled up in my eyes. A hand extended out to me. I grabbed it without question and squeezed it with all my might.

"What would have happened... if ..." I trailed off as my hand tumbled from hers and wrapped around my torso. My body shivered hard as I peered out into the dimly lit swamp. What time was it? What day was it? How long had I been out? I stared out into the shadowy treeline. "I guess it doesn't matter much now."

"Cecelia, you have to know how utterly astounded I am with you. I am at my peak power, and I still did not see the monster's attack. I didn't see it in enough time to save Quinn, and I've helped raise her. Your power is miraculous and amazing, and something you shouldn't fear." Serias beamed. She illuminated the night with a toothy grin.

I stumbled back a step. My eyebrows shot up on my face as I gawked at Serias. "What?" I choked.

"When I was your age my visions were small or incredibly obscure. Most nights I spent hours trying to decipher them, or they were dull and simple everyday occurrences. You saved someone; your visions saved multiple people!" Serias stepped forward and clutched my biceps. In the low light that came from inside the house, her jacket exposed more of the tattoos that crawled up her skin—a wispy smoke design along her throat with a hand that broke through the smoke. That hand held a dagger that was shattered in midair, a thousand eyes decorated her wrist and forearm in silver ink, I almost missed them. My eyes narrowed in on it and Serias let go of my arm. She opened her leather jacket and exposed her entire neck. "It was a vision. They all were."

I jerked backward with a blink as I studied all the tattoos covering her skin from her neck to her covered midsection, all the way down her arms and even across her exposed feet. Designs swirled into one another, all different in shade and meaning but somehow all a cohesive design. "Don't worry, my legs are still pretty empty and so is my lower back, in case I need more."

"What are they for?" I gasped.

"A reminder of the worst ones," she murmured as she rubbed the one on her neck. "Of the nightmares I've witnessed. It's how I cope."

"Would I have—" I cut myself off as I grimaced. The idea of physical pain for art was never on my wish list. I loved the look of tattoos but only on other people. Jess swore up and down she would get a tattoo one day when she could decide what she wanted.

Serias broke my train of thought with a chuckle. "Oh no! Just because it's my coping mechanism does not mean you have to choose to do this. But it is an option. Mira, a friend of mine on the west coast, she paints her dreams. Eggsy makes dolls of the faces he's seen. There are a thousand ways; each seer has their release." Serias shrugged as she pulled the leather jacket back over her shoulders.

"I write down all of my dreams so I don't forget." I breathed as my arms hugged my torso. Serias reached out to soothe my arms with a soft rub. When she dropped her hands, I peeked at a dark tattoo upon her right hand. "Which one is that?"

"This?" She held up her hand as she exposed the back of her hand to me—a box cut in half while flower petals and stems fell out from its gash, the bow on top made of wiry ribbon. "The first nightmare I had was when I was eighteen. A fellow high schooler's birthday present, she wanted to walk the gardens at night with her boyfriend, to see the fountain light up. She said her romantic dream was to be kissed under the waterfall and stars... She was murdered there," Serias confessed with a thick swallow. "I gave the police the evidence they needed to put Edgar Moreson away for life."

"You couldn't stop it?" I whimpered as Serias shook her head.

"I was with a few friends on vacation in Miami. I did everything in my power to stop her but it was too late, she was dead before sunrise. This tattoo is a reminder, that I can't always save them... but sometimes, I can get them justice." She shrugged as she stepped back to lean against the railing of the porch. I examined her while my heart sank to the floor of the swamp.

"Is it always like this?" My words trembled as they fell from my lips.

"No, not always. I get lottery numbers a lot; I write those on sticky notes and put them in random places when I can. I also see a lot of people living their lives, unaware. I catch onto their thoughts and we connect for a small time. A week ago, I was in the head of a woman in Washington State; she works for an art gallery and I was there for opening day of an exhibit. It was beautiful." Serias blinked away fat tears as she smiled, her eyes down to the porch below her.

"I saw Emma Featro's window screen invention before she did. I saw her enchant them all and make enough money to pay for her father's surgery and more," I confessed. Serias lit up again as she clapped hands on my biceps and squeezed them enthusiastically. My lips curled into a smile, unable to hold back.

"So you were the seer!" Serias let out a loud laugh; it bounced off the windows and wood and filled the night air. I smiled with a weak shrug.

"Yeah, she was the first witch I'd talked to before Quinn. I got so nervous to meet someone like me that I kind of...ran." I deflated as Serias laughed harder. She bent at the middle, her hands on her hips as she laughed. When she stood up, she wiped tears from her eyes as she nodded.

"Cecelia Montreal, I want to teach you." Serias giggled through her words.

"What?" I blurted out.

"I think I can teach you how to use your magic to its fullest extent. Cecelia, you saw a monster attack and ran head first to stop it. You are courageous! With a severe lack of self-preservation, but you are powerful, and it would be a shame for you not to be taught how to use your magic. If you would sign to join our family, I could teach you how to use your magic, truly use it and probably save more people." Serias beamed as she stepped forward.

"Join our family?" I furrowed my brow.

"Well, of course, it would be expected if I teach you that you would join our coven when you come of age. Quinn was raised with Darlin and has agreed to join when she comes of age; even Emma is a part of our coven."

I studied her face. There was no glint of mischief, or even a wicked smile, a genuine excited grin upon her lips. Serias couldn't be more than thirty-five, her nose was broken in the middle but healed over, and she felt... honest. If there was something Gretchen instilled in me early was to catch a liar in the act. No bullshit, as she would say, only the truth.

"What would I be signing up for?" I grimaced, my arms wrapped around my torso tight like a boa constrictor.

"Well, much like a college, you want to join a coven that lines up with what you want for your future. Each family wants different things and believes in different rules, but we are all built for the same purpose—to support one another and keep witches safe from the outside world. Amendir, Darlin and I are the elders of our coven and would provide you with a place to live, a job to work that benefits you and the family. And you would inform us of major visions, aid us in keeping others safe in return for aid and teaching. Cecelia, you would never be alone again," Serias explained with a softer expression, her tone even as she moved her hands with her words.

"Do I have to?" I cocked a brow, and my arms loosened and fell to my side. A coven sounded nice—a family who wanted what was best for me. If Serias taught me to use my magic, maybe I wouldn't feel useless. Maybe I could actually help!

"Of course not, no one has to. But it is safer in numbers, Cecelia." Serias nodded.

"Safer from what?"

"Cecelia, that monster is only one outcome of magic being abused. There are many out there who believe the world should be on fire in order for it to be comfortable. There are witches out there who would kill to make their wicked dreams a reality." Serias sighed, her head hung slightly. When she looked back up at me, I saw her one hand rub her bicep and I wanted to know what tattoo hid underneath the leather. But she didn't pull it off again as her eyes trailed the swamp under the moonlight. A breeze tickled both our faces. When I brushed my hair from my face, Serias had her back to Leo Ashwood.

My heart jumped into my throat as I saw him through the branches that danced in the wind. A yard or two away, just behind a broken stump covered in moss, he lingered under the starlight. Leo Ashwood smirked for a moment, his skin sunk around him as if it would fall off his bones like boiled chicken skin. Then he ducked back into the shadows and I stumbled back into the side of the house.

Serias shot a look at me with concern before she whirled around. "Who was it?"

"Um... The..."

"Amendir! Darlin!" she shouted.

Torches lit up the night as three witches dove into the swamp from the porch. The world a whirlwind of motion as the door flew open and light illuminated the porch. Before I knew it, Quinn stumbled out the door. She halted beside me as we stared out into the night. The flames went out and we were both left in the silent night. The three witches' torches snuffed as the wind kicked up around the house. A pressure fell upon me and Quinn as we were backed up against the side of the house more.

"A protection spell, of course," Quinn huffed. "She's still pissed I fought him on my own."

"Who?" I squawked.

"My aunt Darlin—she pretty much just put an electric fence around us. If we put one toe outside this porch, it'll hurt. If Leo Ashwood sticks his nose out too far toward us, it'll *really* hurt." She rolled her eyes.

I groaned under my breath as I leaned my head back against the house. For a long moment, we stood in silence as the world held still.

"What did she talk to you about?" Quinn whispered.

"She asked to teach me," I stammered. "Then, I saw Leo Ashwood."

"Damn!" she growled.

"What do you mean, 'damn'?" I squeaked.

"He's getting smarter, playing games..." Quinn scrunched up her face. It softened as she beamed at me. "But I'm glad she offered to teach you, that's cool."

I furrowed my brow. "Wait, just a min—"

"Usually Amendir does the teaching, but Serias is the best Seer I've ever met. She'll be good for you. Now come on, we have to wake up Maggie. We need the siren." Quinn snatched up my wrist and tugged me toward the front door.

"Whoa, hold up! What do you mean?" I huffed with my arms tossed out to my sides and out of her grip. "I thought you just said she put up an electric fence!"

"We've got to go get Ashwood; we can't let him get stronger. Especially now that he has a taste for blood and is playing mind games. And besides, I know a thing or two about getting around electric fences." Quinn scoffed as she snatched up my arm again. "I thought that was obvious."

Chapter Twelve

Maggie Hates Flying

Dull, slow flashes lit up behind my eyes, the night in stop motion before my eyes like a poorly edited movie on a dial up connection. Pain no longer existed in my body but left a reminder in my posture through my dreams. Bent over in pain, tears in my eyes, blood on my lips, every picture of me screamed pain. Yet, I floated in bliss and rewatched my death. Then I woke up.

I woke up to Cecelia with her frosty fingers dug into my armpits and Quinn hovering over me. A scream broke from my lips mere seconds before Quinn cupped my mouth with her hands and Cecelia dropped me roughly. My body crumpled to the floor as Quinn knelt over me, hands firmly on my mouth. "Shh!"

I grumbled into her palm. Then I swiftly ran my tongue up the inside of her palm. She jerked backward; my eyes lit up with evil, childish glee. My head flopped back against the floor as Quinn jumped to her full height.

"What are you? Six?" she hissed.

A smirk flashed on my lips as I propped myself up on my elbows. "What are you? A psycho swamp beast? Oh wait, you are!" I snapped. Not my best work, but Kitty tended to be the creative one. Quinn recoiled more as rage fueled my body from my toes to my scalp. I scrambled to my feet. "What are you doing?"

"Trying to wake you up, you ungrateful siren," Quinn retorted with a snarl. I stood up straight, my shoulders squared. If I threw a punch, Quinn would probably use some witch nonsense and knock me on my butt. Plus, my body was still weak, not as scrappy as usual. Sense cleared me of my anger as I whirled to look at Cecelia.

"Why are your hands so cold?" I put a finger in Cecelia's face. She put her hands up with a grimace.

"Sorry for having cold fingers in late winter!" she retorted. She rolled her eyes.

"Don't get smart with me," I growled, my hands to my hips.

"Says the one with an attitude." Quinn snatched my upper arm and whirled me to face her. "I saved you, remember?"

My lips pinched tightly, twisting up my face at the center. Quinn pressed her lips into a thin line. She didn't back down as she cocked her hip out and crossed her arms. We locked eyes. I stepped back from the situation and calculated my position. Reality sank in as my eyes adjusted to the room around me—a round room, the walls stacked floor to ceiling with books and things in jars. The walls were made of bookcases, scrolls and novels the size of college textbooks burst from the shelves. There was a whole shelf full of tiny items in jars of oddly colored liquid, and another with wood carved in the shape of animals all embedded with a jewel in the foreheads of the creatures. My eyes followed the shape of the room and found no windows, only one carved door. This room was carved into the side of a tree, the rings of a large tree covered the floor and the ceiling. I stopped to stare at the floor, which was covered in a sand and burnt wood design, much like a pentagram although not exactly, as the major shape was more oval and the star was drawn from curled lines, like knots in the side of bark. I didn't miss the large Maggie sized spot in the middle, outlined with candle wax, illegible words carved into the warm wax.

"Well, to be honest, you kind of created the problem, Quinn," Cecelia interjected. My head snapped up from the floor to Quinn. Quinn shot a glare over my shoulder toward Cecelia.

"What!" I whirled to face Cecelia.

She squeaked and jumped backward in the hallway. "Quinn made the monster!" Cecelia blurted out, hands up. She stared past me with an apologetic grimace. I whirled back to Quinn who glared directly at Cecelia but caught my eyes in seconds.

"You made the monster?" My words reverberated low and gravely.

"It's a long story," Quinn snapped before she shot Cecelia another look.

"Don't glare at her!" I snapped my fingers in the air, and Quinn's eyes flickered to me. "Why would—"

"I said it's a long story." She bent down and grabbed a candle from the floor. My eyes followed her movements. The design filled my vision in fuller detail. I spun to see the whole shape. Snakes made the outer oval, two entwined in a dance with their mouths over the other's tail. There were at least thirty candles on the floor in a multitude of shapes and sizes. Wax glued many of them to the floor, and others looked dropped to the floor with little care. All the candles but one were out. The one in Quinn's hand crackled. She held it out to me. "Hold this."

"Why! What is—" I jerked from her only to have it shoved back in my direction

"You want to die?" she spat.

I fell silent. The candle landed in my hand. It was thick and white with no smell, carved with the same symbol as the floor. Quinn wrapped my fingers around it, our eyes locked the whole time. I pulled the candle closer to my chest and relief spread through my body. It produced the same ease that Quinn did the night before. I sighed and pressed it against my exposed collar bone. The candle didn't drip, burn, or singe my body. It was neither hot nor cold, but a comforting warmth that eased the tension in my shoulder. Then Quinn produced a small kitchen knife from her waist and held it up. The tension returned in an instant as she eyed me expectantly. I sputtered to life. "What are you doing?"

"I'm a blood witch—I use blood. It's kind of my thing." She shrugged before she snatched up my free palm.

I yanked back from her; my feet stumbled over air. A wash of nausea moved over my stomach. "I don't think so!" I squawked. She cocked a brow in my direction as I tucked my free hand behind my back. Cecelia brushed past me softly.

"Use mine," Cecelia sighed as she put out her hand. Quinn hesitated, the steak knife iron gripped in her right hand. Cecelia jutted her hand out a second time toward Quinn and put it into her open hand.

"Wait, Cecelia—" She whipped her head toward me over her shoulder.

"Leo Ashwood followed us here; he's out there in the swamp right now." Cecelia spared an apologetic grimace before she twisted back to Quinn and nodded. My heart dropped. I swallowed the vomit that turned to thick chunks in my throat. Quinn put the knife against Cecelia's forefinger and jerked it fast. A hiss filled the air as Cecelia recoiled, her face scrunched up in pain as her eye twitched. Quinn poked Cecelia's finger in her mouth, her eyes glued to Cecelia's face. Until I shot my hand out at her.

"Maggie?" Cecelia cracked an eye open at me as I glared directly at Quinn.

"Look, just don't do my fingers—I need those for guitar," I whined as Quinn straightened up. She held the knife down at her side as she examined me. If there was ever a time in my life that I thought it couldn't get weirder, this took the cake. Quinn was right, she saved me. She took me here, and despite the weird candles and chalk, I felt better. The horrific death that filled me held at bay by her and now the pillar candle. Life returned to my cheeks, stronger than before, and my legs held me up without a single tremble. "Get the outside of my hand or something..."

Quinn took my hand and ran the knife swiftly along the back of my forearm. I clenched down hard. The sting ran the length of my arm. Despite my muscles rigidness, a shiver ran down my spine as she licked across the back of my arm like a body shot. If I survived this, I wanted tequila rose, and the good kind. Maybe Bootleg Kevin would pity me and slip me a bottle of the good stuff if I paid him the price of it. Quinn pulled back, her lips pressed into a thin line on her face. "We need to go."

"Whoa, wait, you never explained the candle. Why am I carrying it?" I blinked as Quinn brushed past me and launched out into the hallway. I whirled to face her as she glanced both ways and set on the right side of the hallway. Cecelia and I followed after her with confusion.

"It's keeping you alive—don't let it go out. I thought that was obvious." Quinn furrowed her brows.

"Quinn," Cecelia huffed, hands on her hips.

"What? It's like she wasn't raised a witch." Quinn tossed her arms out at her side.

"Excuse me! I was raised Baptist." I recoiled.

"Ew, I'm sorry," Quinn grimaced as my mouth hung open.

"Maggie, Witch isn't a religion—it's what we are. Quinn, Maggie's parents aren't witches." Cecelia stepped in between us.

"Really? I found the only two teenage witches in all of Idabel who don't know they're witches? What are the chances." Quinn scoffed as she whirled on her heel and charged down the hallway. I lunged after her only to stop when the flame on the candle flickered. Instinctively, a hand up went up in front of the flame. It licked my palm and I smiled at the soft comfort. Then I peered up at Cecelia, her eyes darted from my candle to my face.

"I'm going to slug her right in her smart mouth." I snapped to Cecelia. She sighed as she linked arms with me.

"Please don't," she muttered as she marched both of us after Quinn.

Quinn stopped at the first doorway in the circular hallway and pushed it open slowly. A room full of floating candles filled my vision as Quinn dove into the middle of the room. She grabbed a glass bowl from under the edge of her bed and hid the knife under her mattress.

The room was long and ended with a wall wrapped in drapery. Candles floated around the room, lighting up the dark crimson color of the wood with sheer black fabric that fell around the room in low dips. A large vanity took up one wall; piles of books and papers covered the edges of the room. Clothes tucked into the corner and a full recliner was drowned in other clothes. A door on the exterior wall lit up by the moonlight with red stained glass of different colors all in the shape of a rose.

"Here, this ought to keep it lit." She turned and held out the betta fishbowl sized glass vase. "Keep it close, don't let it go out. I don't know how to cure you yet."

I gently lifted the candle and put it in the bowl, unafraid of the flame even as it licked the sides of my hands, like the tongue of a kitten against my palm. I pulled the vase close to my chest. "Cure me?" I eyed her, my back straightened tight. She softened her face as she looked up at me with a soft smile.

"Your cancer—I don't know how to cure it yet, but we will have to find one after we deal with Leo." Her voice wobbled out as a whisper. . She would find a cure? The doctors couldn't even find a cure! But she was a witch, after all. I was a witch! I could sing people to sleep, and I made a man stab himself with my words. If I could do that, then the witch who licked my 'tainted' blood and punched Frankenstein's monster clear across town could cure me. It sounded asinine but it was the only thing that felt probable.

She clapped her hands clean as a wicked smirk grew on her lips. "Oh, there it goes... I can feel it."

"You can feel our blood?" I gagged. "Gross!"

"Smell it too," she chirped with a wide grin. I rolled my eyes as she wheeled around to the door against the exterior wall. Her hands slowly lifted toward it as she inhaled a slow breath in.

I leaned toward Cecelia with a cocked brow. "What's she doing?" I whispered.

"We're locked in. To get to Leo, we have to get out," Cecelia replied with a grimace.

"What!" I spat under my breath. "If we're safe in here, why are we leaving?"

"Because *he's* out there, hurting people." Quinn turned just an inch to catch me in the eyes. "Those murders? It's him! He's killed at least ten people at this point, and I won't let him kill more."

I straightened up, the candle vase hugged to my chest. "Shouldn't we just, I dunno, tell the police?" I shrugged as my eyes darted from Cecelia to Quinn.

"The human police? Who are, what? Under the impression that these murders are done by some kind of mutated bear?" Quinn tossed her arms out at her side.

"Jess thought it might have been a mutated bear too," Cecelia interjected as she leaned toward me. "But then again, she also thought it had to be like, Hulk-level mutated kind of bear."

"Ah, yeah, Messy Jessy, the pillar of sanity at our school," I spat back without a moment to think of it. Regret seeped into my veins and glued my lips shut instantly.

Cecelia furrowed her brows and crossed her arms under her chest. "Do you guys really think she's messy? Jess is just as anal retentive as my mom about cleanliness. Have you seen her truck?" Cecelia scowled, her body twisted to stare me in the eye.

I chewed on the inside of my cheeks. The truth tumbled out of my clenched jaw as I looked over Cecelia's lemon sour, twisted face. "Messy as in messed up in the head," I muttered.

"What does that mean?" Cecelia dropped her hands.

I scoffed. "Seriously? She lost it in the lunchroom and Hulk-threw a bench through a window. I would call that messed up—"

"She lost her mom!" Cecelia screamed and the whole room died. My heart sank as she tossed her arms out to her side. "How would you feel if you lost the one thing in this world you love the most? I doubt any of you jerks would know what that feels like? Yeah! Jess has anger issues, but she's dealing with them, and you have no right to judge her! None of you do! You made a girl cry in gym locker room when you told everyone she sounded like a beached whale! Kitty slapped the bejesus out of me and then tackled me to the ground like a wild animal because I told Lance she was cheating on him!"

"Whoa, whoa, hold up— Kitty did what?" I blinked. Kitty? My Kitty? My very 'the only time I'm allowed to be sweaty and bruised is at cheer practice', couldn't be bothered to swat a fly, Kitty tackled Cecelia? Everything in my mind stalled. "Did you say cheating?"

"Look, this all is riveting but, like, we have much bigger—" Quinn's interjection was killed as Cecelia and I put up a hand in unison to her.

"Yeah! I had a vision that she was sleeping with Tommy Jet and I told Lance! He broke it off with her and she attacked me!" Cecelia huffed; her bottom lip jutted out in a pout.

"I... I... What..." I stuttered as I blinked rapidly. "Kitty?"

"Yeah?" Cecelia deflated for a moment, her anger dulled to confusion.

"My Kitty, the 'Lance and I forever' notebook Kitty Justin?" I repeated.

"I don't understand what's going on," Cecelia murmured as I stumbled back.

"I'm a horrible friend," I blurted out with a sigh. "I didn't even— I didn't know...When did this happen?"

"Like, Monday." Cecelia recoiled as I slapped my hand to my mouth. "What?"

"I-I made it all about me, I wasn't even thinking," I stammered. Silence fell over the room. My eyes moved to Quinn, arms crossed and eyes shifted between both of us. She stopped her stare on me and cocked her head. "Nothing, let's just get this over with. I'm done playing monster hunter."

A loud rattle broke through the room. We all turned to the door with wide eyes. All of us went dead silent as it trembled, the glass cracking like a spider web.

"You do realize I don't know how to do this," I muttered.

"And my visions won't help us here," Cecelia whimpered as the door rattled harder.

Quinn stepped up in front of us, her hands out to the door. As it flung open, the room became void and we were sucked from it. My heart and stomach turned to weight in my toes as I screamed. Cecelia clung to me, and I clutched the candle bowl to my chest as we flew out into the night's sky.

Mad laughter filled the air as Quinn snatched me by the arm and jutted out her other arm toward the night. She caught onto something in the darkness and we swung through the air. I screamed harder. Cecelia screamed higher than me, and I was a soprano, and we flew through the air. Quinn laughed harder as we slid down. Our screams died as Cecelia and I touched the ground. The candle lit up only the small space around my face in the dark canopy of the swamp. Water seeped into my shoes and I shivered.

"I... really... hate...flying." I panted as Cecelia shivered against me.

"Leo Ashwood! Show yourself!" Quinn shouted.

"Ah! Yes, please, just shout out to the darkness for the body munching monster witch guy that holds a grudge against you. Perfect planning." Cecelia's teeth chattered as her fingers dug into my arm.

"Slow down the sarcasm, Birdo Baggins. She's high on the power of blood," I scoffed.

"Ha, ha." Quinn cocked a brow at both of us. The dark grew quiet as she peered around the trees. I spared a look back to the house we were ripped out of. Her door was wide open on the side of the house, candles flickered in the doorway to light up the night. My eyes followed the willow tree up to the sky. It was too dark. Extremely too dark. The moon was gone. I swallowed hard. There were no stars and no moon.

"I might not be an expert, but, uh, wasn't there, like, a moon?" I stammered as Cecelia shifted against me.

Horror filled her features as the candlelight lit up her face from below her chin. Cecelia gawked at me, eyes wide and mouth ajar. "No, no, don't you give me that face!"

"That's what I meant when I said his powers were returning," Quinn whispered as she shuffled closer.

"The monster controls the moon!?" I squawked as quietly as possible.

"No, much, *much* worse," she muttered as she grabbed both of us by the bicep.

"What could be worse than controlling the friggin' moon!?" I snarled between gritted teeth as Quinn huddled us all in together. Not that I got an answer, because as soon as Quinn looked at me, a hand shot out of the darkness and ripped her up into the air. My heart stopped as Quinn was flung behind the monster like the wrapping paper of a present of an overly excited toddler.

"There you are!"

A whistle note left my throat. Cecelia dropped to the mushy ground around my ankles while the sound filled the air. Sharp tingles ran up my spine as pressure filled my chest. Leo Ashwood, the monster, whatever he was, jerked backward. His hands flew to his ears. The skin on his face twitched and fell off his bones in flakes. The light of the candle flickered, and I clamped my lips shut. I clutched the glass vase close to my chest out of fear.

"Your death is already within you."

"Go away!" I spat, the pressure on my chest ran up into my throat. "Go! Away!"

The monster stumbled backward as his arms waved to his side. Then his head snapped forward and he lunged forward. *"Siren—"*

"Punch yourself!" I demanded as his fists swung inward. Power filled my veins with excitement as I put one foot out in front of me. "Harder!"

He swung again, right fist then meaty left fist, inward against himself. My throat grew tight as he swung but stopped short of his face. Skin peeled away from his face and exposed rotten, putrid meat underneath. I choked on vomit as a rotten smell filled the air. My hands flew to my nose, but the stench locked into the insides of my nostrils and along the lining of my mouth. Rotten trash had nothing on the smell of acidic death that came from his face. *"Parlor tricks!"*

"How about this?"

I stumbled backward as Cecelia flung herself away from my leg. Hands crawled up the beast like spiders, and a blade sliced through his chest. Vomit projected from my throat and onto the ground before me. The second half of his face peeled off of him. A howl filled the air as Leo Ashwood stumbled to the left. The blade pulled back from behind him and Quinn stepped out into the candlelight.

Leo Ashwood lingered silently as bony fingers stabbed into his flesh. Quinn wielded a sword the same size as her made of a thick, dark red substance. Horror filled my body as blood dripped from Quinn's exposed arm into the blade that shimmered in the candlelight. "Is that?"

"A new talent I've discovered." Quinn grinned as she dragged the blade across the moss-covered ground. Bones crunched together on the chest of the monster; they dug into him and ripped chunks out. Quinn lunged forward, blade out as the monster smashed the bones like mosquitos and tossed them from him. The blade sliced through his arm and it plopped to the ground. My knees turned to jelly as I tried not to lose everything in my stomach all over the swamp floor.

Quinn dug her heels into the ground and spun with the blade, putting all her momentum into the swing. Her blade embedded itself into the truck of a tree as the night flooded with moonlight and stars. Leo Ashwood clutched Quinn by the back of her neck, his hand fully intact.

"Illusionist tricks," Quinn coughed, and blood splattered across the front of the tree.

"Quinn!" Cecelia cried out.

"I've had enough of your childish magic!"

He squeezed, and I lurched forward, my mouth open. I froze in place as something came over Quinn. Her eyes rolled back in her head, the whites of her eyes soaked with blood that glowed like a jack-o'-lantern in a horror movie. Her teeth were exposed in a wicked grin as her back tensed up against his squeeze. Leo grunted, his face sloppily hung to his skull. The world exploded in sudden movement as creatures exploded out of the ground. Blood rained over Cecelia and me. I shoved my hand over the flame to protect it. Bodies shot at the monster and stuck to his skin. Quinn spun around, blade in hand, same possessed grin upon her face.

"Cecelia, we should go," I muttered.

"Uh! You're probably not wrong!" Cecelia wheeled backward toward me; her hands scrambled to grab hold of me. Quinn buried the blade into the leg of Leo Ashwood and twisted it with a mad laugh. My foot slipped backward a step into slime that shifted. I jerked upward as something slithered through the darkness. Many shapes shifted in the night into a large mass. They clambered together and lunged at Leo and Quinn.

"Probably?" I scoffed as we back pedaled from the spot.

We backed into a tree and a soft yelp erupted from both our mouths. Dead snakes dropped from the branches into our view and snapped at us. They tangled with one another and hissed at us. Bones crunched together and snapped into place until a creature large enough to rip us to shreds dangled before our faces. My mouth hung open as it struck toward us. Teeth broke bark off the tree seconds after Cecelia jerked my head away and both of us into a muddy sinkhole. In the dark, Quinn's eyes snapped to us and her head turned inch by inch in our direction. She stepped toward us, her teeth exposed. "Oh no."

"Quinn?" Cecelia whimpered.

The monster smacked Quinn across her shoulder blades with his meaty left hand. Her head snapped back to him. She ripped the blade out. She swung across his chest and dropped it. She raised her hands to the sky and the corpses flung up into the air, the snake monster with it. With the clench of her fists, they swirled together till a new beast formed, made of mushy fish scales and leftover tissue and long uneven bones. The new beast lumbered before us, six feet tall and ran a rotten arm straight through the collar bone of Leo Ashwood. Leo howled as the creature wrenched backward and ripped a bone straight out of Leo's chest. Quinn lunged for him, her hands wrapped around a leg. Darkness filled my vision before a sharp brightness blinded me.

"Quinn!" I slapped my free hand to my eyes and forced my eyes open again.

Cecelia froze as three women flew out of the tree line; bright lights ricocheted through the dark. The lights blinded me and I whirled from them into Cecelia. My eyes clenched tight and I hugged the glass vase with one arm and Cecelia with the other. Cold swamp water soaked up to my shins. Blood dried against my cheeks as I choked on my breath. Finally I gasped for air and peeled my eyes open…

Leo Ashwood was gone. Bits of him remained but Leo Ashwood no longer towered over the swamp. Quinn arched backward, three feet off the water's surface, her mouth unhinged as a will-o'-wisp floated around her like a single moon beam. A woman with short, choppy brown hair hovered over her with a look of worry carved into her face.

"Serias, where did it go?" Cecelia broke the silence.

"Don't worry, little one." A new woman stepped into view. The dark purple streaks in her hair filled my sight as she brushed hair out of Cecelia's face. "We need to get you girls home."

"What happened to Quinn?" I blurted out.

"Don't worry about anything but getting home." The woman named Serias smiled, but my stomach hung in suspended twists and knots in my torso. I craned my head to see Quinn, bloody tears dribbled down her cheeks from her eyes. I spared a glance to Cecelia clutching to my side.

"What about me?" I whimpered.

"Quinn was smart, transferring the spell to candle... keep it close, and keep it lit, and you'll be all right until we can find you a cure." Serias whispered, a leather covered glove raked the hair stuck to my forehead to behind my ears. "We have a healer in the family, we will have him rush home to see you as soon as possible. The candle should keep you safe for now."

"I have a feeling that I'll be calling out tomorrow," I muttered under my breath.

"I have a feeling we'll both be grounded for life." Cecelia added and we both groaned in unison.

"I am in *sooooo* much trouble."

Chapter Thirteen

Quinn Visits the School

There is little in the world to compare to the experience of losing control. Every time it worsens, and the power is a nightmare. For a few moments, even mountains feared my strength. Death came with the snap of my fingers—no survivors. The magic pulsed through my veins in acidic waves and crashed through my brain. I drowned in my own power, unable to decipher up from down. Then I awoke in my aunt's arms, drenched in swamp water and her tears. Blood caked around her face and in my ears. Darlin clutched me and muttered whispered apologies. Then Amendir peeled me away as Darlin worked to collect herself. She peered at me in fear through wet strands of hair. Not afraid of me, but for me. My mouth was a desert, cracked and full of sand, unable to ask why.

Amendir refused to look me in the eye as she whisked me into the house and into the healing circle. She lit every candle with a soft blow in the direction of the wick. I lingered at the center, my eyes glued to my elder's form. She picked the candles up one by one, careful to place them exactly where she wanted until she encased me. I furrowed my brows as she finished. "Wait, Amendir—that doesn't look right."

"I know what I'm doing." Hoarse words floated around me as the candles wept blood. I jerked backward; my hands scrapped around the dirty floorboards. The candles bled until their overflow crawled toward me like a snake toward its prey. I hit a wall as firm as concrete and flung back toward the center.

"Amendir—"

"Do you trust my judgement?" Amendir snapped.

My eyes jumped from my new prison. Tears welled in my eyes, and traitorous fat drops trickled down my cheeks. I touched my cheeks only to pull away inch by inch. Horror crawled up my spine as I witnessed fresh blood trickle down my fingers. Amendir's first lesson chanted at the back of my skull—all power comes at a price.

"What... Why am I..." I trembled as my eyes crawled up to Amendir. The air tightened as the blood reached its destination. Tendrils of magic latched onto my form. Wax crawled through my pants and bit into my skin. Pain radiated from each spot on my flesh until wax the strength of steel yanked me back to the floor and forced my eyes upward, my chin locked in place.

"You are a blood witch, Quinn—that's what blood witches do." Her words were a scalpel to my sensitive skin; there was nothing to numb the sharpness of her tone. Disgust hidden in a sneer, she stepped into my view with a face twisted up in rage.

"I don't understand," I whimpered as the magic tendrils crawled over my face. My body lurched against the tendril's touch. Magic forced my lips open as it crawled inside me, and wax tickling the roof of my mouth. Then my lips snapped shut and locked my mouth up tight. My eyes shut without my permission.

"Rest up, Quinn. You've had a long day."

And my world shut off, like a switch within my skull flipped. I tumbled into darkness. No pain, no fear, no tendrils of magic. Behind my eyelids, soft bulbs of light floated through my vision. Ghost faces floated before me, practically transparent and far away. I was stuck, unable to look away, as Darlin stared at me in worry.

Her face was suddenly replaced with Cecelia's and Maggie's just before we were ripped out of the door. Amendir slashed through their faces with her nails and stared me down. A pond disturbed, her image rippled and left me with an aged mirror of myself. My heart raced itself up into my ears as I realized it wasn't me. Gwenevieve Charlotte Foster stared across the darkness at me, her right eye green and left eye blue, a diamond birth mark upon her throat and millimeters above her lip.

Then the switch flipped back on and I launched up off the floor. I gasped for air. A cough rumbled through my chest. My eyes blinked, my fingers twitched, and I opened my jaw to feel its soreness. The room existed exactly in the same shape as before Amendir knocked me out, except the candles—they were gone. I was alone within our miniature library, surrounded by fluttering pages and the symbols burned into the floor by my ancestors. I eased my legs toward my chest and hugged my knees. Tears welled up in my eyes without permission as I clenched my knees harder. My fingers dug into my shins, the pain lit up my system. I desperately wanted to sleep for days, or maybe a week max, my nerves flared with sudden touch.

"Lovely?" Darlin appeared in the doorway. I jumped in my skin as I glanced up to my aunt. Her face crumbled as I sobbed, eyes locked with her. Her hands shot out to grab me and I let her. She wrapped me up into her arms and I melted. "Oh, Quinn."

"What did I do?" I gasped for air. "What did I do wrong?"

"Nothing, Quinn, you did nothing wrong," Darlin rasped in my ear, my nose buried in her hair.

"Then why did she punish me? What did Amendir do to me? What was that?" Hysteria and panic coursed through my veins at top speed.

Darlin peeled backward and examined my face. She studied me for an eternity before she sighed. "It wasn't a punishment," she murmured.

"Sure felt like one!" I exploded. I threw myself out of my aunt's arms.

Immediately regret sank into my stomach as Darlin stared at me with a dejected, broken hearted expression. Her mouth cracked open an inch as her hands settled into her lap. "It was a healing spell. But it's special to only you and witches like you," Darlin whimpered as her shoulders sank.

"Blood witches," I spat.

"Yes, blood witches."

"Why?" I croaked; my tears trickled down from my face to my hands. I jerked as my eyes snapped down to my lap. Relief flooded my system when I found salty water splashed around my palm. My body relaxed as I dried my tears with the inside of my palm. I sat completely cleaned of all dirt and soil, most importantly, blood, like the nightmare of Leo Ashwood never happened.

"It's a cleanse of the toxic blood in your system. Amendir and I realized you ingested blood, most likely from Cecelia and Maggie. Cecelia's blood enhanced your powers, but Maggie's blood tainted your mind. It gave you power but turned you into a nightmare, lovely, you scared us. You attacked Serias."

My mouth hung ajar as I peered up from my lap through my rat's nest hair to Darlin. She nodded softly and clambered to her feet. A hand offered in my direction and I took it out of regret. Darlin beamed as she brushed thick brown locks from my face. My voice cracked. "Is Serias hurt?"

"No, she is fine. You nicked her good on the hand, but you know her, she's slick as a pink pig drenched in vegetable oil." Darlin winked at me as she stepped back from the room toward the hall. "Now, enough about that, you're awake, I bet you're hungry. Why don't you go wash up and change out of those clothes? Huh? I'll whip you up a roast beef sandwich and some fresh fries? How's that sound?"

"Amazing," I confessed with a sigh and a hand to my stomach. Darlin left with only a pat to my head and a wide grin. I waited exactly three seconds after she left to deflate and crumble against the doorframe. A prolonged moment passed as I gazed at the floor. My mother's face haunted my mind. Rage and horror lingered on my mother's face, dripping in blood. Heat trapped in my scalp from the leftover wax, the sticky burn grounded me back in reality.

The tendrils left wax melted to my skin, as if they covered every inch and then ripped off at least two layers of it. I swallowed hard before I mustered up the nerve to swing out into the hall and stalked to my room. My aunt busied herself in the kitchen and I slunk into my bathroom.

I hurt Serias? How was that even possible? Her sight allowed her to stay three steps ahead in a fight. Never in my sixteen years was I able to land a finger on her without her say so. In my moment of sheer power, I cut her hand...and that was only with a lick of Cecelia and Maggie's blood. What was I capable of?

I gazed into the mirror, large and obscurely cut reflective glass framed in pink and silver marble against my ungodly mint wallpaper. The wallpaper was a punishment turned into an inside joke between Winestra and I. What would she think of my newest developments? My tutor might not appreciate the new me. Winestra was not exactly a fan of my interest in thralls and vessels, but she allowed me to try my hand at them. She even helped me perfect the craft until I commanded small creatures without the blink of an eye.

She never let me taste blood, and it tasted so good. It made me so powerful. A wild grin grew on my lips until the chill of reality snatched it back. Dangerous! The word reverberated through my skull. My mother's haunting face, drenched in the blood of her enemies! I almost hurt Serias; I could have done worse. I shook the thought from my head and stuffed myself into the shower.

Once dried, dressed, and the knots combed from my hair, I joined my aunt in the kitchen. My limbs ached and creaked as I slithered around the archway.

Darlin flashed a toothy grin at me. "Oh, there you are, I was worried the drain ate you."

"Drains don't eat, they suck," I retorted with a tongue stuck out in her direction.

"Are you insinuating a drain would slurp you down like a straw instead of opening up to munch on you?" Darlin chuckled as she placed a large plate in my usual seat. I slipped into the chair and smiled up at her with a playful gleam in my eyes.

"Are you insinuating the drain has teeth I am unaware of?" I wiggled my brows at her.

Darlin put her hand to her chin and tapped it with her forefinger. She hummed lowly, the note lingered in the air before she broke into a wicked grin. "Now, wouldn't that be the prank of the century. Say, why don't we play it on Raphael when he gets back into town." She whipped from me as she snatched up the wine bottle off the counter and poured herself a glass nearly full to the brim.

I eyed it with worry before I blinked rapidly and realization hit me. "Raphael? He's coming?"

"Of course, he's the best healer in the family! When you told us of Maggie's condition, we got in contact with him immediately. He should be here in a few days, if the weather is good." She shrugged before she shot a look at me. "Why? Are you upset?"

"Is this another part of my restriction for sneaking out? Auntie, please, pick a different healer," I begged shortly before I stuffed half the sandwich into my mouth. Garlic and basil filled my mouth and warm broth slid down my throat. It eased my stomachache and melted my muscles to mush.

"He is the best," she countered as she took a long sip.

"He's also a narcissist!" I coughed on food as I shot her a look.

"Is that because you had a crush on him for the longest time and he turned you down, or because he truly is—"

"He's full of himself!" I barked, my face exploded in red. "And I don't care if I thought he was cute as a button when I was *twelve*, Auntie. He's a butthole and I hate him." I stuffed more food into my mouth. Raphael's obsession with himself and control complex were the exact reason I begged Winestra to tutor me. It pissed him off to no end that his older sister taught me and not him. She refused him three times before she said yes to me the first time. She even gloated in front of him to the elders of how advanced I was last year at the summer solstice festival.

My aunt snorted into her wine glass. I huffed and chewed with malice. We sat in silence as I ate and stewed on my hatred for my teacher's younger brother. I felt even sorrier for Maggie. She had cancer and now she would have to deal with Raphael for a few weeks while he cleansed her of the illness.

Then my brain flickered back to life and I realized. Cecelia and Maggie were out there where Leo Ashwood could get to them. I brought them into this and I couldn't let them get hurt. Plus, if I was honest, I was stronger with them nearby. Cecelia's visions were a necessity! She also had that nasty ability to peer into my brain; I couldn't let her get too far without my quick removal of that trick from her spell book. Anyone else's brain but mine! I needed

Maggie's powerful blood in a worst-case scenario. Toxic blood might be dangerous, but I needed to have her near should Leo attack again. I would not allow him to defeat me—I would kill him next time!

"Auntie?"

Darlin hummed into her wine glass.

"Can I go visit Maggie and Cecelia? To their school?"

"You want to go where now?" Darlin coughed up a massive swig of wine.

"To their school, Maggie and Cecelia's. I want to apologize." I spoke over the hard lump in my throat. No way of sneaking out, Darlin made sure of that. If I wanted to see them then it would have to be the honest way. My aunt would have to take me to school. Or, at the very least, let me go.

"And you think that is a good idea?" Darlin set down the wine glass and swiveled to look at me. Despite the four bottles in the glass bin and the empty bottle of scotch on the counter, my aunt stood up smoothly and put her hands to her hips disapprovingly. She cocked her right brow as she eyed me up and down. I'd pulled on clean jeans and a t-shirt, the closest thing to regular teenager clothes I owned. Usually, I mixed old clothes I'd rummaged out of the bins at trade shops; my style was nonexistent as compared to every teenager I'd seen in town. Clothes are clothes, and their function is to cover my skin—what did it matter if they matched?

"Just for a little bit, and it'll be at the school; our monster friend wouldn't chance it with hundreds of people around. He's made it clear he wants to get me alone," I explained, my hands tossed out to the side.

"Oh! Our monster friend? Since you brought him up, I should tell you his latest meal!" Darlin snapped around her chair. I stumbled back a step as Darlin marched up to her book and flipped it open aggressively. My aunt scowled as she turned back toward me. She was angry, but I wasn't sure if it was at me or at Leo Ashwood.

"Auntie, I—"

"Sheriff Thompson, Jared Scott, Agatha Straight, Bean McGee, Brian Little, Justifina Clearwater—"

"Auntie!" I choked on my own voice as she glanced up from her book. She set it down on the kitchen table, and my heart sank into the depths of my stomach. Twelve photos sat upon its pages with sticky notes on each of them. Names, dates, families, small information scribbled in thin ink—my aunt wrote it all down. Another journal would be made on just Leo Ashwood.

"What do you know about this monster?" Darlin whispered. "What happened in New York? Why did you leave in the first place? Why does this monster hunt for you? What aren't you telling me!?"

Tears welled up in my eyes as I grasped the closest photo to myself: a young woman, Justifina. She was a banker with thick curls pulled behind a red and white polka dot headband. Half-devoured and left out on the streetlight. My throat closed up as I set her picture down with hands that trembled. "Auntie, I..."

"Quinn Gwenevieve Foster, don't you dare lie to me." My head snapped up to see her stare right at me. It'd been years since she'd used my full name. Gwenevieve was my middle name only because it had been my mother's first name. She never used it, never talked about it, and I accepted that she'd never open up those wounds.

"There is a police investigation; the coven is concerned now that it's become clear the monster has magic. He was once a witch, and now he's a beast with a thirst that grows every day. You better start talking to me, young lady."

My mouth fell open as my knees buckled. I sank into a thick oak chair; my hands shook as I stared up at her. If I told her the truth, she might forgive me but they never would. When the coven found out, they'd deny me. Necromancy, true necromancy, is "impossible." Yet I'd brought him back, demented and blood thirsty but alive, as I found him.

"I, uh, used the library computers to join a social media site. I wanted to see the outside world, and I just wanted to see, just to talk to others. That's where I met Berry..." I trailed off as my tongue turned to ash in my mouth. My mouth faltered as Berry returned to the forefront of my mind—olive skin, long silk hair like raven feathers, thick fake lashes that covered up the pink eyeshadow on her lids. I swallowed hard. "She said she was a witch. Her parents were broke and her family was on the brink of homelessness or worse because of some millionaire. I just wanted to help her! So, I snuck out to New York to help her take back the money he'd stolen from them."

Darlin's face was marble and cold as she sank into the chair. "Go on."

I folded my hands in my lap as I struggled to sit still. "She said he was supposed to be at some huge function, and that we were just going to get enough cash out of his safe or whatever, that we were going to be in and out, but he was there, and he was out of his mind. He thought we were there to kill him! He put a knife to our throats, there were all these people there, and he lost it!"

Darlin put up her hand, a long sigh breaking her silence before she stood up. "Is this man you went to rob the monster?"

"His name is Leo Ashwood," I confessed.

"Did you curse him? Did you change him?"

My mouth faltered as I peered up at my aunt. I wanted to tell the truth, but the words hid behind my molars. So I shook my head slowly. "No! You know I would never. I tried to reason with him, but he freaked out on us. We interrupted some sort of ceremony of his. Then he hit me in the head, and I blacked out. When I woke up, he was gone." It wasn't a complete lie. My head hung down as my shoulders slouched. "I freaked out when I saw him again. I was panicked... I'm sorry, I lost control."

Soft hands cupped the sides of my face to lift my eyes to her. The anger seeped out of her face and left a sadness in her eyes that stung. "Quinn, you can't lose control like that again. You have to start telling me things instead of acting rashly. Things like this have consequences and it feels like you never learned from your first mistake."

I shrank in my chair. My throat closed in on itself as I stared at my lap. Power whispered sweet nothings into my ear as she locked eyes with me. Losing control meant power I never dreamed of ...and hurting my loved ones. "Did my mother... ever lose control?" I whimpered as I fiddled with my shirt. My eyes ventured toward her face and my chest clenched down.

She bit her lower lip as she stared anywhere but me. "Oh, lovely, that's a—"

"Auntie! You never talk about her!" I blurted out as her hands fell from my cheeks. "You don't have any books on her or my magic, it's like you don't want to remember."

Darlin backed up a step and sank down into her chair. Her hands inched toward the wine bottle but stopped an inch short. "Quinn, honey, it's not that. I... your mother..." Darlin trailed off in a sigh as she lay her face in both hands. Her shoulders slouched and she crumpled into a pile of body parts in her chair. I held my breath as she took exaggerated breaths in and out of her palms. Her fingers raked through her chestnut waves steadily and brushed them behind her ears.

"You didn't even tell me how she died," I croaked as tears welled up in my eyes.

"That's not a story you want to hear." Darlin swallowed hard, her voice barely recognizable to my ears. Her face drained of color. I slithered forward in my seat and reached out my hand to cup her knees. Darlin took a hold of my hand and squeezed it.

"I keep discovering gifts that I should have known about. I wake up and find out more things that scare me. What else am I capable of? Why don't you have any information on witches like me? Did you know I could smell blood? Or that I could taste the disease in Maggie's? I have so many questions, but I can't ask them because they all lead back to her!"

Darlin looked up into my eyes, but she wouldn't tell me. Sadness sparkled against the tears that trickled down the side of her face, her nose scrunched and lips quivered. "I'm so sorry, lovely, but I can't..." She slipped out of my hands and stood up with her book. She flipped the pages to a well-worn section and sat it down on the table. A transportation spell stared right at me. Soft swirls of color with thick lines of ink on a page I'd seen many times. It was the same spell I used to get to New York. Darlin took up a spool of thread out of the junk drawer and put it on the table next to me. "Just be back by midnight. Tomorrow is the blood moon ceremony, and I will need your help."

"Auntie, please—"

"I love you, sweetheart. Please be careful. I'll be watching over you." Darlin bent down and pressed a kiss to my forehead before she tucked a needle into the spool of thread.

My body was a marble statue with my eyes glued to her retreating form as she left the kitchen. Inch by inch I crumbled away until only my soul lingered in pieces on the kitchen floor. I flipped the book shut with one swift move of my hand and took up the spool and needle. All the eyes snapped to me and I grimaced.

"Don't give me that look. I know the spell," I murmured as I poked the needle against my thumb. A drop of blood bubbled out of my thumb and broke over the needle. I ran the needle up the side of the spool; the blood sank in and branched out along the thread instantly. It cracked the surface of white thread, dark red spiderwebs out in sharp jagged lines. Words formed on my tongue as a tingling sensation ran up my spine. Magic pumped behind my ears and my thumb burned liked the sun. "*Je Moechte Voyerisa.*"

I stood up with a gust of wind behind me. With one inhale, I existed in my kitchen full of pots and pans and plucked chicken feathers. Then I exhaled and landed outside in the crisp winter air. Snow crunched under my sneakers. My feet slipped to the side until I steadied my stance. I shivered; my arms instantly wrapped around my torso. The swamp was always warm—partially magic's fault as it pumped through everything that lived in the swamp, imbued with our magic and presence.

Now I was in the middle of town, inches inside the school yard fence. Snow dirty with footprints all over the yard and concrete. Cars and busses loitered in haphazard lines, and the ice was only partially cleared. One man in a plump camo jacket stood near a large clump of snow, the only line of defense against the cold as he shoveled away. I stepped closer to the school, my eyes following him. His eyebrows knitted down low as he dug into the ice and growled profanities at the snow.

My feet crunched as I ducked my head and stomped through the snow. The spell would last until I pulled the spool of thread and ideally, will plant me back in the kitchen. Warmth spread through my jeans from the spool as I peered up to the large building. Rumor had it that the high school was built from a prison that didn't pass inspection, and it sure looked like it—slate grey brick, windows only on the top floor, scratches along the base with chunks of brick missing, a long stone walk-way that leads nowhere.

I stepped up to the building and found one of the side entrances open. A few teenagers let out joyous laughter as they lingered by the doorway. My hair fell down purposely around my face as I ducked my way up the steps toward them. They didn't even notice me as I slumped past them into the building. I hugged myself tighter as I marched down the hall.

Then I stopped as a realization hit me like a stupid train headed at my forehead at top speed. How was I supposed to find them? Would they be in the same spot? I heard teenagers complain in the marketplace that they weren't in the same classes as friends.

Lilac flooded my nose, and a smirk grew on my lips. I could still smell them. My heart thundered in my ears as I snuck down the dull lit side hallway toward a large foyer. The school exploded in noise as I slunk through open doorways into the massive cafeteria. Chatter from all sides filled my ears as my eyes scanned the crowd. The soft murmurs died down a notch as my eyes fell on Cecelia. She looked absolutely horrified. I grinned from ear to ear.

"Quinn?" Her voice wobbled in the air. I beamed as I practically sauntered over to her table. Cecelia sat at a table mostly by herself. Another teenager sat in front of her, eyes narrowed into slits in my direction. She had bright green eyes, flame red hair in soft curls pulled up on top of her head, thick flannel shirt, and a sprinkle of freckles across her face. If she didn't glare at me like I'd killed her family, she might be cute.

Cecelia gasped as I slid into the long bench next to her, my hands folded in front of me. "How?"

"Simple transportation spell," I whispered lowly as I leaned toward her.

"She means how did you get in the school; you're not exactly a student," the ginger haired girl growled darkly.

"Jess," Cecelia whispered.

"You all are incredibly trusting of other teenagers. I simply walked in. I expected a much bigger fight," I chuckled.

"Quinn, you should go home," Jess snarled, her fist clenched around a flimsy plastic fork. It snapped in her grip. My eyes followed the pieces of plastic as she released her hold and let them fall to the table before her.

"I just got here," I scoffed.

"You almost got her killed, twice!" Jess leaned across the table, her face twisted up at the center. Her lip was curled up in a barbaric snarl. I cocked a brow up as she inhaled short breaths through her flared nostrils.

"Jess, we talked about this," Cecelia whispered as a soft hand reached across my vision and took up Jess's hand. Cecelia dusted off the plastic pieces. Jess kept her eyes locked on mine. I cut the look to turn to Cecelia.

"You know it's forbidden to discuss witch business with humans, right?" I tilted my head to the left.

"What did you call her?"

"Do you ever shut up?" I snapped my eyes to Jess before I glanced back to Cecelia.

"Quinn, be nice! Jess, it's not a bad word. It's what I am." Cecelia swallowed hard as she recoiled back into her spot. I eyed the both of them. Cecelia folded her hands on the table, her face pale and dark lines under her eyes. "No, I didn't, but I tell Jess everything. She's my best friend."

I straightened my shoulders as I turned back to Jess. She met my eyes with fury. Obviously, Cecelia had not slept. Even more obviously, Jess blamed me. I didn't blame her, because I blamed me too. A sigh fell from my lips as I shook my head and swiveled until I straddled the bench. If I fixed Cecelia's exhaustion, it might ease the tension in the room. Though, I had only done the spell once, to the lawyer in the precinct. Back then, I didn't know what I did or how I did it, but I touched him and made him shut up and feel paranoid. If I applied that magic to Cecelia to feel well rested and calm, she might feel better. The trick would be to do so without killing her or the spell to disintegrate after I pulled away. I reached out to Cecelia, despite Jess's lunge toward me. My right hand ran across Cecelia's hands and I clutched them hard.

My magic trickled across her body like a slow disease. Her skin lit up with life inch by inch until it touched her cheeks. She gawked at me strangely as the dark circles faded and her cheeks turned a sharp pink. Tingles ran up my spine and through my fingers. My temperature fluctuated and made goosebumps pucker across my arms and legs. Lilac filled my nostrils painfully—it choked me. I shifted toward her, unable to stop my body. Magic grabbed me by the muscles in the small of my back and pushed me forward.

Stop!

"What are... how..." Jess turned breathless as I yanked my hand back sharply. Cecelia studied my face. I shot back on the bench and nearly toppled myself off of it. My teeth took hold of my upper lip and sucked it down for a long minute as I pushed the tingle away from my fingers.

"It's hard to explain." I coughed; my hands flew to cover my mouth.

"You never cease to amaze me," Cecelia murmured, her mouth hung open just an inch.

"In a good way, I hope." I grinned.

"Well, you did scare us there for a moment." Cecelia shrugged as she tucked her hands into her lap. I forced my eyes not to follow and linger on the tabletop. My magic still picked at the ends of my hair, my goosebumps grew in number. "I thought you might go after us too."

"I'm sorry." My lips turned numb as the words fell out of my mouth. "I don't remember what happened."

"What?" Jess barked with a palm slapped to the table.

"Oh no—Maggie is coming!" Cecelia gasped.

I jerked my head up to find Maggie with a tray full of food headed in our direction.

"Excellent! I had hoped to catch both of you!" I grinned, my stomach settled once again. Tainted blood filled my nose and cleared out the floral scent.

Chapter Fourteen

Cecelia Tries to Hide Quinn

"Who let her in!?" Maggie hissed under her breath as she slipped down onto the bench next to Jess. Jess motioned at Maggie with the same exasperated glare and scowl. My mouth hung agape, unable to form words. I shared a look with Jess in my disbelief. Both Quinn and Maggie at our lunch table. Just the week before we were shunned to the edge of the lunchroom by social hierarchy. Then with the appearance of Quinn, it seemed the world now revolved around our corner table. The lunchroom stared with soft murmurs, all eyes on us. It most likely had less to do with me and more Maggie—the talk of the school, and this time, she seemed to hate it.

News spread like wildfire of her video. People called her clickbait and whispered sharp words under their breath at her. That lasted till she coughed blood all over the cafeteria floor before the first period. Then it was a pity party. I wasn't sure what pissed her off more. Things should have gone back to normal, but the world refused to turn. Lance was iced out by every girl for Kitty's revenge video, then he was the man to all the football players. The school split right down the middle.

When I walked into school, Lance waved me over. I almost pretended not to see him until he called my name. Jess stood to my right as he apologized for the incident again. Awkwardly I avoided thanking him. I didn't want to even acknowledge him. Then something miraculous happened and it left me in awe the whole day. Maggie appeared out of a crowd of people and slapped Lance hard enough to spin him into Ethan Piper. I watched in horror and amazement as Maggie stood at my side: "How dare you do that to Kitty!"

"She cheated on me!" Lance defended with fury I'd never seen him express. He stumbled back till Maggie slapped him harder with her opposite hand. She dropped her bag into my arms with a swift demand that I hold her stuff.

"So?! Break up with her, sure, tell her off, you have every right! But you had no right to expose her like that! You distributed revenge porn on Kitty!" And with a deep inhale, she snatched him up by the front of the shirt.

Something flipped on a switch in my head and I lurched forward. It was too late. Maggie's chest rumbled audibly, and a cough shook her to the core. Then she coughed hard enough to drop Lance and cover her face. Blood trickled out of her mouth and she gasped for air. She snatched up her bag and held it to her chest as she wiped blood off her lips. Maggie looked Lance dead in the eye as she talked through bloody teeth, "Delete every photo you have of Kitty, Delete every text message. And if you so much as put a snapchat of her pinkie toe, I will *fuck* you up! Got it, McCalister? You disgust me."

And Maggie changed the atmosphere of the whole school. Boys called her psycho and clickbait and a bunch of other horrible other names, but for the girls, it was like the world shifted. Kitty walked the hallway, arm in arm with Maggie as if the breakup never happened and every girl in the school unified behind them.

Maggie had the power, and I stared at her in marvel as she loomed over our table. She eyed me with confusion before she shot a dirty look back to Quinn. "Look, you can't be in here."

"Why not?" Quinn scoffed. "Why is no one happy to see me?"

My sanity arrived ten minutes late and flicked me at the back of the head. I stammered, "You're... a... you're..."

"A witch." Quinn smirked, her lips curled up on her face. I swallowed as she winked at me, a mischievous glee in the way her eyebrows wiggled. Her eyes glistened, accentuated the difference in their color in the bright lights of the cafeteria. "Like you and Maggie."

"Stop calling them witches!" Jess snarled.

"Keep your voice down," Maggie spat in unison with Jess. They shared a long moment of silence with eyes locked. I stared Jess down as she fiddled with her lunch tray aggressively, her lower lip trapped between her teeth. Rage turned to steam that poured out of her ears as she darted her eyes between both. Change was not Jess's strong suit. If Maggie sat with us, then Kitty might follow. I leaned left and right but couldn't see Kitty in the crowd. All eyes watched us. Then Maggie caught my eyes and whirled to face the cafeteria. The other students jumped and looked away in an instant.

"How'd you keep the candle close?" Quinn folded her hands on top of the table. Maggie turned back with a scowl. I mouthed an apology to Jess who shoveled mashed potatoes into her mouth sourly. She nodded at me before she returned her glare to Quinn. Quinn didn't spare a glance her way which stung. Jess was my best friend—I valued her opinion of people. She did *not* like Quinn, especially not in person. It would be hard to convince her to hear Quinn out and help her.

"It's in my backpack." Maggie pulled the satchel bag off her shoulder and slid it onto the table. Maggie flipped the top on it to expose an illuminated center. The candle sat in a Tupperware, aflame and carefully tucked between books and notebooks. "Found out it doesn't melt plastic or burn, and even with the lid shut, it still stays lit. I just poked a hole at the center and it burns."

"Excellent. That will extend our timetable." Quinn beamed. "And hopefully allow for better options."

"Our?" Maggie huffed.

"What timetable?" I squawked under my breath as they all snapped their eyes to me.

"Maggie's disease is aggressive, and with her skills it will only aggravate it. Ironic that the siren can't sing or risk damaging her body." Quinn shrugged nonchalantly.

"So it wasn't just click-bait," Jess whispered softly, her eyes scanned Maggie. Maggie scowled, but closed her pack and threw it over her shoulders. "I thought the blood was for dramatic effect. I liked it, like some new metal phase or whatever."

"I'm not some cheap vlogger," Maggie sneered with a sharp glare sent Jess's way.

"I'm sorry, a cheap what?" Quinn scoffed with her right brow cocked halfway up her forehead. Maggie spared me a glance to me first, in disbelief. And for a moment, we shared a moment of mutual confusion and exasperation. After a twenty-four-hour period from hell, I couldn't imagine how Maggie fared in it all. Did she go home to a family who scolded her or cried over her? The Waltons were pretty private with their personal life, even with Maggie's social media. I didn't know her well enough to ask. Besides, in between her threats to Lance's life and her need to fight off pitied onlookers, there was no time to talk to her.

Gretchen cried when I came home, and I'd never seen her cry, especially over me. For a moment it scared me, until she hugged me silently. I soaked up all the affection hungrily as I sat on the couch while Gretchen buried her face in my shoulder. Her frizzy red hair tickled my nose, but I left it be. She never said a word, didn't even mention the accident or the car or my absence. Then she made me lay down in her arms, in which I did not sleep. I couldn't drift off with the worry of Leo Ashwood on the edges of my mind. I reached out for him, like I wanted to see the monster standing over my bed.

Then I had to return to school and remember that I was Cecelia 'Birdo Baggins' Montreal. Not a witch on a monster hunt, not wrapped up in a magic mystery of my powers, but a weird teenager. Kitty still glared at me as if her irises could stab me. Lance avoided me, especially after the Maggie attack, and most of the football team sneered at me from across the hallway. I found my locker full of bird feathers while opening it this morning— chicken feathers, to be exact. Here I wasn't some mystical being like Quinn. Here I was Cecelia, the nosy, goody-two-shoes weirdo with an affection for farm fowl.

Then Quinn looked to me with a beaming smile. "Have you seen anything? Anything we can use?"

"What?" I swallowed. She reached out and suddenly my skin lit up with life again. A wave of soft comfort rolled over me, a warm breeze and the taste of green tea with honey at the back of my throat. She clutched my hand as I blinked hard. "No... nothing."

I ripped my hand away, but her face stayed unfazed. "You need rest. You will do best when well rested. Is there anywhere you can nap in this building?"

"Ha!" Jess let out a bark of laughter. "This is high school."

"That seems hardly fair to humans; naps are very important." Quinn pursed her lips as her eyes scanned across the cafeteria. Then she landed those magic eyes back on me with that wide grin and I tried to bite back tears. Her eyebrows knitted as she scanned my face with those magic eyes. "Cecelia?"

"I'm sorry, I'm kinda useless—" My mouth faltered as she blinked rapidly.

Quinn cut me off. "Nonsense."

"It's not nonsense; all I do is see stuff. I'm not a fighter, like you are. Like any of you. What do I do? I nap and I know stuff. I'm useless in times like this—"

"Cecelia," Jess hissed.

"What?" I pouted. My eyes followed Jess's eyes, soon followed by Maggie's concerned gaze. Quinn examined my face with concern, but all eyes focused on the blood that trickled out of her nose. Two thick drops dribbled down her upper lip. I jerked to life and snatched up one of my napkins. Quinn held still like concrete as I dabbed the blood away and swiped it from the edge of her nose.

"No witch is useless," she murmured as she took the napkin from my hands. That's when the blood dribbled from the other nostril and she swallowed hard. "This is a new development."

"What do you mean, new?" Maggie cocked a brow as she leaned across the table. My tongue expanded and took up the whole of my mouth. Quinn stared at me with such worry while blood trickled out of her nose like a leaky faucet. I snatched up a new napkin and stuffed it into her hands. I winced as her fingers grazed my palm, a sharp breeze ran down my spine. Her magic swirled within my stomach, butterflies formed and flapped gusts of wind against the walls of my torso. She stayed silent. I cocked my head to the side as her eyes fell to her hands full of bloody napkins.

"Quinn?" My voice trembled.

"Well, it may come as a shock to you to hear that I'm still learning to control my, you know," she murmured as she dabbed her nose again.

"But you were raised in that...school." I cleared my throat as I fixed my words. Quinn gazed up at me through her eyelashes before she shrugged.

"A school not meant for me," she whispered in short, raspy breaths. I reached out with a new napkin. One hand pushed her hands down and the other dabbed her face with new napkins. I cleared her upper lip of blood and applied pressure to her nostrils. Then she broke the dead silence around us. "Cecelia, you shouldn't feel useless."

"Oh, uh, I guess I did say that. Just, you know, forget I said it." I laughed nervously as I licked my lips.

Jess caught my moment for a second as she shoved her tray aside. A warning in her eyes as her eyes darted between me and Quinn. She'd been painfully quiet this whole lunch. Usually, Jess turned into a fountain of conversation, and yet she sat dead silent.

Then I spared a look at Maggie, who stared me down with daggers for eyes. "What?"

"You don't get to play the victim card here," she said with tight lips and clenched hands.

"I wasn't—"

"If anyone is useless, it's me," Maggie huffed. "I can't even last longer than one scream before I'm all gag and blood."

"Whoa, wait, backup, what?" Jess jerked to stare at Maggie.

Quinn let out a sigh. "No one here is useless, let's make that clear. Besides, both of you are intensely important to my plans."

"Oh, you have *plans* now!" Jess tossed her hands up.

I opened my mouth to stop the downfall of the conversation, but the shrill chirp of the bell cut me off.

Maggie glanced to Jess before she sighed and stood up. "You're still bleeding there, Quinn." She pushed away from the booth and pulled her backpack over her shoulder.

Quinn stared down at the napkin as blood trickled out of her nose.

"Well, Montreal, don't just stare at it. Take her to the nurse." Maggie barked.

I jumped in my skin as I gawked at Maggie who scowled at me. "But she's not a student."

"But she's a teenager, and if you don't tell the nurse, the nurse won't notice." Maggie sighed. "Look, get her checked out, get her out and we should talk about this later. I still want to know about that Ashwood monster, but we can't here."

"I agree, school is not the place," Jess confessed with a sigh.

"Where, then?" Quinn chirped nasally as she leaned her head forward.

I looked to Maggie expectantly, ready to ask if we should meet at the farm but stopped. She licked her lower lip nervously as she pulled out her phone. Wouldn't she suggest it if she wanted it at her house? She wanted it at my house, away from her family. Gretchen would be at practice all day; the note had been on the fridge this morning. She often stayed late the week before a huge performance. This weekend was a church in Tulsa. Given that I called her to talk as if everything was fine, she should stay out. No need for her to know I hid a witch in plain sight, right?

"Well... Gretchen won't be home after school for a few hours," I blurted out.

"Perfect, Montreal's house, directly after school!" Maggie wheeled on her heels and marched from the table. The crowd of students dispersed within seconds, Jess included.

I watched her leave with a scowl on her face and her eyes zeroed in on me. However, she headed toward the band room. She left me behind. It left a strange sting in my chest to see her walk away without me. Quinn and I sat on the bench as people shuffled by. I swallowed over the lump in my throat as I twisted back to Quinn. Her eyes were focused on the blood that slowly trickled out of her nose.

"Come on—"

"Miss Montreal."

A cold blade ran the length of my spine as I hovered over the table. Vice Principal Justin formed in the reflection of the glass across the cafeteria. He lumbered up and behind my shoulder. Quinn cocked a brow, her focus on him instead of the bloody napkin. "Yes, Vice Principal Justin?"

"Not getting ourselves into trouble, now are we?" His eyes narrowed, pale skin showing signs of missed sleep. I backpedaled as I grabbed Quinn by the shoulder.

"No, sir," I laughed nervously. "I was just taking Quinn here to the nurse; she suffers from nosebleeds, sir."

His eyes turned to slits as I jerked Quinn up onto her feet. My hands quivered as I yanked her toward me and away from the bench. A queasy feeling filled my stomach as I stared over his face.

Vice Principal Justin straightened out his tie, his thin grey eyebrows quirked up in my direction. He stepped past me and strode across the foyer with a sneer. "Make sure not to dribble on the tile; it is a slipping hazard."

"Yes, sir," I squeaked. Silence devoured the air as I dragged Quinn by the bicep across the floor. Panic filled my veins and adrenaline lit up every nerve ending. My heart thundered in my chest. Quinn snatched herself away from me, eyes wide open as I stumbled into a brick wall. I gasped for air, my back frozen against the main office wall. The queasy feeling slipped out of my pores like sweat while I stayed completely dry.

"What was that!?" Quinn hissed. "Who was that?"

"The vice principal," I wheezed.

"Those words mean nothing to me." She blinked slowly.

"He's like, second in command, here, and he also happens to hate me." I closed my eyes, and a groan slipped through my lips.

"You want me to curse him? Make dead fish come up his drain pipes? I can make his lunch come back to life—"

My eyes snapped open as she grinned from ear to ear. "No!" I scoffed.

"Why not?" She cocked a brow, her hands to her hips. Blood dribbled out of her nose faster. She stuffed the napkin into her nostril only for blood to pour out of the other. I watched in silent horror as she ripped the napkin back out and blew her nose as hard as she could into the closet trash can. Bloody snot-rockets filled the bin but blood continued to trickle from her nose. Quinn pinched her fingers over her nose and turned to me. "I don't see the problem."

"Because I don't want you to." I sighed. Quinn eyed me but said nothing as I rolled my eyes. My heart regulated itself but the panic that once burst through my veins found a new home at the bottom of my stomach. "Why is it every time I touch you, I feel wonky?"

"Well, that is also a new feature I'm working out." She tossed her head back, nose pinched between her fingers.

"Do you know anything about your gifts?" I let out a small snort. My face fell as she frowned deeply, with a hard swallow she looked right at me and let go of her nose. Blood ceased to flow.

"No, I seem to be the only one of my kind" Her voice wafted through the air in a low hush.

"Oh? What about Serias and them?" I cocked my head to the side.

"The family was there my whole childhood, but I am not like any of them. The only other was my mother."

And I knew better than to push that subject. So we stood in silence, in the hallway, both eyes downcast until the sound of footsteps filled my ears.

"Students should be in class!" Vice Principal Justin's voice bounced off the walls.

Quinn burst past me. I flew around her and pushed open the doorway to the West wing of the school. The murmurs of students in math and science class filled the air as we ducked around a corner into a new hall. A loud crack made me jump in my skin, but Quinn tossed herself in the doorway of a classroom. Magic flung my body with all its momentum, into Quinn and tossed us both out of the doorway and into a collection of lockers. The thud and rumble of items in the locker filled my ears as I pinned Quinn up against the steel.

"Miss Montreal?"

I spun around and beamed a nervous smile up to Miss Myles, the chemistry teacher, her face covered in soot. Miss Myles still styled one full eyebrow and one eyebrow drawn on her face to cover up the massive scar horizontally across her forehead. Her lab glasses always rubbed it halfway off and showed how deep and squiggly the scar was. Despite her efforts to cover her eyebrow up, she always started the year off by "blowing it off" with a contact explosive. Every year she told a different story about how she received the scar. At the PTO meeting my freshmen year she told me that she lost it in a bad card game. Then on the first day of class she warned us about the dangers of playing with knives without protective glasses, and that's how she gained the scar. Jess told me Miss Myles told her that she made the mistake of having a seamstress wax her brows, and that the woman pulled a seam in her face.

"Miss Myles." I laughed, hands firmly planted behind me with my back to Quinn, who was still pinned to the side of the lockers. "Is it fire safety week?"

"It's *always* fire safety week here." She cackled with a wide grin that lit up her face. Crows feet prickled the skin next to her eyes, and it made the soot shift and fall off her face as she let out a snort.

"Sorry about the disturbance. Quinn and I were just leaving," I squeaked as I backpedaled away from Miss Myles.

"Quinn? I don't recall ever seeing you. Do you go to this school?" Miss Myles cocked her head to the side.

"What?" My voice pitched in my throat as I tossed my hands out to the sides. "Of course, she goes here, Miss Myles, everyone goes here. It's such a small town."

That's when my eyes caught Quinn shift beside me, her eyes narrowed in on a shadow behind Miss Myles. My eyes flickered to the corner and my heart roared against my ribcage. Vice Principal Justin lingered at the corner, his lips pressed thin and beady eyes narrowed on Quinn.

"You're right, how silly of me," Miss Myles chirped. "Well, go on, get to class, Miss Montreal, wouldn't want you to be late again."

"Miss Montreal, I believe you were headed to the nurse!" Justin's voice bounced down the hall as Miss Myles whipped around to face him.

"Vice Principal Justin! Great timing—why don't you join me this session? I have some science questions I could use your help answering." Miss Myles grinned from ear to ear. Quinn's hand wrapped around my bicep and squeezed, and a sharp wave of calm ran through my body.

"I am busy, Miss Myles. Maybe another time."

I clamped my lips shut as Quinn and I edged ourselves away from the lockers and down the hallway. Vice Principal Justin eyed the both of us from the corner of the hallway before he slithered away from the wall and back out of the west wing.

My heart thundered in my chest as Quinn and I inched down another hall. Then we burst into a run down the hall toward another side door. Quinn barreled into it with her shoulder before she flew and tumbled down the steps from the school. Long legs meant my jump off the top step was a tiny hop, and I landed beside her. She scrambled to her feet.

"What is he? A wolf?" she snarled as she broke into a new run across the parking lot. And for some reason, I followed her.

"I would honestly prefer a wild wolf as my vice principal," I muttered as we ran across the snow. The crunch filled my ears, and I didn't spare a look back at the school. One minute I was convinced I needed a nap in the middle of the lunchroom, and the next I abandoned my school to chase after Quinn.

Chapter Fifteen

Maggie Visits Cecelia's House

The last time I stopped by Cecelia Montreal's house, I was eleven. Gretchen Montreal agreed to teach me to play piano, and Cecelia sat in the living room with a book the whole time. The Montreal house was the *only* place I wanted to learn to play from. If it wasn't Gretchen, it wasn't good enough. Her skill is known all over the Bible Belt. She played at mega-churches for Christmas and Easter; she also played for a traveling orchestra when she was sixteen. There was no one else in my eyes, and my parents paid for her to yell and smack my fingers for four years.

Then she cut me off, and I never stepped foot in the house again. Gretchen Montreal said I needed to continue on my own and threw me from the nest. That's when I started playing on Facebook and YouTube. Started my own channel to play around on the piano, fiddled with my own songs. I taught myself guitar and to sing and play at the same time, but Gretchen Montreal is the true reason that I unlocked my musical talent.

Which is a shame, because Gretchen Montreal is an absolute jerk. She is rude, she is mean, and she often talked about other students behind their backs. As the front door to the house opened, my mind instantly returned to the day Gretchen shut the door in my face. My mother was livid as I slumped back to the van. Except, this time as the door opened, Cecelia stared at me in disbelief. She wore a long faded gray scale shirt of a Monty-Python film over a pair of acid washed jeans, her long onyx hair trailing down to her hips.

"You actually came?" Cecelia blinked as she stepped aside.

I scooped my blond waves off my shoulder and readjusted my bag. Kitty, after hearing I couldn't hang out after school, turned aggressive when I explained who I ditched her for. Ever since I returned to school, she devoured my personal space. Usually, it never bothered me how clingy she was, until I saw her glance at me in worry and silent concern. The whole day we never spoke of the cancer; we didn't speak about my video or about how I dropped off the face of the earth for two days. We especially didn't speak about how I ditched her at lunch to sit at Cecelia Montreal's table. We also didn't talk about Lance—a silent agreement, that what happened last week stayed in last week.

"I said I was." I rolled my eyes as I brushed past her and the door. Quinn sat on the dusty waiting couch, notebooks spread around her and a pen between her lips. Jess hunched on the wooden rocker, eyes nailed into the side of Quinn's head. Cecelia closed the door behind me and all the memories came back. The scent of fresh paper and sweet tea filled my nose. Light trickled through the front window onto the grand piano that sat dead center in the room. Thick jade curtains pulled back against the deep crimson walls, and there were golden accents on jade furniture and thick oak floors. I dropped my bag onto the piano seat and ran my fingers across the frosty keys.

"So..." Cecelia trailed off as she lingered halfway in and halfway out of the room. One thing that always caught my attention was the lack of pictures anywhere in her house. My family filled the house to the brim with badly taken photos framed along the walls. Cecelia's house existed out of time and space, bare of anything but her and the piano.

She joined Quinn on the couch. Her long limbs curled around her. The snow outside the window made the light more intense. It lit up the spotless top of the piano, unlike the piano my parents saved for years to buy me, dusty and covered in fingerprints with a small slope in the middle from where Martin sat to dramatically sing Christmas carols poorly last year. Gretchen Montreal's piano sat spotless, slick, and stunning.

"Are we going to talk about the fat elephant in the room?" Jess snapped, her teeth bared.

I rolled my eyes before I twisted back to all of them. "Now that's no way to talk to Quinn," I sneered.

"Whoa!" Quinn jumped in her seat, her eyes shot between Jess and me. "Elephants aren't fat—they are naturally voluptuous."

"Stop trying to distract from the fact that all of this started because of you." Jess shot up in her seat. I crossed my arms as Jess tore across the room. Cecelia lunged forward to grab Jess a few seconds too late. Jess snatched up Quinn by the arms and hoisted her up into the air.

Quinn tossed herself out of Jess's hands and landed with a loud thud onto the living room floor.

"I was doing fine until Cecelia interjected herself!" Quinn spat.

"Whoa, sorry for trying to help," Cecelia whimpered, and her shoulders slouched more.

"And what about Maggie? She ran into danger blindly; she put herself in this situation." Quinn flashed a hand in my direction.

"I was only at the hospital because I hit that stupid monster with my truck in the first place!" I barked.

I swallowed hard as Cecelia stepped toward me with concern. Quinn interjected herself as she wheeled around the coffee table covered in notebooks. "You faced Ashwood alone? Prior to that night?"

"Yeah! I did! I was upset and a bit volatile, so I took a drive and I... well... I kinda crashed into him then screamed my head off," I murmured as my heart sank into my feet.

"Why were you upset?" Cecelia cocked a brow.

"Does it matter?" I croaked. I stumbled back a step. "I was diagnosed with cancer. Doctor Higgins... Oh god."

I crumbled onto the piano seat and my hands shook, as if the mention of his name brought it back. My skin turned to ice as I stared to the wooden floors, my snow boots made tiny puddles underneath me.

"Maggie, Dr. Higgins death hit us all hard, but that's no reason to beat yourself up over it. He was the only doctor for the whole town; he was dealing with a lot at home." Jess sighed, her arms tossed out to her sides. I peered up from the floor as tears trickled down my cheeks and both Cecelia and Jess's faces fell.

"That's the thing," I whimpered. "He didn't kill himself. I was there."

"Maggie, you didn't." Cecelia crumbled to the floor in the living room.

"I didn't mean to! I was upset! He just said we would have to do surgery on my throat, and my vocal chords might not survive the chemo if we went that route. I was ruined! And I didn't mean to! I didn't know I was a witch, or a siren, or whatever she calls me. I was just a girl who was told the one thing she loves was ripped from her fingers and I... well..."

A pen could drop, and it would sound like a bomb. My body trembled as I replayed the moment in my mind. Tears fell from my eyes as I heard him run the pen through his body like a hot knife through butter. The blood on my hands appeared again as I shuddered on the floor of the examination room. My father screamed for help and shock took over my body.

"That happened less than two weeks ago! How did no one know about this?" Cecelia broke the silence with a whimper. Her eyes caught mine and brought me back to reality.

"Because she's the town sweetheart and no one would ruin her reputation over the likes of a simple family doctor, right? That's why the police said he committed suicide?" Jess barked. "What did you do?"

"I didn't!" I cried out.

"You didn't know," Quinn interjected and my eyes jumped to her. "Some sirens have been known to talk people over a ledge."

"But I didn't talk him into it; I just was crying and I..." I trailed off. My throat tightened. A pressure tickled at the back of my throat. My lips clamped shut and I grabbed for my bag. The Tupperware of the candle tumbled into my shaking hands.

"And what? Did she just tell him to stab himself? Or did she throw a temper tantrum and force his hand?" Jess growled as she rounded the table to glare at Quinn.

"It doesn't matter what happened; it was a learning moment." Quinn sighed.

"Hell, it doesn't matter! She killed someone!" Jess snapped her eyes to me. "You killed someone, Maggie! And we thought he was depressed! We thought he committed suicide, and it turns out you just witched your way—"

"He was my doctor, too!" I shouted. "You think I wanted—"

Quinn launched across the floor and clamped her hands over my mouth. The damage had already been done. Jess flung across the floor, dragged by the force of my words, her hands clamped to her ears and body curled up. Cecelia rushed to her side and pulled Jess into her arms. A dent stayed in the wall where Jess's back collided with it. A large crack ran the length of the wall; the plaster exploded around her in a cloud of dust. The lights swayed and her crack exposed the space between the drywall and boards. My eyes widened and tears streamed down my cheeks as Quinn ripped her hands back from my face. "Indoor voice for you, for like, all of the time."

"I didn't... I didn't...I didn't." My brain shattered into a million pieces. I did it again. What would have happened if Quinn didn't stop me?

"You see, right there, the panic and fear, realizing you just did something stupid and wrong and you didn't mean to..." Quinn sank down onto the piano seat in front of me as she tucked her hands between her legs. "That's how Leo Ashwood happened."

I swallowed hard and clutched the Tupperware candle to my chest. "What?" I whimpered.

"What do you mean, how he happened?" Jess growled from the comforts of Cecelia's arms.

"It's a long story." Quinn sighed. Small fingers tucked in between her thighs as she slouched her shoulders forward. Quinn looked like anyone else, dressed in a tank top under a faded, open button up draped over ripped jeans tucked into ankle boots. Then she glanced up and stole the air from my lungs. The green and blue eyes glistened; she could bewitch anyone with them. Lips opened an inch, she took a long breath in. "Buckle up, because I think the clue to defeating him is somehow in how I made him."

"Made him?" I squeaked under my breath. Her palms pushed against the bottom of the seat.

"There is something you should know about me. About what I am." Quinn fell silent for an eternity before she shot up off the piano seat and walked to the coffee table. She picked up the first notebook on it. She etched a pentagram etched into the page. Then she labeled all the points, labeled a few inner corners, and then the center.

"So witches are humans that became divine. My aunt used to draw this for me all the time, and it's the best way to show it. We are all born with a specific area of gifts. Most witches fall along one of the points of the star of magic. Seer, Siren, Spellslinger, Herbalist, Illusionist. Most magic falls into these categories, like Cecelia who is a seer, and Maggie a siren, my aunt is a spellslinger. Then there are more specific magic sub-sections that are very powerful, but their gifts are specific and not as vague. Enchanters, for example, are able to imbue items with magical power, and like a potion, give it specific properties, but they can only enchant. All this magic makes up the star of magic, where the center is blood magic. The magic where all of us came from, the kind of magic that I use." She lay the notebook down with a sigh. Her fingers traced the star in slow motions before she shoved it away from her and poked her hands into her lap.

"So you're what, some kind of Super Saiyan witch?" Cecelia cocked a brow.

"Seriously?" I quipped.

"What?" She shrugged.

"Once again, those words mean nothing to me." Quinn shook her head. "But what that means is I draw my power from the original source: blood magic. The kind of magic the first witches drew their powers from. You see the further out on the star you are, the more stable and controllable the magic. You can learn to direct it, to control it, to wield it like a weapon you've been trained with all your life. It takes time, but I have heard of many sirens from many other covens and families who live long lives in music and show business, who have a few skeletons in the closet but are all around good people. I've never met them, but Darlin assures me that they aren't a problem. Now just like everything, there are always a few bad eggs in the batch, but those we can talk about later."

"And so what about you?" I said. My body had stilled, and my blood warmed up around the candle's light that flickered across my face.

"I am a whole other animal," she grumbled. "Which sucks because I could sing stories of great Sirens through history and talk about Seers who have stopped wars. I have read and memorized history and stories from all over the world... and yet I know nothing about me and those like me. We are far and few between and... there's very little written about us... and I'm starting to see why. Because there are a few impossibles when it comes to magic. Or at least there were One of those was complete reanimation, or true necromancy. It was impossible. I can make monsters out of the dead. I can reanimate bodies and parts like minions or zombies but not like Leo Ashwood. I shouldn't have been able to bring him back."

Silence returned as she sank down into the rocking chair, her hands folded in her lap. Jess emerged from Cecelia's arms and stood up to her full five foot three height. Hands clamped to her sides, fingers clawing into her side. Rage radiated off her as she stared Quinn down.

"Why did you?" Cecelia cocked a brow.

"I didn't mean to. He wasn't the person I wanted to bring back." She clenched her eyes shut tight and took a long breath in through her nose and out through lips that quivered. Then Quinn opened her eyes. "So, it might have come to your attention that I'm not very socially acceptable. I have never gone to public school, I live out in a swamp, and I'm not up to date on social media at all. I honestly don't know how to work the internet very well."

"Noticed." Jess rolled her eyes. She stretched and rolled her shoulders, but she avoided eye contact with me.

"Well, a while ago, I ventured into the town library just to see if maybe the humans had some information on my mother or me and my kind. My aunt was being difficult, and I may have reacted in kind. But then I found someone was logged into a blog site, I think that's what they were, and there were blogs from all over. I kind of have this habit of obsessively seeking knowledge and there was so much to read.

"Before I knew it, I came across a blog from a girl in New York. Her name was Berry and she was upset because this rich, heartless man fired her father from his large company and completely bankrupted them. Apparently, he fooled them and there was no money and they were evicted. She was distraught and just wanted to take back what was owed to her. She openly posted about being a witch, and I was foolish enough to believe she was actually one. So I reached out to her, as a witch, and well... I had a friend. Finally, a friend that wasn't an adult in the coven and wasn't my aunt. There was another person to talk to. For weeks we talked while I dug around on the internet for information. Then I did something *very* dumb." Quinn grimaced as she hung her head.

"You decided to go meet her," Cecelia blurted out. Quinn snapped her fingers then pointed at Cecelia while another finger pressed into her nose. Quinn fiddled with the hem of her shirt.

"Well, what happened? Was she Leo Ashwood in disguise?" I cocked a brow.

"Oh, I wish, but no, Berry was very real. She was also *very* human. She was one of those play-pretend witches—you know, they like the look and sounds of being a witch but no idea we truly exist. But I had already snuck out to meet her and transported myself to her. I also still liked the idea of being her friend, even if she was human. So we made a plan to go to his home and steal back the money he owed them. Just enough to fix their problems. I felt like I was on a hero mission. We were going to sneak in while he was supposed to be at this huge charity auction, which she told me is where he was supposed to be, mistake number three at this point. I broke into his home and that's when I met Leo Ashwood, illusionist witch and complete paranoid piece of trash. He thought we were there to kill him."

"What!?" Jess interrupted.

"Well, it would have been easy for me to wiggle and lie my way out of it, say we were just in the wrong place and apologize if Berry wasn't actually there to kill him." Quinn pouted. "He found the knife she had on her with his name carved into it. Apparently she was convinced if she killed him with a ceremony knife, it would fix everything he'd done to them. After that it gets really blurry."

"That's bad." Cecelia muttered as Quinn placed her hands over the back of her head.

"He was so angry! And he just wouldn't listen to me. I panicked, and there were so many other people there, but some of them weren't there. I can't remember their faces, but there were so many bodies. I began to panic and then he stabbed her. Cut her open and had them grab me. I couldn't escape and I panicked... I didn't..." Quinn trailed off as she raised her head and caught my eye.

"So you killed him?" Jess licked her lips nervously.

"I killed all of them, I think. Then I tried to bring Berry back...and brought him back instead." Quinn's hands shook as she clutched them in her lap. "I don't know the rules, and I'm not even sure how I did it. It's not supposed to be possible! I winged it, you know, went without a script and no idea what I was doing and winged it right out the window. Now he's a monster who can talk and hunt and use his magic again, and he wants nothing more than to destroy everything...but mostly me."

"Well, that settles it, then," Cecelia murmured.

"Yeah, we gotta hunt him back. Leo Ashwood is a monster, and he just stumbled into hunting central. He's gonna wish he'd never been brought back!" Jess slapped her hand against the couch.

I shook my head with a sigh. "I hate to say it, but they're right."

"I just don't know how, we're going to do it, quite yet, which is why I need you two." Quinn leaned back in the chair.

"Hey! What am I? Chopped liver?" Jess huffed.

"You will be if you try to help," Quinn retorted.

"Jess is a part of this now, and besides, she's the only one of us that's gone hunting. She stays," Cecelia countered.

"Hunting a deer and taking down a monster with magic are two different things," Quinn quipped, her arms crossed over her chest. Jess and Cecelia stared Quinn down until she sighed and let out a groan. "Fine! But she's your responsibility!"

"Fine!" Cecelia snapped.

"Fine!" Quinn shot back.

"Fine!"

Words swam in my brain. I ripped the top of the Tupperware off and scooped the candle out. Flames licked my skin but left only a soft tickling sensation. The candle helped. Without it in my hands I existed as a tiny raft on the water, holes poured with thick dark water and sharks circled me. Then the light of the flame lit up the night and my boat floated above water again. I heaved a heavy breath, candle pressed against my skin.

"Maggie, how are you holding up?" Jess's words softened in my ears as I glanced up from the candle.

"Well, I have cancer, I'm sixteen, I tanked my YouTube career by posting about it only a day after I killed one of the nicest people with my voice, and I can still see his face when... and I now have to carry a candle around with me in Tupperware like bad leftovers. I have no idea how I'm holding up, but so far I'm not dribbling on the floor, so I suspect that's a plus." I blinked.

She scowled, but not in my direction. Her eyes shot to Quinn before they softened on me and knelt in front of the piano seat. "Sorry for going slightly psycho on you there," she muttered.

"Yeah, well, I've known you since kindergarten, Jessy," I teased with a smirk. She cocked an unimpressed brow as I snickered. "I was there the day you Hulk tossed Eric Johnson across the playground and into the steel slide for tugging your pigtails."

"Good times, good times," Jess muttered under her breath with a warm gleam in her eyes. I rolled my eyes, my hands cupped around the candle to soak in all its magic. "So what's with the candle?"

"It is keeping the cancer from wrecking me, apparently." I shrugged.

"Weird." She eyed the candle.

"You're telling me. This whole week has been weird." I looked down to the candle and inhaled. Soft wicker scents wafted up into my nose, the kind of wooden wicker rich people put in cheap candles to add to their experience.

"I don't trust Quinn," Jess whispered as she turned on her knees to stare at Quinn and Cecelia in a stalemate in front of the jade couch. Cecelia stared Quinn down who kept her hands on her hips and kept her eyes locked.

"I do, strangely enough."

Chapter Sixteen

Quinn Returns to the Swamp

I held the spool of thread between my thumb and forefinger, home in my mind, but the spell stalled. I didn't want to go back. A sigh tumbled from my lips as I pocketed it and sank down into the backyard grass. The buzz of confession still under my skin. Cecelia and Maggie needed to know the truth, but my aunt could never know.

The night replayed behind my lids as I stared out into the yard. His door, heavy, thick white wood with golden accents as I pressed my hands against it. Berry picked it with two bobby pins and a thin metal rod, as if she'd done it a million times. For a moment I worried that I'd made a mistake. Then Berry thanked me for the help, that she would have never done this alone. She made me feel accepted. It didn't matter that she wasn't a real witch.

My eyes closed long enough to see her just outside the train station, wide eyed and eager, a thick plum jacket pulled tight against her. Her hair stood up in tight curls like golden wire threaded through with fake flowers that exploded out of her hair. The pictures she posted of herself were nothing compared to seeing my friend in person. My only friend, as I stepped out of a train I snuck into the last stop. She rushed up to me with a squeal and a hug. I shivered in my sweater, and she offered a coat out of her tote. There was no snow, but in her messages she said that it might later that night.

"Spell got your tongue?" Maggie sneered just an arms-length from my left shoulder. I opened my eyes and dabbed away any moisture that betrayed me. The sounds of the house trickled out into the yard as I composed myself. Bare feet crunched the grass beside me.

Cecelia babbled over the phone with her mother, all smiles and laughing with Jess in the background. I ran my thumb along the spool in my pocket, my other hand tucking as far as my opposite pocket would go, about two inches deep. Damn fake pockets—no one needs imaginary pockets! I scowled as I turned my head a hair toward Maggie. She slid down into the grass beside me carefully, the candle tucked in between her fingers.

"You ought to be careful, that candle could go out," I whispered hoarsely as I peered back out to the large, solid oak fence that climbed up six feet from the grass. There was a clean cut, small garden with a couple of scattered rose bushes. Strategically placed vines with thorns grew up the side of the fence and over its sharply cut top. I eyed it suspiciously the first time I saw it, until Cecelia showed me the rest of the house. Neat, clean, not a speck of dust or item out of place. Cecelia said her mother cleaned the house continuously.

Darlin and I cleaned when it was convenient, enough to keep it livable, but nothing organized. Books were strewn about, blankets and pillows everywhere but the kitchen, bottles of potions and experiments on ledges with notebooks nearby. Home, my comfortable disaster.

"And would that really be a bad thing?" Maggie sighed as she tucked the candle between her thighs and put the pads of her feet together.

"Very," I spat. "You seem very lackluster, despite your clear fight for survival instincts." I cocked my head to stare at her profile. She kept her eyes on the trees that rose from the backside of the fence, where dense oaks and pines full of moss grew, full of sound as wildlife fluttered between the branches. Despite the screams of insects, light chirps of birds, the noise of life around us, it felt dead in the yard.

Maggie folded her hands on top of her feet, her face empty of emotion. "I have kind of a warped sense of life, I guess," she murmured as her eyebrows furrowed.

"How so?" I chuckled.

"If cancer took me, I guess I wouldn't be so angry. It's what I deserve, after what I've done." She scrunched her nose. "But I refuse to let that monster take me out!"

I cocked a brow as she tightened her hands around each other. She inhaled sharply and let it out gradually until her face eased. My eyes fell away from her face, they wandered back to the fence. "I don't think you deserve death."

"Ha! Funny!" Maggie barked harshly as she dropped her hands behind her. Her fingers buried in the grass as she stared at the fence with me.

My hands slipped out of my pockets and pulled my knees up to my chest. "Why is that funny?" I scowled.

"Says the girl who brought something back from the dead. The same girl who has confessed to more than one murder," she retorted with a short snort and a roll of her head backward. I glanced back toward her as she hung her head toward the grass and stared back at the house.

"I don't think you deserve to die by some illness for a mistake," I stated through firm teeth.

"Oh? And what do you deserve?" Maggie popped her head back up to catch my eyes.

"I... I... I don't know." I jerked my head back and tucked my chin between my kneecaps. The sound of the outside filled the air as I bore my eyes into the fence line. "I've made a lot of mistakes..."

"You know, I can be kind of mean. I know what everyone in school says—I'm a grade A bitch. I'm the one who gave Cecelia her nickname of Birdo Baggins. Kitty spread the rumors about Jess, and I let her. Everyone online thinks I'm sweet and kind, but the truth is, in person, if you really knew me, I'm... I'm a monster."

I straightened my legs out and twisted to look at her fully. "You are not a monster," I growled.

"Then neither are you," Maggie shot back. "I'm not exactly a good judge of mental health right now. I'm kind of in the middle of my own crisis, you know. I hate myself and then I don't, I'm afraid and angry, and boy, am I angry. Like, ready to melt the next person who says they're so sorry that this happened to me. Like, like I'm some stupid kid who broke their arm skateboarding in a freak accident. I have cancer! The only person who should feel sorry for me is me and yet I don't! Everyone else is *sooooo* sorry but I'm not! I'm livid! I'm pissed! I'm so... so damn scared. So I'm not gonna lie to you, Quinn, I'm shaking in my boots about Leo Ashwood. But when I look at you, when you ran into him head on, I'm not scared for some reason. You make me feel brave and rational...

Monsters don't do that. So, I'm absolutely certain you're not a monster."

I swallowed hard as tears welled up in my eyes. "What if, in some twisted, horrible way, I like the power?"

Maggie shuffled till she was sat hip to hip with me, candle in one hand and the other linked through my arm. The sun set inch by inch over the tops of the trees. The sky turned pink and orange around us in soft waves. Birds quieted down but the insects only grew louder. Lightning bugs speckled the tree line as one flew into the yard like a stray comet. "Like you like feeling powerful?"

"No. Yes. Maybe." I tucked my forehead against the back of my hands. "It's different. I've always felt out of place, my magic doesn't always work the same as it does for everyone else. The spells can go wild, and I lose control. But when things are the most chaotic, when the power is dark enough to scare small children, I feel the most in control. I feel at peace and strong, like I could face the world. It's this force that comes over me and makes everything possible and everything is calm within me. Then I wake up and I see what I do to everyone else."

Tears dripped down my face. "I like it. I like how it feels to use my magic. It's like being free enough to fly. I like it! Then I feel bad, because when I let go, people get hurt! And every time I try to control it, every time I think I've got it this time, it gets worse. And there are no answers for me. There are no teachers, there are no books, there is nothing. No information, no nothing, it's just me and how I feel and I can't trust myself. I just can't."

Maggie squeezed my arm. "Quinn-"

"We have a healer coming to eradicate the illness from your body. Soon you'll be back to full health. Since you're a siren, and you'll be back to full strength soon. If I lose control again and turn into a monster, you have to stop me," I blurted out.

"What?" She recoiled, disgust scrunched her nose and twitched in her mouth.

"If I become a monster, I want you to use your magic and force me to stop. No matter what it takes."

And Maggie stayed deadly still and silent, her fingers dug into the candle as her eyes searched my face. I hardened my resolve. Maggie is a siren. She made the monster stop in its tracks even weakened and in pain. When fully healed, who knew what power she could possess. It had to be her. Cecelia might not see it happen, Jess was too human, and my aunt would be too biased. She could never hurt me; she could never do what had to be done.

"It has to be you," I murmured. "You're the only one with the resolve to do it."

Maggie said nothing as she nodded silently and put a hand to my shoulder. I smiled weakly then I pulled the spool of thread out of my pocket. She eyed it suspiciously before I sat it in my lap. Gradually, I pulled myself up to my feet and waved to her. Maggie struggled to stand as I pulled the thread and released the spell. I snapped back to the front porch. Once again, wild magic with no control. If I had performed it correctly, I should have returned to the kitchen.

Darkness filled the swamp from top to bottom. The familiar bog smells of stagnant water and moist trees filled my nose. A sharp crackle of blood floated through the air toward me from behind the door. My aunt was home and close by. Crickets sung late into the night and frogs joined in as bass. My hand stopped inches from the knob.

I could trust Maggie to stop me. The power was not worth hurting my loved ones, not again.

"Quinn?" Darlin called out for me.

I came through the front door, the sunset dipped to barely visible between trees. Darlin sat on the large collection of pillows with journals all around her. She had her hair pushed back behind a thin scrap of fabric with a clip and a pen wedged between her lips. She read over passages from paper in her right hand and then ripped the pen from her lips to write with her left hand. Only for a moment did her eyes shoot up to see me, then they went right back to work.

"I said I'd be back," I laughed sheepishly as I closed the door behind me. Her spellbook swiveled from its stand on the floor to look at me with all its eyes. Worry portrayed in a few of them, suspicion in others; it was hard to decide if the snake looked more concerned than the crystal. The house was quiet except for the clink of dishes as they dried and put themselves away in the cupboards and the soft hum of music that played off a record player in her bedroom. When Darlin worked, it felt deadly quiet. Even more quiet after we fought, then she went to work and I whisked myself away to another place just to avoid the dead silence in the house.

"I was worried you might not this time." Darlin sighed as she put another notebook away. She folded her hands in her lap, her pen tucked behind her ear. All eyes were on me as I tucked my hands into my loose pockets. The morning replayed behind my eyelids. She put on a warm smile but it barely reached her cheeks, let alone her eyes. "You learn anything at school?"

"Nothing noteworthy. But I do think something bad is happening with the vice principal; he was shifty in the worst way, but Cecelia swears that's just who he is as a person," I confessed with a shrug. My feet all but dragged my exhausted body across the floor. Within moments of a spot cleared by Darlin's hands, I dropped myself into the pillows. After I melted into the cushions, my eyes closed.

"Well, if you think he is questionable, I will have someone in the coven investigate," Darlin stated, and gave me a firm pat on the back. Then her nails raked across my spine in soft circles, goosebumps deliciously jumped across my arms as I dissolved into the cushions. "I trust your judgement."

My eyes sprang open. With just a statement, my heart sank into the floorboards and forced me wide awake. I struggled to make my body relax, but the goosebumps were gone. "You do?"

"Of course! I raised you, sweetheart; I taught you to see things like I would." Her nails left my back. I heard her shuffle papers and notebook around, right back to work. She muttered a few words to herself as she read along.

My eyes stared across the pillows, my heart thundered in my chest. "And what if I made a mistake?" I shoved the words through my teeth.

"Everyone makes mistakes, hun—it's how you fix them that matters," she mumbled, the same phrase I've heard every year since childhood.

A sigh tumbled out my lips as I cracked my back and clambered out of the pillows. "I stink, I'm going to shower," I confessed.

"Good idea," she replied without sparing a glance to me.

I twisted toward the book, all eyes scattered in different directions. "Maybe I'll summon a demon from the abyss," I whispered with a huff.

"Have fun," she muttered between mouthfuls of pen.

I sighed for a second time but gained no response. I lumbered toward the bathroom. The light switch was a million times heavier as I stumbled into the bathroom and shut it with my rear end. Backed up against the door, I swallowed tears and screams that rushed up from inside me. Pressure built up at the back of my skull as the tears spilled down my face. Blood trickled down from my nose as I clenched my eyes shut. My fingers swiped at the blood but only spread it across my face. The dams burst when I opened my eyes and found Cecelia in my bathroom.

Dressed in only a T-shirt and damp hair, tears streamed her face. She lingered within my shower, arms wrapped around her tight enough to leave red marks on her biceps. I swallowed the lump in my throat as she opened her eyes. "Cecelia, please stop breaking into my head."

"I wish I knew how to," she muttered. I scoffed as tears doubled down the sides of my cheeks. My body went rigid as she stepped out of my shower and toward me. "Why are you crying?"

"Why are you crying?" I snapped back at her with a sharp look.

"Because you're crying, I think," she whimpered as she slumped against the open space on my bathroom wall. Mint walls glistened around her midnight-colored hair—

the only color my aunt hated more than I did. Two years ago, I refused to do an assignment for Winestra. She then refused to listen to me and painted my bathroom. The entire time she told me she would stop the second I did what she asked... Suddenly my bathroom was completely mint colored and I still ended up having to babysit a possum at the kitchen table and recite the magic laws to it with my eyes closed. Cecelia cleared her throat and brought my thoughts and focus back to her. "I was brushing my teeth and then all of the sudden I felt so lonely..."

"Yeah, well, I'm not lonely." I stormed past her; her form wavered for a moment. The tears blurred my vision. My hands stilled over the handles in my tub. The question wasn't if I would act as if she wasn't there, but how far would I go to act as if she wasn't stuck in my head? Stubbornness was a genetic trait, one my aunt instilled deep within me.

"Quinn... what happened to your mom?"

Every ounce of spite in my system turned into sharp rage. "What?" I barked as I whirled around. How dare she! She poked into my head, farther than before. My hands clenched tightly. The roar of the pipes would cover up the sound of a conversation as steam water pumped out of the faucet. My aunt was far too focused to notice, but there was no reason not to be cautious. Besides, I said I wanted a shower.

"You're thinking about her a lot..." Cecelia confessed as her lower lip jutted out in a soft pout.

My heart fluttered painfully as I hugged my arms around myself. My mother, another sore spot. Not only did I miss her presence and regret a life without her, I didn't know a single thing about her, just scraps I dug up about her from others. The only concrete thing I knew was that we were identical, from the choppy brunette hair to the shape of my face and nose. Darlin told me once that even our birthmarks were identical, and she cried for a whole day.

"Stop that!" I croaked.

"What kind of birthmark?" She blinked rapidly as her hands covered her ears.

"Quit it!" I snapped, my hands jerked to my sides.

"A heart shape on the back of your right thigh," she stammered.

I lunged across the room. Solid as a wall, I grabbed her by the arms and tightened my grip around her bicep. "Stop it *now*!" I ground out between my teeth. "Please!"

Tears fell down her cheeks as she shook her head. "I can't!" Her honey eyes glowed as tears trailed down her face. My fingers fell from around her and dangled by my sides. I licked my lips nervously, my hands quivered. She lingered by the wall, unable to move. "I am sorry."

"She died," I muttered. My fingers gripped at my clothes, and the feel of jeans on my fingertips felt foreign as I tried to pump life into them. "My aunt won't tell me anything about her. I don't even know who she was. I don't even know what her favorite color was. I have no memories of her but the only thing I have of her is my magic."

Cecelia slipped off the wall and closed the distance between us. Her form wavered in and out of my vision before it grew permanent again in front of me. Her fingers grazed my cheeks, her thumbs dried my tears. "I was adopted. The only memory I have of my mother is from Gretchen. As she pulled me out of my mother's dead arms..."

Steam filled the bathroom as she hovered over me. Then, without rhyme or reason, I cupped my hands over hers and held them tightly. In quick succession, she pushed her arms under mine, pulled me into her embrace, and buried her face into my shoulder. I broke into a million pieces, my arms wrapped around her and clenched onto the back of her T-shirt. Lilac washed over me, and for the first time, it comforted my nose instead of burned. I inhaled her scent sharply as tears flooded out of my face. "I just want to know her. How is it I miss someone I don't know?"

Cecelia held me tightly against her, one hand against my shoulder and the other buried in my hair. I clung to her. Softly, like rolls of cold air from under the door to combat the hot steam, Cecelia disappeared from before me. The pressure at the back of my head lessened and I let my hands fall down. Cecelia was gone and I was alone. Hot tears fell down my cheeks as I leaned against my bathroom door. Loneliness stung my chest as I struggled to collect myself.

I stripped and tossed myself into the hot water. Time passed slowly as I scrubbed every inch grime off my body. Red as a lobster, I emerged from the shower and dried myself quickly. I wrapped a towel around myself and slipped out into my bedroom. The hole from where the three of us ripped out the door was replaced, like that night never happened. But it had—just like the night in Leo Ashwood's suite happened. I couldn't erase my mistakes; I could only fix them. So I dressed in pajama shorts and a tank top and stepped up to the door.

I pulled it open and sat on the ledge, legs dangled out to the swamp below. Darkness settled over the swamp and I eased myself closer to the edge. The blood was gone from my nose and the tears dried from my eyes, but the loneliness still prickled at the back of my neck. Hairs on my arm rose as the tickle of magic ran up my bones like electricity. He skulked nearby. His toxic blood, the magic within him vibrated through the air. My fingers gripped the sides of the doorway as I stared out into the darkness. A flash of eyes from across the water caught my eye and I nearly jumped out.

"Quinn?"

I tossed myself back from the door as my aunt's voice carried through the house. The door closed with a knock from my left foot as I reached for a book nearby. Falsely propped up on a pile of cushions and blankets, a discarded book in my hands, I lingered awkwardly close to the door as my aunt walked in. "Yeah?"

"How do you feel about coming to the coven meeting tomorrow? Serias asked if you would be joining us. We postponed the festival till we've addressed the problem." Darlin leaned against the doorframe. She held onto a scrap of paper, obviously sent by hawk, a dead giveaway it had been sent by Serias. Amendir only sent mail by fire, while Serias preferred more archaic methods.

I smiled as warmly as I could with a fake yawn. "Sure! I'd like that."

"Excellent. We are discussing the monster and how we are going to hunt it down." My aunt pushed off the doorway and sent my heart into painfully irregular heartbeats. The house closed around me and pressure pushed over every inch of my skin as she ran her fingers down the length of the doorframe: a protection spell, stronger than anything I'd felt before. I swallowed hard as I slunk toward my bed. Wet hair, damp clothes and tear stained cheeks, I toppled into my bed with wide-open eyes.

Chapter Seventeen

Cecelia Meets the Monster Alone

"So are you going to fess up and tell me about the car or am I going to have to ask the Waltons?" Gretchen grumbled from behind her newspaper.

I jumped up from the notebook in my lap like a busted criminal. The whiplash from focus on my homework to my mother made my brain spin. I blinked hard. Gretchen slid her newspaper down an inch to stare at my face from over the brim. My mouth hung ajar like that of the salmon I cooked up for dinner. Jess helped me eat all of dinner as Maggie escaped moments after my mother arrived, and Gretchen was full from her packed dinner. Gretchen did, however, join us at the table in silent judgement as Jess overplayed the normal card the best she could. I did my best not to look like a toddler caught with their hand in the cookie jar.

The hour I took in the shower didn't help my case. I was unable to even justify the tear stains on my cheeks when she caught me in the hallway.

"I thought you didn't care?" I swallowed. After Jess excused herself to go home, I went straight to homework.

I wanted to feel normal for a moment after everything that happened. The accident felt months away when it had only been a few days.

"Of course, I care, but I was worried sick, Cecelia! You ran your car into the Walton's in the middle of the night in another town for no reason and then just disappeared for two days? Then you waltz back in here like the Queen of Sheba with no explanation?" Gretchen snapped the paper down to her lap. Fury etched into her features and fear tickled the underside of my belly. "Care to explain yourself? Why you suddenly talk to the Walton's daughter? Or why you have Jess lyin' for you?"

I winced as she folded the paper up sharply and dropped it onto the table. "I don't have—" Busted. Tears welled up in traitorous eyes as Gretchen fixated her fury in my direction.

"She told me over the phone you were still at her house just moments after the police called to ask why your car was at the scene," she interrupted, her lips pulled thin on her face and arms folded over her lap. I inhaled sharply—my truth choked me. My lips slipped open and I almost confessed. Until Quinn's words repeated in my head, don't tell humans about witch stuff. So I chewed on my confession and swallowed it down.

Her eyes red from crying filled my mind, the feel of her pressed against my chest as she sobbed into my collar bone. Quinn opened up wounds within me I didn't notice until I sat in a room with my adopted mother and tried to forget about myself. I poured myself into homework while everything that happened lingered on the back of my tongue. How would Gretchen even understand?

"It was a dumb teenage thing," I said through my teeth, my face twisted.

"Teenage thing?" Gretchen cocked a brow halfway up her forehead.

"Yeah. At school. Well, it's an out of school thing. I was—"

Gretchen cut through my rambling with a hand put up into the air. "You've obviously come to your senses, and you're ashamed of it, I can see it on your face. So I'm gonna drop it, but I swear to the lord above, if you *ever* do somethin' that dumb or that reckless again, I'm gonna *put* the fear of god in ya, have I made myself clear?" she said in a low voice, her eyes sharply on the newspaper. I stared at her in sheer terror as she took it back up, unfolded it and crossed one leg over the other in sharp precision. Gretchen Montreal didn't give empty threats. "And you will either make up the money to get the car repaired or save up to buy a new one, tag it, insure it, the whole thing."

"Yes, ma'am," I murmured as I ducked my head back down to my work. Tension and silence passed between us as my pencil crossed the paper and her fingers flipped paper back and forth. The world settled down to an unusual environment as she slouched back in her chair and I melted into the couch. I felt ready to spring at any moment, like she would demand more answers and I would break down. It never came.

After I finished, I tucked my notebook into my book bag and closed it up on the coffee table. I stood up, stretched my body and slunk over to Gretchen. She folded the paper in half as I loomed over her. "Mom."

She stayed silent as she peered up into my face. I bent down and pressed a kiss to her forehead. "I love you."

"Love you too, kiddo. Now get to bed." She squeezed my elbow. A weak grimace crawled on my lips as I knelt down next to her chair. Gretchen cocked her head to the side, worry etched into her brows as she closed her paper. "Cecelia?"

I lay my chin on the arm of her chair as I stared up into her face. "Maggie has cancer on her vocal chords," I confessed. Gretchen's face twitched in a sudden look of horror before she masked over it with stone. There was a flash behind her eyes as she tucked her hands into her lap in a slow, smooth motion. I took a long breath in through my nose before it shattered. Tears welled up in my eyes and choked me as I shuddered. Maggie is dying.

"She is not your responsibility." Gretchen stated through gritted teeth. "You barely know the girl. Don't you dare wind yourself up over something you can't fix, Cecelia. We've talked about this, never hurt yourself over someone else!"

"But Mom—"

"No! It's not like a financial problem or she needs help with music, Cecelia. We can't fix this problem. *You* can't fix this problem. Don't you go and put your nose where it don't belong, young lady. I don't stop when you go and wiggle your goody shoes in people's problems with good intentions. I know you wanna help, but don't. With as much trouble as you're in right now—don't go and make it worse!" She snapped the paper open again and lay it out before her.

I clamped my lips shut again as she swallowed and looked away. My eyes devoured her visage, contorted in a mask over the crystal clear pain. Maggie would never know, but she was my mother's favorite student. She spent years on our piano, vocal and chord training; my mother burned a lot of hours into Maggie's talent.

Then my mother realized Maggie was bound to be a star, but her only motivation was to impress Gretchen. So she shoved her out of the nest and made her motivation to prove Gretchen wrong. Boy did that work, because Maggie made herself a star. Took that manic work-a-holic mentality into a business she owned online. Gretchen actually uttered the word 'proud' when I showed her one of Maggie's songs.

With as shut in as my mother was, I doubted anyone would tell her about Maggie. It didn't have to do with her work, and her "best friend" hated the Waltons. I crumbled into a million pieces as my mother inhaled sharply and blinked away tears she would never allow to fall. A hand found mine on the edge of the chair and squeezed hard. "Do you care if I invite Maggie over more?" I whispered hoarsely.

"That's fine; the girl is probably rusty, she could probably use some practice." My mother stated between gritted teeth. I smiled through tears that spilled. She would never cry, so I cried for both of us. I stood up and pressed another kiss to my mother's temple. Gretchen leaned into it without another word.

My feet were numb as I walked toward my bedroom. Everything shifted, the air ice cold as I tossed myself on top of my bed and rolled up into a cocoon of blankets and pillows. Maggie is dying. Quinn said they had a healer, but what if that didn't work? Quinn is lost and hurt. And what about me? Did I even know?

Sleep took me shortly after the lights turned off in the house.

Frost tickled my skin and sent goosebumps up my arms. Snow smashed under my toes. The trees whined as they arched toward me. The sky was a painting of silver and black, stars blurry and undefined. The light shined in sharp beams as they pierced tree lines outside of my house. The world was submerged in water, weightless as it flowed from side to side and I moved forward. With every inhale, I floated further from the ground toward the tree lines. A beam of sunlight shattered my sight and I clenched my eyes shut.

Soft fingers brushed my cheek, and the light died. I opened my eyes. Quinn hovered over me with a wide grin. She brushed hair from my face as the scent of the ocean filled my nose. The air thickened with salt. Quinn dripped with salt water; her long hair stuck to her face. Everything was quiet—no squawks of seagulls, no crash of waves, no words as Quinn moved her lips. She smiled happily as she pulled back and stood up. A black tankini soaked against her, sand over her hands and legs as she offered me her hand. I took it.

I sat up and was greeted by a splash of sea water to the face. Suddenly Maggie, in a flashy pink bikini, broke into my eyesight as she shoved me teasingly. Then another bucket of water dumped on both Quinn and me. Maggie burst through the sea water, head tossed back in a bout of laughter I couldn't hear. My world lingered in absolute silence as the two wrestled happily over the sand only to break toward the water. I gazed up toward the sky, and the sun beat over me. In all the heat, my core stayed frozen. My eyes caught movement and dropped to the water's edge where Maggie and Quinn lingered. The two waved for me to come with them, smiles wide and open. I grinned; my foot took one step forward.

"Is this what you truly want? Is this what your heart desires?"

I blinked, and the world ripped back into the snowy winter. My lungs burned from lack of air. My eyes burned as I stared across an empty yard. Snow smashed under ash and blood, an open field of bodies. I gasped for air. Pain erupted in my skull as I sunk to the ground. Maggie lay in shreds before me, eyes wide open. Tears poured down my face as the world seized. My brain spun within my skull, woozy from visions as faces appeared on corpses before me. Jess, Kitty, Lance, Gretchen, everyone in my life... except for Quinn.

She stood in the middle of the field, head bent backward at the hand of Leo Ashwood. He stood at the edge of my yard, Quinn in between his fingers. Slowly she spun to face me, eyes rolled back and blood trickled out of her nose and mouth. His palm closed around her skull.

"Is that not a much better dream... than the reality..."

A silent scream broke through my lips as Quinn dropped into a crumpled mess.

"I could make it real... I could make that dream real forever..."

I shot up in my bed, darkness draped over my room. My hands slapped for my cell phone but found only emptiness. Horror drooled like dog saliva over every inch of my skin. My throat tightened and my lungs transformed into slabs of concrete as I struggled to come back to life.

My vision told me Leo Ashwood existed just outside my house, his misshapen face half hung off his skull. Eyes illuminated against the dark of night. He stared at my house with malicious intent. Toxins fueled my panic as my phone bumped my fingers near the edge of my bed. I unlocked the screen and the room lit up instantly. Soft bulbs of light danced before my eyes as the flashlight on the back of my phone passed across my room.

"Hello... Seer..."

My heart exploded, and I screamed. Leo Ashwood lumbered over my bed like the ghost of my dead mother. His hands dove over my face and hoisted me up out of my covers with ease. Fat fingers squeezed the sides of my head. My phone tumbled to the floor; the light whizzed around the room and then stopped under me. Leo Ashwood's lopsided face illuminated, the flesh taut against his skull in one spot and loose along his jawline and right nostril. There was bone exposed under his right eye, and foamy pus spilled out from his eye socket. My arms flailed as I slapped at chunky hands around my face.

"What on earth has gotten—" Gretchen's voice cut off in the doorway.

For only a moment, the world froze. My eyes shifted to see Gretchen kick down the door, her curlers alive in the night as her robe blew around her. Leo Ashwood glanced at her; his hands tightened around me. Then, the world spun back into motion as Gretchen lifted the shotgun from her side, planted it against her shoulder, and fired directly through my canopy and into Leo Ashwood's left side in quick succession. I crumpled to the floor as the world descended into chaos around me. A gasp broke my lips as blinking streetlamps danced over my head. His body jerked backward as Gretchen fired at the monster. "Not today, Satan!"

"*Mortal!*"

A final shot tossed Leo Ashwood through my bedroom window. I lay upon the floor, unable to hear or breathe or function. Gretchen rounded the bed and jerked my body up onto my flimsy feet. "Get it together, Cecelia!"

"Yes, ma'am," I squeaked.

"Go get my extra rounds out of my bedside." Gretchen slapped my arm with enough force to wake me up from the shock. Anxiety pumped through my veins and I tossed myself over the bed and across my room. Leo Ashwood broke into my house! He could have killed me! Terror and paranoia slowed my feet as I stumbled into her room. My hands trembled. It took every ounce of focus in my body to pull the bedside drawer open.

Three things faced me as I loomed over the drawer: a new piano sheet music folder, a box of bullets, and my yearbook picture. I grabbed the box of bullets but stopped as my picture shifted to expose many photos. They ranged from candid photos of me as a child to candids of her dressed in military gym shorts, arms full of duffle bags. There was one of Gretchen with a massive gun upon her arm, a photo of her in salute to a woman three times her size. A Polaroid of her with a bazooka laughed at me from the stack. Then I found one of her and a crowd of young people. All covered in sweat and dirt, arm in arm, mid laugh, Gretchen on a tree-giant man's shoulders. Mary on Treebeard, all bright eyed and smiles.

"Cecelia!" Gretchen's voice broke my concentration.

"Coming!" I called out as I slammed the drawer shut. My feet stumbled but my spine forced me upright as

I ran back to the room. The hallway grew longer somehow—it wound more than usual and went on forever. Was my mother really in the military? How did I never know? She was a completely different person back then, full of life and smiles. I came around the bedroom doorway, my heart in my toes. Gretchen, my mother, inspected the broken window with a scowl.

"Well, good news is Frankenstein's monster is gone. Bad news... how that beast got in this house?" she hissed as I walked up next to her. Her fingers snapped bullets into the gun like she'd done it a million times. She snapped the gun back into place and put it up against her shoulder swiftly. Of course, we lived in the South—there weren't many people in this town that didn't own a gun. Yet, now, in her hands, the shotgun gleamed with an alien light.

"Mom?" I swallowed. She didn't answer. Gretchen aimed out the window for a long time before she lowered the gun and scowled harder. "Mom, I have something to tell you."

"Did you let that thing in?" she snapped, her eyes sharp.

"No!" I confessed as tears welled up in my eyes. Gretchen relaxed a bit in her step as she cocked a brow up toward me. "For someone who was just face to face with a monster, you sure are calm."

"Cecelia, I've faced a lot of monsters. Some beefed up druggie has nothing on a man on the opposite team with a gun and no mercy."

I stumbled back a step as I studied Gretchen Montreal. The woman who raised me, never once mentioned something... My mouth hung open as she stared out the window with an animalistic sharpness, they snapped back and forth in fierce concentration. She stepped back up to the jagged window and examined it inch by inch. "Mom... you... what are you talking about?"

"It's nothing, what were you going to say?" she whispered, her shoulders tense.

"Mom, were you in the military or something? What were all those photos in your drawer?" I carefully placed the box of bullets onto my bed. My skin prickled as she refused to meet my eye. "Mom."

"Those are stories best left to die, Cecelia," she sighed as she straightened up. "Now, come on, you are going to sleep in my bed while I wait for the police. The insurance won't pay for wall repair without a police report."

"Mom—"

"Cecelia, do as I say!" she snapped.

"The police can't know!" I whined. Her body jumped into place and her eyes were on me. "His name is Leo Ashwood. He's not human anymore."

"What are you babbling about, Cecelia?"

Quinn's voice filled my head as I looked over at my mother: *You're not supposed to speak to mortals about witch business.*

And yet... "He's a monster; he was dead then brought back to life. He's pissed and is killing people and trying to kill my friends and me because we're trying to stop him." The words tumbled out of my mouth faster than hot vomit, but once they formed, they didn't stop.

Gretchen watched me for a long moment in silence, her lips pursed into a thin line. "I knew this day would come, but I had hoped you'd have more sense."

My mouth dropped open. "What?"

"I raised you to have more common sense then to go runnin' off after some monster with your gifts. I let you wiggle your nose into Walton's chicken business and that weird girl with the screens because you were doin' the right thing, but this is dangerous, Cecelia. That thing lifted you by your skull, do you realize that? And you want me to what? Let you go chase it in your nighties? Absolutely not! No daughter of mine is about to be that dumb and that dead. I'm calling the police and you're gonna march yourself to my bed right this instant. I won't tell them about Leo whatever you called him but I ain't paying money out of my pocket because some magic nonsense decided to break through the window like a bat outta hell!" Gretchen spun me by the bicep and forced me to march through my room and into hers. My head spun as she slammed the door behind me.

I blinked rapidly. Pressure built up at the back of my skull without warning. I didn't want to bleed into Quinn's mind at this hour, but my magic made me helpless to stop it. With the blink of an eye, a yawn filled the room behind me, and Quinn sat up in my mother's bed with a sleepy scowl. Her form wavered like a ghost in a Hollywood movie before she solidified, her eyebrow cocked over her green eye. "Seriously?"

"I'm sorry," I muttered.

Quinn sported a long tank-top, her chestnut hair a wild mess around her face. Her fingers raked through her hair. "It's not even dawn yet," she grumbled but slapped at the mattress beside her. I sprang across the floor and crawled up into the bed next to her solid form. She rubbed her face in slow circles before she let out another yawn. "I owe you one for the bathroom."

Unlike my bedroom, my mother's room stayed clean and precise. There was a queen bed with gray sheets and pillowcases and a solid wooden frame. There were no strewn books or dust on her bedside table. All the dirty clothes were in the laundry basket. Her bed creaked as I crawled into place; the stiff but comfortable cotton shifted and crumpled under me.

"Leo Ashwood was in my house." The words tumbled out of my mouth like hot water. My tongue scorched and stung, and my teeth clamped down and nearly shattered. Even in the darkness the glow of her green and blue eyes lit up the room as she opened them wide.

Quinn snapped her attention to me, and her hands snatched up mine. "What!"

"He was in my room, he grabbed me—" My words died as her hands moved to my cheeks. Flashes from the beach haunted me. She looked so happy, drenched in beach water. Her skin glowed, her smile warmed even the frost around me. Dream Quinn looked at me with wonder and happiness. Reality crashed on top of me as she brushed a piece of hair from my face. Worry etched into her features as she ran her fingers over my temples and cheeks. Her lips cracked open an inch. I beat her to the punch. "My Mom shot him."

Quinn choked as she jerked her fingers back to cover her mouth. She coughed to clear her throat. "She what?"

"She shot him, four times, hit him dead on," I confessed.

Her face twisted, as if she physically processed the information. Brows knitted down low before she swallowed hard. "Well, damn." She worried her lower lip. "Are you all right?"

"I don't know—it all happened so fast, and she wants me to sleep..." My words jumped around as the shock settled back into my bones. Skin cold as ice, my heart skipped beats as I sank down onto the pillows. The world became surreal, the ice and snow, the bodies that filled the air. His voice bounced through my ear canal and removed all other sound. The grave tone of his words ran shivers down my spine as I replayed the moment over and over. My visions were never unnerving—they were a movie, a scene or a short play just for me to see. That vision was a game he played over in my brain. What vision would I have had if he didn't mess with my head? Was his whole game to kill me... to kill us? The questions piled up as I stared through Quinn, my fist clenched tightly over the pillow.

Quinn hovered over me for a moment before she slid down under the blankets and lay next to me. Her eyes brought my focus back to her as she examined my face. Her pinkie slid through my iron grip and twisted its way around mine. "I promise, that monster will never hurt you. I will keep you safe."

I inhaled sharply as she slid closer and clenched her pinkie around mine. "Quinn—"

"I've been told pinkie promises are sacred, and you should know, as a blood witch, I am sworn to obey all vows

I take." She beamed widely as she put her forehead to mine.

"Really?" I blurted out with a nervous giggle.

"I have no idea, but what if I was? Who's to say I don't have to fulfill all my promises?" she teased as she pulled back. My eyes watered as she reached over and soothed my hair in repetitive motions. She drew designs into the side of my head, it lulled me into a puddle. "But I will stop Leo Ashwood whatever it takes. I will keep you safe."

Every time I closed my eyes my hands trembled and my skin grew colder. My eyes snapped open and I relaxed to see Quinn still in the bed. She smiled at me softly and squeezed my hand.

"Get some sleep; Seers work better when they're well rested," she whispered as she rested her forehead against mine again. My eyes fluttered closed and they stayed closed. Fireworks went off behind my eyes as the pressure eased on my skull.

"Birdo Baggins, pay attention!" Maggie's snap of her fingers made me open my eyes, her form entered my vision. I sat on the other side of a lunch table. "Hey! In there! Tell me what you saw."

Her face swirled, like a puddle rippled before my eyes. As the water settled, I found her face, twisted up in pain; blood dribbled down her lips that parted to gasp for air.

I opened my eyes to find myself at Maggie's farm. She knelt at the center of a large field of grass at the edge of her property. Tears streamed down her face, and her shoulders had fallen back. A scream fell out of her lips. The farm shook, goats screamed, chickens flew over her head. I watched as she screamed hard enough to break eardrums. Leo Ashwood lingered before her, his hands lunging out toward her.

Gretchen opened the bedroom door, and I opened my eyes. Alone, for the first time all night, in the bed; dawn broke through the drapes and I sighed.

"You're going to be a smidgen late, but you can tell Vice Principal Justin to shove it where the sun don't shine," Gretchen grumbled.

"Yes, ma'am," I whispered, my hand closed and opened where Quinn held it earlier in the night. The shock tickled at the back of my neck, but I sat up gradually and let Gretchen pull me out of bed softly. Then my vision of Maggie returned to the front of my skull and I leapt into action. My body buzzed with terror and energy as I threw myself into the hall. "I gotta help Maggie!"

"Lord help anyone who tries to stop you."

Chapter Eighteen

Maggie Reminds Herself She Has Friends

"And then my mom was all, ooooh! There's a serial killer on the loose! You can't possibly go out tonight!" Kayleigh whined as she tossed her hands up around her head.

My mind whirled in and out of concentration as I put all my reserved energy into my feet. Kitty lingered a centimeter to my right like a barrier between me and the lockers. Math, in my mind, existed a thousand miles away at this pace instead of just down the hall.

"Well, let's be honest—the police aren't catching anything but the flu sitting in the cold looking for this crazy killer," Daisy Lee retorted with a roll of her eyes. She swerved in front of the pack of us to stop at her locker.

I sighed with relief at the stop of motion. My bag clutched to my chest, the effects of the candle weakened. Vomit threatened my composure at every sharp turn or downward step.

"You sure you're all right, Maggie?" Daisy Lee cocked her head to the side as she shimmied a textbook out of her locker.

I nodded pitifully and dug my fingers dug into my bag. If I opened my mouth more than an inch, motion sickness would coat the hallway walls.

Kitty snaked an arm through mine and tugged me up against her. "Yeah, it's the meds, ya know, how crazy doctors are these days with overprescribing," Kitty lied through her crystal clean teeth with a wide grin.

My lips glued together as I leaned into her shoulder. God, what did I do to deserve my best friend? A hand rubbed the inside of my forearm in soothing circles. Daisy Lee and Kayleigh nodded, hands full of books and notebooks.

"You know, Mama says that the doctors are making money on all the prescriptions they write us that we fill out. Like the more stuff they make us take, the better their bonus!" Daisy Lee chirped.

"That is a flat out lie, Daisy Lee," Kayleigh scoffed, her eyebrows furrowed. "Your mama thinks anyone who charges more than five dollars for anything is a conspiracy to pay the government for mind control!"

"Does not!" Daisy Lee spat.

"Does too!"

Thankfully, both Kayleigh and Daisy Lee continued their argument down the hallway toward the classroom. I inhaled sharply as Kitty slammed Daisy Lee's locker shut with a flick of her hand. "I swear, that one would lose her head if it wasn't stitched to her neck."

"She's got bigger thoughts to think," I murmured; my legs wobbled. Kitty said nothing as she moved us forward. Everything turned numb. I moved through the space with no feeling in any inch of my body. My fingers loosened around the bag as I came to the painful realization: the candle went out. I blinked rapidly as my throat grew hoarse and my insides clenched down. Pain erupted like a bomb within my throat and pulled all the feelings to my neck. Kitty clenched down on my arm and whisked me up and into the classroom. Eyes bore into me as I stumbled to my desk and tossed myself into the seat. Life oozed out of my toes; puddles of my soul flooded the linoleum.

"Pop quiz!"

The sound didn't register until a paper was shoved in my face. I slapped at it against the desk and stared at dancing numbers. Even as I forced a pencil into my hands, I couldn't feel the pressure between my fingers. A cough rattled my ribcage and forced me to clamp my lips closed. Faces twisted, a pair of hands clamped on my shoulder, a breeze blew against my face. I didn't recognize any of it. I existed in a blur. Tears welled up in my eyes as I shrunk into my seat.

Time passed and I pushed my hand across the page to no avail. No math equation kept my attention. My eyes skimmed the pop quiz that blurred together to one big smudge on the paper. I wavered in and out of focus. With a hard blink, I hugged myself and snapped to my feet. Everything spun as I stumbled down a row of desks. Was this it? Was this my end? Panic choked me at my desk as my eyes swam in tears.

"Maggie Walton—"My teacher's voice reverberated in my ears.

"Nurse," I muttered as I slammed into the whiteboard. Something pressed into my hip, yet the pain dulled immediately. I waivered, my legs transformed into rubber. The sound of sneakers slapping against the floor bounced around my skull as hands reached for me.

"Kitty, take her."

"Yes, ma'am."

I barely recognized the feeling of Kitty's hands wrapped around my arms. News of my health filled the school like bees in a hive full of megaphones as I deteriorated. Everyone stared at me with pity in their eyes. They packed my locker full of 'get better' cards with little written in them. I tried as hard as I could not to look at my comment section, up until this morning when my manager called my mother and made me face the noise. My community was up in arms—there were two kick-starters for my medical expenses, and at least ten reaction videos. The guilt ate at my insides as the reality kicked in.

I had cancer.

The magic candle died on me.

I was going to die.

"Come on, one foot in front of the other." Kitty's whisper brought my soul back into my body.

Then, there was Kitty. The day I returned after the swamp, she refused to leave my side. She stayed quiet, which stung. Kitty never shut up, not even when her aunt died. The whole funeral she talked and murmured to me, in between tears and sniffles. However, with me, she stayed quiet.

This morning must have been the last straw. We stepped out into the hall and I broke into a fit of coughs. She hugged me close as I clamped my hands over my mouth. I lived on pure spite; I refused to look weak, despite how clearly I lied. As I pulled the hands back from my mouth, palms full of saliva and blood. A napkin dropped into my palm as Kitty pulled away from me.

"Maggie Walton, why didn't you tell me?" she muttered.

My vision cleared enough to avoid a long collection of lockers. I forced Kitty to stop as I leaned into the cool metal. A fire exploded in my throat. "Everyone knows, Kitty," I croaked as I hugged my arms around me.

Kitty shifted as both mine and her bags rested on her shoulder. "No, I'm talking about before that stupid video, and before everyone here started gossiping like a bunch of nuns in church. When you got the news, why didn't you tell me? You scare the crap out of me when you text me you're going to the doctor for your throat, then you ghost me! A day later you put up some thirteen reasons bull-crap on YouTube and disappear off the face of the planet? I thought you died! How could you not tell me?" She put her hands to her hips. A proper, world-famous Kitty Felicity Justin temper tantrum. Her blonde hair was pulled up taut in a ponytail that fell down her back. She wore a scrunchy wrapped around her wrist, and she had her hands to her hips. Her lips scrunched and lipstick cracked with how severe her pout was. Even as drained and woozy as I felt, Kitty stood crystal clear before me. Though, usually, it wasn't me she threw these tantrums at.

"Sorry, didn't feel much like talking,'" I muttered as my lungs grew heavy.

"Maggie Winifred Walton, I have been your best friend since we were in Barbie panties and plastic shoes, don't you dare—"

"Have you?" I interrupted, a sharp knife cut through my insides as she stumbled back a step. A burst of energy filled my lungs and muscles as I straightened up. My vision steadied and my back straightened. "Because a best friend would tell me if they cheated on their high school sweetheart."

Betrayal loosened up her twisted face. Her mouth fell open and her hands dangled at her side. "Maggie—"

"Do not spit righteous bullcrap at me, Kitty, when you know good and well you've kept secrets from me too," I snapped, my nose scrunched and hands planted flat against the lockers.

"That's hardly fair!" she squeaked. "My... affair with Johnny is nothing like you having cancer, Maggie," she snarled through clenched teeth. I rolled my eyes as I pushed off the lockers only to fall back again. Kitty shot across the hallway and caught me by the bicep and eased me back into the metal before she dusted my jean jacket off at the sides.

"You can't even admit it to yourself that you cheated," I murmured.

Her mouth flopped open, huffing and rolling her eyes. I watched her stomp her left then her right foot as she worked through her words visibly through her head. Was she trying to lie to me? I cocked a brow. She pouted.

"I'm sorry that Lance is about as fun as a bowl of off-brand Cheerios," she huffed in my ear as she settled into the lockers beside me. I wanted to laugh, because it was true. Lance may be white bread toast with fat free butter boring. When we went out as a pack, he never added to the ambiance. The life of the party was Kitty. She always talked, always made me smile, always wanted to do things. Lance merely joined along for the ride.

"Then you should'a broken up with him!" I snapped as my eyes drifted to the ceiling. I was pissed at Lance for the video, and he refused to look me in the eye since I slapped him, but I was just as pissed at Kitty. Out of everyone, I thought she would know better. If she didn't want something, when did she start to hang onto it? The Kitty I grew up with dumped guys when she didn't like them anymore. It might hurt in the moment, but at least she left before she ruined their trust. Then Lance broke into the picture, a guy she never should have dated and then she ruined it. "He's a piece of crap for what he did, and I'll stab him in a heartbeat. But the idiot didn't deserve that. And you groveling and asking him to take you back, what was that about? I've never known you to beg for anything, especially boys."

"How ... how did—"

"I heard about it and watched it on Facebook before they took it down. I also saw you slap the mucus out of Cecelia Montreal." I turned my head to stare directly at her.

Kitty grimaced as she clutched a hand to her chest. Her face twisted up tight before it steadily eased and she sighed. "Yeah, I still kinda feel bad about that. I didn't realize she had told him to be nice. I thought she was tryin' ta, ya know, steal him." She shrugged. "Guess I ought to buy her a 'Sorry I slapped you in the lunchroom' gift. Do you think she likes Starbucks?"

"Kitty, maybe you should just *say* sorry." I cocked a brow, my arms crossed under my chest.

"Nah, nobody likes real sorrys, just gifts," she chuckled.

My lips broke open as we fell into a soft fit of giggles. The pain eased, my mind cleared, my chest relaxed. Kitty's laughter cleansed me. She smiled as she turned to face me. In slow movements, she took up my right hand and clutched it in hers. "You still didn't tell me you made a video."

"I was in a weird place. I kinda did a bunch of rash things I'm not proud of. I should'a never made that video. But then again I also shouldn't have tossed myself in my truck and crashed it on the high—"

"Maggie Walton!" Kitty screeched. She flung herself off the lockers, my hand still clutched around hers. "You crazy heffer, what were you thinkin'?"

"That I was gonna die." The words fell out of my mouth and I swallowed hard. Her heartbreak played before my very eyes. "That I'm still going to die."

We both lingered in dead silence. Her face fell, her grip tightened. The sound of her sneakers as she shuffled closer to me. Tears welled up in both our eyes as she stood an inch from me. I sniffled and we broke down. She tossed herself into my arms. Wrapped up in her embrace, I clutched her close to me, the buttons of my jean jacket dug into my torso. Kitty buried her face in my shoulder and her fingers dug into my back. Then the bell rang over both of our heads and we ripped apart. She dipped as if to put her ponytail back up and I ducked my head. Bodies burst into the hall and shuffled around us.

"Are we still going to the nurse?" I murmured.

"Are we?" She cocked a brow in my direction, her face perfectly put back into place. I shrugged. "Lunch, then?"

"Thankfully, it's nacho day," I teased.

"Yessss," she hissed as she linked arms with me and dragged me through the hordes of students. The woozy spell passed in and out of my body but with Kitty, I managed to walk forward and keep my balance.

Kitty slid us into the small line that formed in the lunchroom. Thankfully, the noise softened around us, until Cecelia Montreal entered the room and everything died. Jess lingered right next to her, books clutched to her chest, wearing a mash-up T-shirt and dusty jeans. I nearly broke across the lunchroom to her side but stopped myself. Everyone stared at the large bruises on the side of her face.

Like that of fingerprints.

"Leo Ashwood," I snarled.

"What? Who's Leo Ashwood?" Kitty whispered in my ear.

"A problem," I grumbled. Cecelia sat down, but her eyes were glued to me. Even through the crowd, she stared me down. I made quick work of my order and paid for the food then wheeled Kitty and I straight for her. Cecelia's eyes shot open wide and Jess eyed me with suspicion as we both clattered to the table.

"Well, this is a turn of events." Jess cocked a brow.

Kitty glanced between me and Jess, her tray still in her hands. I set my tray down and swung myself onto the bench despite the look of utter confusion on Kitty's face.

"What happened to your face, Montreal?" I snarled.

Cecelia wheeled backward in her seat as Jess narrowed her eyes to slits on me. Cecelia sat in a rumpled mess. Never in my life had Cecelia been less than presentable. I looked at a girl with her long hair in a messy bun, a wrinkled polo over khaki pants, one earring in and the other missing, and a massive bruise on her jawline.

"Way to be subtle, Walton." Kitty took a long sip of her water bottle. I flashed a glare at her as she winked at me.

"Says the girl who launched across the lunchroom to slap Cecelia," Jess snapped, her hands slapping against the lunch table.

"Whoa, when did this become about me?" Kitty scoffed as she set her water bottle down upon her tray.

"Isn't it always?" Cecelia teased with a bemused look. The glow of life returned to her cheeks as she spoke.

"I wish," Kitty snickered as she stabbed into her pile of chips and chicken and melted cheese.

Cecelia flinched a bit as Kitty stared her down. "Are you here to hit me again?"

"Do I look like that big of a bitch? Can it, Jessica Grace Harris!" Kitty jutted a finger out at Jess with a sharp look. The table went silent as Jess ducked her head and poked a small collection of gummy bears in her mouth. Cecelia stirred her small bowl of potatoes and chicken, obviously leftovers, in her container over and over.

"Cecelia, what happened to your face?" I reiterated.

"You know what happened to my face," she muttered between large chunks stuffed into her mouth. I scowled as I shoved a chip or two into my mouth. Instantly I regretted the food as it churned my stomach. Kitty eyed me as I nearly sucked down every drop of water in my bottle in one sitting.

I dropped my bottle onto the table and slapped my hands against the surface. "He's back, isn't he?" I hissed.

"Whoa, who is back? Is this Leo Ashwood a boyfriend of yours?" Kitty interjected, her back straightened sharply.

"Nope, worse, he's a monster," Jess answered. Cecelia nudged Jess in the arm hard. They shared a concerned look as Cecelia put her finger to her lips. Then she peered up to me with a sigh.

"Maggie, we can't talk about it here," Cecelia murmured as she stuffed pieces of potato into her mouth. Her eyes glazed over. The conversation died again. I forgot about the pain, and as I took another bite of my nachos, my face twisted up in the middle. Kitty pulled my tray away from me and handed me a stick of gum instead. She practically shoved it in my mouth before I chewed it angrily in silence.

"Look, Cecelia, I'm kinda sorry for the whole attacking you thing," Kitty blurted out. A soft smile crossed my lips as I shook my head. Kitty nudged me hard in the arm as she folded her hands on the table.

"Kinda?" Jess snickered, a wide smirk upon her lips.

"Yeah! I did mean to attack you in the lunchroom, but that was my bad." Kitty let out a long groan. She unfolded her hands to ruffle her loose hairs back behind her ears and hang her head back.

"Why did you cheat?" Cecelia interjected. "If you love him so much."

"Whoa, who said I loved him?" Kitty chuckled nervously, her hands tucked into her lap. "But he's the guy my parents like."

"I knew your mom set up y'all's first date, but I didn't think you would date him solely because your parents like him." I turned to Kitty. She stuffed her hands together, fingers folded between her knees with a huff and a pout. She finally exposed the unhappiness in her eyes for the first time. When she first started to date Lance, she never said a word. She smiled and laughed at his dry jokes and hung on his arm like she was in love. Suddenly I doubted every memory of her and him.

"Yeah, easy for you to say. Your parents would die for you to date someone, anyone. My parents only want me to date Lance, and only him. They talk about our relationship like it's some sort of business deal, and Lance and I just don't, you know, click. He's just not for me, but I didn't want to not date him. It's the first time they talked about my future like it was a good thing." She shook her head, her shoulders rolled back. A moment of weakness, a fracture in that perfect shell only to disappear within seconds, healed and smoothed over like it never happened. She took a new stab of her nachos and munched it with a bemused look on her face.

I worried my lower lip with my teeth. With everything from Thomas Higgins to Leo Ashwood, I never thought to check in with Kitty, and she was right. She had been my right hand woman since we were children. She went to every recital, joined choir just to sing next to me despite her tone deafness and her talentless vocal chords. She even filmed a few music videos when we were young and without help. I should have called.

"I'm sorry." I whispered. "I wasn't here for you—"

Kitty cocked a brow. "Oh shut your lip, I wasn't gonna tell anyone about Johnny anyway. He was just fun—dumb as a box of rocks, but that was nice. Now that's ruined and Lance is ruined so, like, now I'm just another disappointment." She shrugged.

"You? A disappointment?" Cecelia scoffed and both Kitty and I snapped our heads to stare at her. "I mean, come on, you're Kitty Justin, you're head cheerleader, you have a near perfect GPA, your uncle is Vice Principal, and you're gorgeous. If anyone is a disappointment it's—oof!"

Jess jabbed Cecelia hard in the ribs. "We're all goddesses, okay, no one is a disappointment for makin' mistakes!" Jess growled between gritted teeth.

Kitty blushed as she tucked loose side hairs behind her ear. I'd never seen her blush before. "Well, Birdo Baggins, if I didn't know any better, I'd say you were buttering me up to ask me out," she teased with a wiggle of her shoulders.

Cecelia sputtered and her face turned completely red. With a cough and a flash of hands, she swallowed hard but Kitty already split at the seams. Kitty reached across the table and squeezed Cecelia's hand softly with a wide grin. "I'm just messin' with ya. Besides, as pretty as girls are, I'm not sure I'm, ya know."

"It's not that you're not my type. Not saying I have a type, and you're really pretty but it's— I'm not—"

"Cecelia," Jess and I barked. Cecelia's lips clamped shut. I rolled my eyes as Kitty sat back and continued to munch upon her nachos.

"Man, we should have sat with you two more often—this is great!" Kitty beamed, a chunk of chips and queso stuffed into her mouth.

Jess eyed Kitty with a cocked brow silently. Cecelia trailed her eyes off into the distance, her face twisted up in worry. The life at the table snuffed out between the four of us. Silence gnawed at my flesh. I sighed as I reached over the table and took up Cecelia's hand.

"Cecelia, have you talked to Quinn about—" I cut off as her eyes glazed over. "Cecelia?" I tugged her hand, but her eyes drifted down the table with a cold sadness.

"Hey! Birdo Baggins, pay attention!" I snapped my fingers in front of Cecelia's face.

That's when her face ran pale and her mouth hung open. I leaned back, my grip tightening on her hand. That face! I knew that face well enough, horrified and scared as she stared at me dead on. "Hey! In there! What did you see?"

"Maggie, he's going to try to kill you again today."

"Whoa!" Kitty's cries fell on deaf ears as Cecelia's eyes welled up. Tears trickled down her cheeks in slow, fat drops. My heart plummeted into my shoes.

"When?" I choked through shock.

"I don't know," she murmured. "I only saw what happened when he tried."

"What's going on?" Kitty choked through food in her mouth.

"Witch stuff." Jess cut across the table.

"Excuse me!"

"What happened, Cecelia?" I growled.

"You made everything shake," she said haltingly. "The chickens and the goats... and the ground... There was so much screaming." She jerked her hand back. Cecelia scrambled to her feet, her items stuffed into her bag. "I have to go get Quinn. She can help!"

"How are you going to possibly get to her? She lives in the actual swamp, Cecelia!" I snarled as I scrambled to follow her. Cecelia fled across the lunchroom with me in tow, Jess and Kitty charged after us. The four of us slid around the West wing corner and down the hall toward the side door. I hit the breaks in time to watch Cecelia smack face first into the door and fall backward.

"Ce!" Jess called out as she flung herself forward in order to catch her before the floor did.

"What the— That door—"

"Has since been locked! I find that too many students use it to leave the premises early. It has occurred to the school that certain students aren't applying their all to their academics. And there are rumors that a stranger walked upon the premises. We can't have unusual characters harm our students. Wouldn't you agree, Kitty?"

A cold chill ran my spine as I swiveled around. Kitty cocked a brow up to her uncle as he slunk out of the shadows of the west wing hallway. I glanced toward Cecelia still hung in Jess' arms, then back to VP Justin as he lingered by the corner. His usual tailor fitted suit seemed to swallow him whole today. A man I'd seen every weekend at Kitty's, a man I'd seen laugh when no one else had, suddenly felt like a stranger. My eyebrows furrowed as a chuckle trickled off my lips. "Isn't that considered a fire hazard, VP?"

"Well, then let's not hope for a fire, Miss Walton." The words carried sharp malice as his eyes narrowed at me. My mouth unhinged in his direction. Kitty's face fell as she leaned into my bicep, worry scrunched her forehead. Even at school, I was Maggie or Magpie. Vice Principal Justin never called me by my last name. I stared at his sunken in eyes, the yellow tint of his skin as he adjusted his suit at the front. "I do believe you were at lunch and should return immediately."

"Yes, sir," Cecelia laughed nervously. The four of us edged along the wall, but I couldn't rip my eyes from him. Cecelia broke through the group and marched back to the lunchroom. I stayed, arm in arm with Kitty as her uncle eyed us before he whirled on his heel. The vice principal marched down the darkened hallway, swallowed up by the shadows. A hand grabbed me by the back of the shirt and jerked me backward.

"What the hell was that?" Jess snarled.

"Did you see how much weight he's lost?" Kitty whispered, her mouth hung open. "I've never seen him so skinny."

"He knows something, no way he would just lock the doors. VP never acts that suspicious of kids." I crossed my arms under my chest.

"I beg to differ." Cecelia put her hands to her hips, her head cocked to the side.

"He's never been that way to us." Kitty shrugged.

"Says his niece," Jess huffed.

"Whoa, judgey," I scoffed.

"He *hates* me." Cecelia enunciated every syllable for emphasis.

I eyed her for a long moment, before I turned to scan through the wing. Tingles crept up my spine as I put my fingers to my lips. "You were right, Cecelia. We should finish this conversation later." A wave of calm crashed over me as my scalp lit up with goosebumps. Cecelia ducked her head and we walked inch by inch toward the lunchroom. I shifted to stand next to her and pushed up on my toes to be near her ear. "Text Quinn, have her come to my farm."

"She doesn't have a cell phone. There's no service at her place," Cecelia muttered with a pout.

"Amish freak," I grumbled.

"Pretty sure the Amish burn people at the stake for being what Quinn is," Jess snickered as we rounded back into the lunchroom.

Our table was cleared of the trays we rushed off without. There were already students sitting in that spot. Cecelia grabbed a new edge of a deserted table. Jess produced a bag of Doritos from her bag and offered it to the whole group. I sat down and tossed one in my mouth. My stomach churned and I swallowed it despite my body's wishes.

My mind whirled around the vice principal. He was like family—all of Kitty's family was family. I spent the night at his house with Kitty and the others in church choir. He bought me Christmas presents. Yet, in those few seconds in the hallway, he hated me—disgusted, even betrayed and livid at me. My eyes landed on Kitty, already enwrapped in a text conversation with her mother. She had no idea who Leo Ashwood was, or what I'd done, and I wasn't sure I wanted to tell her either.

Chapter Nineteen

Quinn Murders Again

The city stunk of a whole new level of death. A scent changed from a small lingering aroma to a waft of death drifting from local clinics and small graveyards—all of which I am banned from. The streets mixed a noxious cloud up into my nostril with every step. Blood surrounded me as people bustled down the street. Their veins pumped vitality through their entire bodies. Their life force was visible to me, my magic an x-ray scanner within my eyeballs. My brain physically sparked as I whirled in the crowd, unable to choke down the smell and stop my visions. Every person that rounded me on the sidewalk smelt strongly of blood. Spikes of cigarettes and undertones of butter filled the air. The local diner gave off the fresh pop of biscuits in between all the blood.

Overwhelmed as I suddenly came to face the facts— my powers enhanced since the last time I stepped foot into town and I didn't know how to handle it. Woozy and nauseous, I spun within my own body. Thick smells of copper and graveyard soil never bothered me until this moment.

A woman with a pink blouse stopped to my right. "Sweetie, are you all right?"

My eyes wide and wild snapped to her as I stumbled back into the hot glass of the post office Darlin stepped into. With every step into town, sickness devoured my stomach lining. I stood on a tiny thread of sanity, my palms flat against the glass as panic rose up within me fast and hot. My teeth gritted over chunks of vomit as I gazed up to a complete stranger. Fireworks exploded behind my eyes as I absorbed everything about her—thin blood, not enough iron, she stunk of cheap, floral perfume and chives. My throat closed up as she stepped forward. Blood pumped through her temples. A sharp noise ran through the sound of my heart on fire. One long, sharp, high note made to deafen me to the soft words that tumbled off her lips.

"I'm sorry?" I swallowed hard.

"You look sick—"

My hands launched out from the glass toward her face. She backpedaled as I trembled and jerked my hands into my armpits. I stammered, "I'm so sorry. I'm not feeling well."

Darlin appeared from the doorway of the post office. "You ready, Quinn?"

"Yup!" I barked as my feet flew across the sidewalk. Fear pounded the insides of my temples; a headache stabbed a fork into my skull and spun it around at top speed. All I wanted was to hold onto Darlin for support but something held my hands in my armpits. Magic surged through my body and my stomach flipped itself into a knot below my ribs.

"You all right, sweetheart?" She cocked her head as I lumbered directly beside her.

"I think my... It feels like... I'm not well." My words tumbled from my mouth in between gritted teeth and quivering lips.

Darlin crept in front of me and bent down to one knee. She examined my face and I tried my best not to spew hot vomit on her soft visage. Darlin smiled up at me softly, her hands reached out to cup my cheeks. I stumbled back and shook my head vigorously. "Please don't touch me."

"Quinn?"

"Something bad happens when people—" My head dropped, and I heaved. Every disk on my spinal cord ached as I recoiled inward.

"I see—you've come into your stronger gifts early. "Your mother was an early bloomer too."

"Why do I feel..." I lurched and my hands flew to my mouth.

Darlin chuckled softly as she pulled silk gloves out of her Mary Poppins purse, which was made of black satin and fuzzy accents of velvet, with purple straps and dragon eye crystals that dripped from the sides. There were flashes of the spell book inside as the glowing eyes stared back at me. Darlin said Amendir made it for her when they were eighteen and first joined the family together on the same day. She dusted the gloves and smoothed them out. They were made of black lace that stopped at the wrist, with tiny crystals dangled from the cuffs like charms. I furrowed my brows as Darlin extended them out to me.

"These were made for your mother, but I think they'll help you."

"Did she never wear them?" I asked as I held out my hands for them. Darlin slipped one onto my left hand without hesitation. My body jerked upright in response, like an iron rod was strapped to my back and forced my body to adjust. I blinked wildly. The vomit disappeared from my throat, and my magic zapped out of my heart and down into the lower levels of my stomach. My head cleared and the scent of blood dissipated from the air. Darlin set the other glove in my left hand.

"She never got the chance, I'm afraid," Darlin sighed. "I'll let you decide if you want to wear the other one. Together they will make that feeling submissive; they are a suppressant. But like any other medicine for the symptoms, they will not cure it. You will have to face it head on, but like everything else, with training, you will learn to control it. But I think maybe it's best if I take over your lessons from Winestra. It's clear you're going to need the extra strength instruction."

My mouth unhooked and tumbled open as she beamed at me. Her knees cracked as she straightened up and pressed a kiss to my forehead. Words slithered out of my mouth, "These aren't a punishment, are they? Can I take them off?"

"Of course, you can, sweetheart. They're merely gloves; I won't make you wear them." She passed a hand through my hair and soothed it behind my ears. "But I would encourage you to wear them in public. Not only are they stylish and in season, but they will help with the power surges I'm sure you'll run into."

I snorted as I rolled my eyes. The other glove fit in my jean pockets easily, and I sighed in relief. My brain cleared of fog and panic as air returned to my lungs. After a flex of my fingers, I held my hand out before me. The crystals swirled with hints of green and purple with specks of silver at the center. "Is it the crystals?"

"Come, let's get to the meeting, I'll explain it inside." She laced her fingers with mine, and a spark tickled the inside of my palm against the glove.

Darlin tugged me ahead and we walked down the sidewalk. The sidewalk cleared around us; the air buzzed with insects as the day heated up under the beams of the sun. Around the corner, we came upon Honey Boulevard. The only things upon Honey Boulevard were two apartment complex buildings and one two story brown brick building with no sign, no company, and no street number. It sat by itself on the right side with two large open plots of land on opposite sides of it with 'sold' signs staked in the middle. A large black iron fence surrounded the house, with a curved gate of a giant snake wrapped around an apple in the middle of lace shaped iron.

Darlin pushed the gate open and motioned for me to enter. As she shut it, a breath of fresh air breathed over me. The house creaked with life, and the door flung open. Serias beamed from the doorway. Her hair was braided in a large loose braid on the right side, flowers pinned into the purple locks. Amendir lingered inside the doorway, arms crossed and lips curled up in a knowing smile. "Just like Darlin to come to her meeting late."

"The traffic was intense," Darlin snickered as she nearly skipped across the large stone walkway up to the house.

Amendir opened her arms to accept the hug from Darlin. Amendir glistened in golden robes with pearl accents, her tan skin made to look like warm honey in the sunlight. She wore her long black hair pulled back by her classic lotus pin; its wings flapped in the air in lively excitement. My hands tucked into my pockets as Serias bound down the porch stairs and scooped me up into her arms.

"Hey!" I cried out.

"Is for horses!" Serias broke into mad laughter as she spun me and threw me onto the porch unceremoniously. My lips curled up into a bright smile as another familiar face came around the corner.

"Winestra, save me!" I called out. Winestra whirled to the left and lit up like the stars in the night sky when she saw me.

"Serves you right to get tormented! You skipped out on lessons last week!" she teased. Winestra Bouton was a gorgeous person inside and out, with long dreadlocks tied back by a vibrant red ribbon, skin dark as night, and eyes like purple ice. She was a spellslinger who specialized in old school spells, like Darlin, but her book was a scroll wrapped around a metal snake that hissed and bit at any who dared opened it. It hung from her hip on a leather belt that also adorned a handsmithed dagger, spells etched into the blade. Winestra Bouton had been my personal tutor for the last year, as she was two years shy from graduating at OU with a major in criminology and a minor in psychology and Spanish.

"To be fair, she skipped out on a lot more than lessons last week." Darlin shot a sharp look my way. I grimaced; my cheeks lit up red.

"Ooooh someone's in the doghouse," Winestra teased as she sauntered toward the doorway. She enveloped me into a hug. Her blood wafted around her like a soft perfume. Her blood was sweet, like mint and cane sugar mixed in with iron and sweat. My hands wrapped around her only to freeze as she instantly snatched up my hand. "What is that?"

"It's, uh, a glove?" I raised my gloved hand.

"It's a suppressor. Why are you wearing one?" Winestra scoffed with a hint of suspicion. My eyes moved to Darlin who stared at me with an unsuppressed question. This was a test, to see if I would tell the truth. Her expectant stare said it all in the way they watched me, but her face softened. Amendir and Serias rounded my shoulders to look at my hand still clutched in Winestra's grip.

"I'm starting to feel intense power surges," I confessed as I weaseled my hands from Winestra. Darlin visibly relaxed, her shoulders slouched, and her face fell into a soft smile. "In town, I could smell everyone."

"Well, that's not hard, most humans forget they give off B.O.," Serias snickered.

"No, Serias..." I stammered.

"Did you smell their blood?" Amendir questioned. Amendir, my teacher from the beginning, everyone's first teacher. When I was little, whatever Darlin didn't teach me about basic magic, Amendir did. As if it were a rigorous school system, she taught me text and vocabulary, and she trained me to focus. She was the first one to teach me to harness the buzz within my skin and turn it into magic. Even when she found me waist deep in an empty grave, fingers covered in soil and face muddy with a failed experimental magic, she never winced. Amendir never looked scared until that moment in the house.

"Yes," I whimpered.

"Well, you are a blood witch," Winestra cut in. My eyes snapped to her. She grinned at me and ruffled my bangs with her long fingers.

"What do you mean by that?" I recoiled to fix my hair.

"That blood witches tend to do stuff with blood, or else we'd call you the boring witch," she teased, hands on her hips. "You'd know that if you came to your lessons last week."

I huffed. "Oh yeah! Any other sage advice, oh smartie pants? Like how you sling spells or else you'd be called the dingus witch?" I sneered.

"Come here you little brat—I'll show you a dingus witch!" Winestra lunged with a wide grin upon her lips. I squealed as she grappled me to the floor. I flung us across the threshold and nearly toppled the two of us down the stairs.

"Come on, girls, please act more your age!" Amendir sighed.

"Says the—" Serias was cut short with a glare from both Amendir and Darlin.

"You speak one number, Serias, and I doubt you will see what happens next." Amendir narrowed her eyes.

"Ha! Good one," Darlin snickered.

"Oh, go sling yourself off a cliff," Serias retorted with a tongue stuck out. Darlin replied in kind with her own tongue stuck out between her lips.

"I'm surrounded by children." Amendir rolled her eyes. I howled with laughter as Winestra dug into my sides with her fingers.

The world exploded, full of laughter and joy, and for a long moment I forgot Leo Ashwood. I forgot the lawyer and the monster, I forgot the blood and the panic, I forgot my mother. I was a witch at a coven meeting, and I was surrounded by people who cared for me. Bliss settled into my body for the moment spread out before me until peace suddenly wrenched itself from my body. Lightning struck my bones and horror replaced my insides as a stranger approached the gate. Danger.

A stranger to everyone but me.

"Miss Foster?"

I scrambled out of Winestra's hands and onto my feet. Detective Smith stood on the other side of the gate arms crossed over his chest. What was once buzz cut blond hair was now shaggy locks against his chiseled features. He was dressed in a button down, sleeves rolled up past his elbow, slacks and leather shoes. Out of place. He was an outsider. The scowl dug into his face.

"Who's asking?" Winestra leapt to her feet. "This is private prop—"

"Um, y'all should head inside. I'll take care of this." I laughed nervously, my hands up to Winestra. I spared a pleading glance to Darlin. Her face drained of color as she watched me walk backward down the stairs.

"Quinn, you sure?" Winestra growled, her face twisted up.

"Yeah, we'll just talk through the gate. Go on inside with the others. Darlin needs to start the, uh, you know,"

I stammered. Winestra inched back through the front door into the house.

"Quinn?" Darlin growled, more of a demand than a question. All eyes darted from me to the gate as I smiled sheepishly.

"I got this, it's uh, it's a part of New York," I added, Darlin's eyes narrowed. "I'll tell you everything inside. Kind of hard to talk about it around certain company."

Recognition filled her eyes as she glanced to Detective Smith with sharp eyes. She jerked Winestra by the arm and slammed the door shut. I knew I was lucky that she took my word and gave me the space. If it had been any other time, she might have pressed the issue. Humans could see the gate and the house, but rarely felt the urge to stare. That was thanks to a spell: A human with no prior knowledge of the house or of the people, would just walk by and assume nothing of it. No human may enter without approval. Without permission, they were banned to the other side. Witches might press their way through, but it had been years since a witch tried hard enough to break in. The last time that happened, Darlin said she was young, and the witch was murderous.

"Miss Foster, you left the state of New York after you were told not to—" Detective Smith's words snapped my mind back to reality. Flashes of Berry and the rage in Leo Ashwood's eyes returned to the forefront of my mind. New York could burn and I wouldn't shed a tear.

"I'm not going back, Detective Smith," I snarled as I whirled to the gate. I stormed up toward the iron, my arms crossed under my chest.

"You have no choice. This isn't an embassy; you don't get diplomatic immunity," he scoffed. I furrowed my brows. Strange word choice for a cop. Smugness filled his face up until the moment he realized the gate did not open. His hands searched for a handle or opening and found it shut entirely. I smirked as he pushed and jerked on the gate. It stayed completely shut.

"You have to be escorted in, and I under no circumstance wish for you to enter this premises," I stated firmly.

His face pinched at the bridge of his nose as he slapped his hands against the gate. "Your witch tricks won't work on me," he snarled as his fingers attempted and failed to wrap around the bars of the gate. My body lurched backward as I eyed him in horror. "Yeah, I know what you are."

"I doubt you do," I huffed as I threw my arms out. My eyes searched his face. He stared me dead in the eyes. He meant it; he knew. Horror settled into my stomach as I stepped forward. Detective Smith knew! My intuition had been right. That danger sense in the precinct, the twinge of danger when he stood at the gate- I was *right!* Which only meant one thing. "Who told you?"

"I will return with back-up, and we will force you back. You are under arrest," he snapped out, his eyes sharp. Wicked glee crawled up on my lips in the form of a grin as his body language gave his true intentions away. He looked like a predator. The way his eyes searched the yard, the knitted brows upon his forehead, his shoulders tense and engaged.

"I don't think so." I shrugged teasingly, my hands jutting out to the side. "I don't think you have *anyone* coming to back you up."

Strange for one of his kind to hunt alone. He must have a personal agenda, or his grudge against me weighed heavier than his respect for his superiors. Detective Smith would be my first Hunter.

His face paled for only a moment as he backed up. "Resisting arrest and for the murder—"

"Does your captain know you're on a witch hunt? Does he even know you're here? Did you tell Alvarez that you're a brainwashed puppet to some scared of the dark, misinformed idiot? Do your friends know you're in a cult that hunts innocent people?" I laughed as his hands slid to his sides. My fingers tapped against my cheeks as I eyed him up and down. There were no tattoos, no markings, but the furious stare, the knowledge and hatred of me, there was no mistake. "Detective, I don't think you have what it takes to take me in. You're lacking in manpower."

"You are resisting arrest for murder—"

I rolled my eyes. Typical. "I didn't kill anyone!" I barked as I stepped up to the bars of the gate. Hands away from the gate, I lingered far enough that he couldn't push his fingers through to touch me. "Leo Ashwood did that."

"Leo Ashwood was murdered by you just like Erik Lawyson—"

"Who is Erik Lawyson?" I scoffed as I cocked my head to the side.

"Your lawyer that you cut up and tossed in a dumpster down the street. Trying to cover your tracks? Huh? No coven members in New York? No one to cover your tracks... or was that their way of masking your kills?" Detective Henry asked, his head cocked to the side.

"Not me." I shook my head. "Come on, Detective, confess what you are, and we can stop doing this dance."

"We have your fingerprints on both bodies," he snarled through his teeth.

I rolled my eyes with a sigh. Then my spine straightened suddenly, and a spike of recognition shot through my heart. "Wait... what?" I recoiled, "Both?"

"Your fingerprints are all over Ashwood's body. The lab brought back enough of your DNA to fill up a tub on his body and the lawyer's," Detective Smith scowled. "Now open this gate and come with me. I'm taking you back to New York myself."

"Leo Ashwood doesn't have a body." I barked, my hands dropping to my sides.

"What are you talking about, of course, he does." Detective Smith swiveled to stand at the bars of the fence. He tried to slip through them and found himself too big. Every slice of gate he tried to fit through, he only wiggled a few fingers in. A growl tumbled out of his throat. "Damn illusions."

"No! Because his..." I trailed off as I looked at Detective Smith. Leo Ashwood must have planted an illusion in the station, but that meant he had to keep that magic up consistently until they got rid of the corpse. When did he have time? How much magic did he own? Horror licked the back of my spine and raised all my hair on edge. He was an illusionist, but his monstrous form must have expanded his powers...because of me. My teeth clenched down as my hands trembled. I made him stronger!

"Quinn Foster, stop this and come out or I will be forced to go in there and get you!" Detective Smith called out and my eyes jumped up to him. The detective determined I needed to put me away. Confession or not, I knew what he was. Hunters were a danger to all of us; it would be a mercy to take him out before he could hurt anyone.

"How many witches have you actually put behind bars, Detective?" I snickered as my eyes sharpened to slits. "Or do they all have accidents before they even get a fair trial?"

"None of you deserve a trial," he whispered harshly from the other side of the bars. There it was—all the proof I needed. My nostrils flared as fury pumped through my veins.

"Then neither do you." I could not afford him to spill his beans to Darlin or even talk to her. If she knew I lied, she would never trust me again. Only a matter of time before she realized the extent of my powers. The Family would not allow me in; I would be labelled as a murderer. This was a secret I had to take to the grave... or at least Detective Smith's grave.

I ripped the glove off my left hand and slid it into my pocket. The gate swung open and I broke into a run. His shoes echoed against the dead silence of Honey Boulevard. I pumped my arms as I bolted for the backside of the empty lot. Detective Smith's blood pumped through my nose. The sour taste of lemons and iron filled my nostrils and made my eyes water as my feet kicked up loose dirt under my sneakers. On the backside of the lot a lot of underbrush bit the ankles of teenager's who liked to run through town. My brain spun in time with the pounding of my feet against the concrete.

Then I dove for a bush and flipped just in time. Detective Smith flung himself into the bushes. My hands jumped up and snatched him by the chest. He tumbled in the thick bushes and sharp thorns. Blood trickled out of scratches up my legs and arms as I landed hovering over him. In the tumble his hands scrambled to snatch mine up. A howl of animalistic panic filled the air as I slapped my palms flat against his face. "I'm sorry, Detective—you won't be bringing anything back to New York."

Explosions went off behind my eyes, and my ears filled with the roar of waves that crashed against a rocky shore. Magic thrummed within me. Tingles ran up my arms, the scent of lemon disappeared and only blood remained. His eyes rolled back and his mouth fell slack.

He jerked as I crawled over his body. His hands flailed wildly as I dug my fingers into his scalp. The sun beat over me, and my back grew sweaty against my T-shirt. Detective Smith's fight died down until his body lurched in sharp movements. Energy pumped through me as I sucked him dry. Then, without even a blink, he died— mouth hung open, eyes rolled back, tongue flopped in the back of his mouth. I hovered over him in shock as I inspected his body.

Detective Smith turned into a corpse hidden in the underbrush. I pushed against his chest and clambered up to my feet. A rush of adrenaline filled me to the ends of my hair, and electricity tingled under my skin. I stepped back from the bush, breathless with a wide smile upon my lips. My feet inched backward up against the soil.

It happened so fast. His life, his spark filled my veins and my magic expanded within me. I grinned as I whirled and ran toward the gate. In seconds, I tucked myself back within the fence and shut it behind myself.

A smile tattooed to my face as I stared at my fingers gripped around the snake on the gate.

"Quinn? Are... you all right out here?" Winestra hovered on the porch, arms crossed.

"Yeah! He's just from the school." I shrugged.

"School?"

"Oh, yeah, I made friends with two witches who didn't know they were witches, they go to public school!" I chirped with a toothy grin. My body thrummed with energy as I forced my feet to meander back across the stony walkway.

"Ew, public school. Didn't you say it had to do with New York?" Winestra snickered.

"Yeah, he was a guidance counselor or whatever, trying to figure out why I wasn't in school too. Nosy social workers, you know," I lied through my teeth. It flowed out easily as Winestra nodded and waved for me to follow her inside. I tucked my hands into my pocket, the glove harder to put on from within them.

"Yeah, CPS once came snooping around my house because I blasted myself through the side of the house by accident. Scared the snot out of some nosy neighbors. Humans, what can you do?" Winestra let out a snort as she gave her elbow. I looped my hand through hers, hip to hip as we walked into the house. I adjusted the glove as nonchalantly as I could, but Winestra shook her head. "Look you don't have to wear that thing if you don't want to."

"You know... I am feeling a lot better now that I think of it. Darlin just gave them to me to help when I'm overwhelmed." I shrugged as I pulled them off by the fingertips and tucked them away. Winestra shook her head again but said nothing else.

We ducked into the house and headed into the main dining room. A large round table with Darlin, Amendir, and Serias at the front; all three stood and demanded attention. Winestra and I tucked into the last two seats toward the left side of the table. I smiled up at Darlin, she nodded at me warmly before she glanced over the rest of our family.

"Witches, it's been a while, but it seems we have a monster on the streets." Darlin sighed, her hands put to her hips.

Chapter Twenty

Cecelia Comes Upon a Birthright

There were two absolutes in my world at the moment: Leo Ashwood would strike and either kill Maggie or cause her to kill others; and Quinn was the only one who stood a chance against him hand to hand. Panic pumped through my body as Jess launched the car down the backroads toward the swamp. I held onto the door handles with my nails as she swirled us around a sharp corner. My eyes peeled for any piece of the swamp that appeared familiar. How did I find a witch who spent her whole life hidden from the rest of the world? The sun bore down onto the top of the rickety truck, the windows rolled down and air roared in our ears.

Jess gripped her fake cow fuzz covered steering wheel and lurched us around another bend in the road. "Anything?" she asked.

I searched the horizon and nothing. Even if I wanted the connection, the pressure at the back of my head, I couldn't grasp a hold of it. Quinn never existed far from me up until the moment I needed her. I begged Maggie to stay away from her home as long as possible.

Until the moment school let out, her mother sat in their farm van, ready to pick Maggie up. A mother daughter surprise, she called it. Maggie asked if they were going out, just the two of them. Mrs. Walton nearly cried in happiness as she nodded her head and Maggie jumped into the van.

Then Maggie told me to find Quinn, and find her ASAP. That would be easier if she wasn't *a swamp witch*! How do you find a needle in a haystack? Or in this instance, a specific tree home in the middle of a swamp that spanned hundreds of acres. Even with my elephant's memory nothing clicked or reminded me of my stay in the swamp. We hit a dead end with a heavy-footed break. Jess whipped the truck around and slammed it upon the gas pedal back up the road.

Nothing screamed familiar to me. Panic rose in my chest as reality set in. If I didn't find Quinn and bring her to Maggie, the monster would get her. My chest vibrated with hysterics as tears welled in my eyes. Every breath transformed into cement in my lungs, I trembled in my seat as I searched frantically.

"Ce, breathe—"

"I can't remember! I can't—"

"Ce! Freakin' out over it won't help a lick! Calm down!"

"No one in the history of ever has ever calmed down when told to do so!" I shrieked as we came around another bend faster than the first time. My voice pitched and turned shrill half-way through.

"Maybe you should be the first!" Jess shouted back.

I needed answers, I needed control, I needed—"How—" My voice caught in my throat as my body tossed back in the seat. Jess slammed on the breaks, but I stayed arched back in my seat, my body craning backward, my spine curved at the middle as my hands clawed at the sides of the car. Jess screamed, but I only heard it from under the water of a vision. Darkness swallowed me as my eyes rolled back in my head. I swam in a pitch-black ocean, nothing but liquid and abyss.

I managed to put all my strength in my limbs, barely able to keep myself afloat. Salty water filled my mouth as I bobbed in and out of soft waves.

Feng Mian Su, what is it you seek, collector of eyes?

The abyss lit up with fireworks of red and green. They sparkled behind a shadowed figure. I kicked my feet hard, and my hands slapped against the ocean. Fireworks illuminated a sea of wispy human forms, twisted figures that danced underneath the liquid. My mouth cracked open in horror, but liquid filled it quickly. I sputtered and spit out the liquid. Two loud cannons cracked off and shot a new collection of fireworks into the sky. The figure before me held no solid shape but wavered over the water like the Loch Ness Monster upon the lake of souls.

What is it you seek, collector of eyes?

"Why are you calling me that?!" I squeaked as salty water filled my mouth a second time. I spat it out and slapped at the water more. Almost the texture of jelly fish, the souls brushed past me and tickled the tips of my fingers and toes. I jerked in the water.

Is that what you seek? Information upon yourself?

Panic pumped through me, despite how calm the water settled around me. A calm washed over me as I scanned my abyss. I didn't know how much time I had here, but as I lingered in the water, I realized something. I knew this place! But I didn't know it completely, but there was a sense of familiarity to it. An odd sense of déjà vu filled my veins. I stared up at the figure. This place could answer me, I needed to ask the right question.

"No! Maybe a different time. I... I seek Quinn. I need to know how to get to her! I need to know how to contact her!" Panic rose in my voice, my body trembled. No temperature, no sound other than their voice and mine, an endless abyss cast in absolute darkness.

One question allowed, collector of eyes, you know the rules.

"What?! Fine I-I need to find Quinn. How do I find Quinn?" I did not have time to play games with a spirit created most likely inside a panic induced coma or something. Quinn was all that mattered.

You will find her with your sight, use your magic, collector... you already know how.

"There's no time for this! I don't—"

Use your sight.

And like a collision in a car wreck, I launched from the seat into Jess's dashboard. I gasped for air as my eyes whirled to see the world before me. Jess lurched to grab me too late. My hands collided with the dashboard and I knocked my forehead into the windshield. No pain, no tears, no words as I stared out the windshield to find Quinn lingered on the other side of the road. Not a full Quinn, but a whisp. Just like the souls in the abyss, she lingered with her back to me. I blinked hard, but she stayed there. "Go, Jess, go!"

Jess threw the car back into gear as Quinn took off down the road. Barefoot, hair loose in the wind, she burst across the road like a ghost out of a graveyard.

"Where?"

"Go forward!" I called out as I shoved myself back into my seat.

I would see her with my sight... nice wizard riddle. My face twisted up in the middle as we chased after a ghost only I could see. Right back toward town. I furrowed my brows. "She must be in town?"

"You askin' me? Are we gonna talk about the exorcist crap that just happened? You turned into some horror movie—"

"I don't even know what that was," I cut Jess off as I pointed toward U.S. 1 that led right back into town. My forehead pounded as the shock fell away and the pain returned. A headache would surely ruin me later. Until that moment, I followed after the wisp of Quinn. She flew down the road with Jess on her tail. "It was just black. Like I was in an ocean with no sky, it was really dark."

"Ooookay." Jess drew out. "And why the head butt to my poor windshield? It didn't do nothing to you."

"I don't know. There was this force... They kept calling me the collector of eyes, and they asked me 'what do you seek' over and over." I scowled my lips pursed into a long thin line. Jess blinked rapidly but followed when I jutted a finger down a side road from the main road. We slowed down to a stop at a stop sign as Quinn's ghostly form crept along the corner of a road down in the middle of town. I cocked my head to the left.

"Why does collector of eyes sound so much worse than witch or seer? I know we joked about you having a sixth sense, but you didn't have to go all Tom hanks on me, you know?" Jess mumbled under her breath.

"Bruce Willis—"

She cut me off with a sharp glare. "Whoever, you knew what I meant, collector of eyes."

"I assume it would mean I have a jar of eyeballs somewhere." I shivered at the idea.

Jess snorted as we floored the truck down the main road. I pointed at the turn and Jess swerved down Honey Boulevard. Quinn's ghostly form lingered by the large, locked gate. A massive house hidden behind an iron gate no one could open. Her form disappeared and Jess stopped without having to be told. "Of course, she's in the creepy, abandoned house."

"That's what you have an issue with?" Jess scoffed. She put the car in park and flicked off the engine.

"I've started to realize that every day of my life is no longer normal, so I shouldn't really be surprised by any of this." I shrugged. With a twist, I freed myself from the seatbelt and spared a look to Jess. "Stay here."

"Don't have to tell me twice." She rolled her eyes as she leaned forward over her steering wheel. Her eyes focused on the house for a long moment, regret scrunched her nose and pulled her lips into a frown. I slipped out the side of the truck and shut the door with a slam. A creak from the stubborn metal filled the air. The second my hands grazed the hot metal of the gate, the front door to the house burst open. My heart dropped into my toes in shock as Serias burst out into the yard.

"Cecelia! Did Quinn tell you about the house?" Her purple hair was braided against her head and turned ultraviolet in the afternoon sun. Black leather boots kicked up the loose dirt as she sauntered to the gate.

"Well, I was trying to find Quinn. It's kind of urgent." I blushed hard enough my chest lit up in fire.

"Cecelia? What's wrong?" Like the devil herself, Quinn appeared at the sound of her name. She emerged from the doorway, and her eyes zeroed in on me. Through the fence the glow of her green and blue eyes caught my attention. Accented by her long hair that billowed around her like a cape, a dark ratty T-shirt and jeans, her green eye sparkled.

"It's Maggie," I whimpered.

"Did you have a vision?" Serias asked, palms flat against the gate. I waited in silence as the two of them pushed open the gate like a curtain of beads with no weight. In all of my childhood, this house sat empty and that gate never budged. There were no hinges on it, no handles, no way inside or through the bars. Some boys even tried to climb it and found the bars too slick even after dusted with earth. And it was a house for the coven?

"Saw that coming," Jess called out from the open windows of her truck.

"Cecelia? Who—"

"That's the best friend, her human friend. I tried to tell her," Quinn sighed in Serias' ear. A tired truck horn filled the air as Jess threw up her hands in exasperation.

"Whoa! Rude! I can hear you!" Jess barked.

"I see what you mean," Serias chuckled as she shoved Quinn from her side lightly.

Quinn sauntered up to me, a wide grin on her face. She glowed from deep within her skin, her smile full on her face. Until she looked me in the eye and her face faltered, her hand midway through a brush of her long hair.

"Cecelia?" My name floated through the airlike a fragile piece of glass in the middle of free fall. It shattered as my confession tumbled off my lips.

"He's after Maggie. He's going to attack her at the farm. She freaks out and destroys everything."

The world crashed over my head as Quinn launched across the ground and bolted for the back of the truck. She flung herself into the back and slap at the hood. "Well! There's no time to waste."

"Whoa! Hold up! You don't get to go fly into action, Quinn!" Serias barked. "Your aunt, Amendir and I will follow after you. Do not engage him until we are there? Am I understood?"

"Serias—" I was cut off.

Serias put up a hand to me before she narrowed her eyes on Quinn. "Quinn Gwenevieve Foster, I swear on your mother's grave if you step one toe out of line without my direct order, you will know the true meaning of grounded! Am I understood?" Serias sounded like a thunderstorm as she squared her shoulders.

Fear rattled deep within me as Quinn's face drained of color. Then it lit up again within seconds. "Yes, Serias!" Quinn shot an urgent look at me. In a split second, I flung my body back in Jess' passenger side of the truck with the engine loud and alive. Serias bolted for the front of the house as Jess ripped a U-turn in the middle of the street and took out a trash can that lingered on the other side of the street. She floored it down the road, Quinn knelt behind the back window with her head stuck in.

"You know, you're blocking my rear view."

"What are you talking about? You can clearly see your butt if you turn your head. I don't suggest it though, as you are driving." Quinn rolled her eyes.

"I'mma kill her," Jess snarled at me.

"I'd like to see you—"

"Both of you!" I barked.

"What?" they whined. There was a stretch of silence that strangled my courage as Jess floored the truck through the small section of town we were in. Quinn focused completely on the road ahead with hawk-like diligence.

Then my mind went back to the abyss, like a childish nightmare. I revisited the water, how I tasted salt but smelt nothing. The abyss was no illusion, like the one Leo Ashwood planted in my skull. Among a thousand souls in the darkness, a presence loomed over me. Even as I replayed the moment over and over in my mind, I still couldn't pin down its shape. The voice chilled me to the bone as I rewound the tape and listened to their words again. After a hundred or so visions, dreams I couldn't remember after a few moments, suddenly I couldn't forget. I blinked hard.

"Quinn?" I turned in my seat. She jumped in her skin and jerked her attention to me instead of the road. "Do you know anything about a collector of eyes?"

"A what?" She coughed out of surprise.

"I was called the collector of eyes. I'm not sure by what though." My cheeks burnt to a crisp as I realized how ridiculous it sounded out loud. I glanced at Jess, hyper focused on the road, and knew how strange it must be for her to hear me speak about it aloud. Lips clamped shut, I looked back to Quinn sheepishly.

"Cecelia, are you getting enough sleep?" Quinn cocked a brow.

"I'm serious!" I blurted out.

"In what context? Like a voice in your head or like a vision?" Quinn tilted her head against the window, her arms crossed in the frame.

"Like she went full on paranormal activity, eyes rolled back, body contortionist freak attack and then woke up spewing something about the abyss and it called her the collector of eyes," Jess growled as we slowed down upon a gravel road.

"Well, no, I haven't but we can ask my aunt later. She's the librarian, so if anyone would know, it's her." Quinn reached out and patted my shoulder with a grimace.

"What does the librarian do? What is that?" I turned more.

"Well, every person in the family has a job, but we also give people a title. Amendir is the teacher—she oversees all education for children and witches that enter the family. She also teaches a hard English and professional writing class at OSU. Serias is the collector, for obvious reasons—she collects items and people that are dangerous to the family and well, everyone, really. She uses her visions to stop stuff. Also she is a bounty hunter, like Dog, but like, with purple and leather.

"But Darlin is the librarian. She picks up information on everything and anything and writes it down. Our library is filled from top to bottom of information on just about all I can think of. She is also the one who does research, the one people come to for changes in human affairs, things like that. She would know if there was a collector of eyes and what that means."

I choked on a question that bubbled out of nowhere. My eyes blinked hard as I played with the question in my skull. If Darlin held information, if she was a hall of records... my parents might be on her records. My real parents, the ones who passed down all my strange powers. People I didn't know, had no connection to, and yet wanted to learn about. I thought I knew Gretchen, but then she shot Leo Ashwood and stashed pictures of me in her drawer. What else did I not know?

"Would she be able to tell me who my real parents are?" I blurted out as the truck stopped a foot short of the Walton's mailbox. Jess looked at me slowly, "What?"

"Maggie's already here."

The truck went silent as Jess parked outside the Walton's fence. Chickens clucked from all over the acres of land; gravel paved a one lane driveway down past where the eye could see. My heart sank into my toes as I realized how calm the whole farm seemed to be, except for the van her mother picked Maggie up in idled in the dead center of the driveway, still rumbling with no one around.

"We should talk about this later," Quinn whispered.

Chapter Twenty-One

Maggie Has a Death Match with Leo Ashwood

The chokingly tense silence filled the van the whole ride back from the diner. I stared out the window as my mother focused on the road. There were few days I remember where my mother and I couldn't find anything to speak about. My mother was one of those people who could find a conversation about the clouds. A social butterfly made of rainbows and unicorn farts, that's what my grandmother used to describe her daughter. Deliah Martin, the fifth of six children, the only person in my whole family who only had three children. I loved her, but I'd never felt further from her as I did now.

I'm a witch.

Cecelia's vision hung on my neck like dead weight, suffocating and sinking me further within my shell.

"Mom..." I broke the silence, my throat raw and on fire. The candle in my bookbag flickered on and off, and my vision wavered. I tried to light it multiple times, but it went out every time. I knew that magic wasn't infallible; the candle couldn't completely cure me. Was it selfish to wish it could have lasted a little longer? My body turned to cement in the seat while my brain and soul floated inches above my body. I swallowed hard. "I love you."

Where the hell was Cecelia? She was supposed to go find Quinn and beat us back to the farm! Those two found each other in their dreams, how hard was it to pinpoint her on a map?

"Oh, I love you too, Mags." She spared a hand to my left knee. I was luckier than most. My mother didn't drill into me, she didn't snoop in my life, she didn't even watch my YouTube videos. She subscribed for support but considered it an invasion of privacy if I didn't specifically show her a video I made. Often, she would wait for me to come out and speak on something, even if she knew about it prior to my confession. Until the day I stumbled back from the swamp. She stood at the door in tears, she demanded to know what happened, where I was, and I couldn't tell her.

"The night of the accident." I started my confession as we wound down the road we lived on. My mother slowed down so she could listen over the sounds of the van. "That strange girl and the Montreal girl, they saved me. Mom, I'm a witch. My voice is a weapon and I killed Thomas Higgins, and I used my voice to keep my cancer at bay. Now I can't even save myself and I just don't want to lie to you anymore."

The car crept to a stop along the side of the road. My heart hammered in my chest as I turned my head to peer up at my mother. She stared out across the hood of the car. Her fingers clutched the steering wheel, knuckles pale and lips parted just a half inch. Then, she pushed back in her seat and let her hands fall to her lap. "I always wondered who it would pass down to." Her whisper filled the air.

"What?" I squeaked.

"My aunt, Izzy Martin, never married, never stayed with the same man or woman more than a few months. Mom always said she would settle down. But there was this one day, I saw her. She was a lounge singer for a couple of months, and me and cousin Larry snuck into the lounge to steel a bottle of Jack. Don't tell your father. And I saw her sing; it was like perfection. She was so pretty and alluring, and then, all of a sudden, every person in the audience was pulling out their wallet and paid her handfuls of cash. I almost didn't escape when I stood up and dug in my pockets for something. Aunt Izzy saw me and stopped. Larry yanked me back and it was like it never happened. I thought for the longest time I made it up. That her voice was just good, and I was overdramatizing it..." Then my mother turned to gaze at me with a soft smile. She reached out and took my hand. "Then you were born and even when you cried as a baby, you were just like her."

My mother's eyes welled up with tears as she squeezed it and pulled it to her mouth. She pressed a kiss to the back of my hand. "Mom, you knew?"

"Of course, I knew, you're my child. Every concert, every choir practice, the older you got, the more I heard her in you. So I didn't say anything, in case it scared you. I just wanted you to believe in your magic, real or not," she murmured as she patted my hand. "I saw the same look on Dr. Higgins' face that I saw on those people in the lounge, that look of complete submission, like you had control of him. I couldn't stop you, and I wish I had."

Tears poured down my face as she turned back to the wheel and dabbed her eyes. I sat up in my seat, the words processed like cogs in my brain. Then my body lurched, and I lunged across the seat and wrapped my arms around my mother. She enveloped me without a second thought and tugged me close. My eyes fluttered open and found him, lumbering behind my mailbox. I'd know that silhouette anywhere. Like the shadow of an old oak tree poisoned with magic, he slunk back behind a bush around the front gate. I twitched in my mother's arms, certain of one thing... Cecelia's dream. Leo Ashwood would not harm my family! "Mom, who else is home?"

"Just your dad and Frankie. Frankie wanted to play with the goats, so I expect your father's fast asleep in the living room." I swallowed my tears as I nuzzled my face into her shoulder.

"I'm so sorry."

"There's nothing to apologize for—" My mother stopped mid-way through her words as I yanked the keys from the ignition and tossed myself back to the other side. I flopped with all my might out of the cab and barreled woozily toward the farm. Her shouts filled the air behind me as I bound down the side of the road and around the driveway. Leo Ashwood bolted across the field, a buffalo soaked to the bone and half ripped off from a lion attack. His flesh flopped to the ground in chunks as I pumped my arms.

Where the hell was Birdo Baggins?

What was left of my lungs tightened down to painful husks as I gasped for air. My throat ignited into an inferno and lit my whole body on fire. I dropped the keys onto the gravel. Dots formed in my sight and my world spun. Leo Ashwood stumbled to a stop in our burn pile halfway through the open yard, his hollowed eyes stared at me. I heaved for air.

"Illness has stricken you weak, Siren."

"Eat shit!" I howled.

"Maggie Winifred Walton!" The roar of the van as it screeched around the driveway filled my ears. Fear exploded in my stomach and I turned inch by inch back to my mother. She had extra keys! Of course she had extra keys! Why wouldn't she have extra keys?

"Ma—" My voice dropped as she parked the van and leapt out of the driver's side. Her hands trembled as she stared behind me. I opened my mouth to speak but no words came out. Only a fit of coughs filled the air as tears welled up in my eyes. She saw him.

"Should I kill you first, or make you watch me devour them?"

A switch went off deep in my soul. Fury filled me from my toes to my scalp, every inch of my body covered in goosebumps. My nose scrunched up as I whipped around. Screams tumbled off my lips like no roar I'd ever produced before. It shattered the glass on the barn and sent birds out of their nests in the trees.

Leo Ashwood flung across the field into the roof of the goat barn. He crumpled down the side of the roof and into the pen. Screams of animals filled the air as I dropped to my knees. Muscles shook with rage as red colored in my vision.

My mother tried to console me, to pull me away, but the surge filled me with electricity. Emotions deep enough to drown in clawed up my insides as I struggled to my feet.

Blood splattered the roof of my mouth as I jerked out of my mother's grip. "I'm so tired of him!"

If there was anyone to thank for my impressive temper tantrum that followed, it was Kitty. Like a puppeteer of my body, my emotions ran wild through my body and fueled me across the yard in an endless rage. I skidded to a halt in front of the pen of goats with a howl that splintered wood and split the wire. Leo lurched, his hands to his ears. "Put your hands down!"

His hands slapped to his meaty sides. This Frankenstein's monster held deathly still as I stepped over the snapped wire and into the pen. Pus dribbled out of his mouth and eyes as I stepped up before him. "Claw your eyes out."

My hands vibrated as his hands raised to his face, steady as ever. Plump fingers punctured his sockets, and I listened with disgust as he ripped skin and pus from his sockets. The air filled with a squishing sound as he howled in agony but obeyed. I let out a new screech that flung him backward in the pen. He stumbled, unable to stand up fully, face scrunched up in the middle. His hands covered his face.

"Listen to me very carefully—" A scream filled the air that was not mine... nor my mothers.

Frankie.

My heart stopped as Frankie wailed from the back side of the goat pen, trapped under the wire and the remains of wood, his eyes on the monster before us both. Dirty blonde hair matted with caked on mud and blood, face contorted in horror, my baby brother stared across the pen. Leo swiveled steadily to peer at the back of the pen, a malicious grin on his face.

"Face me!" He was forced to whirl around, but his feet stomped the yard backward. Demonic black holes for eyes stared me down, his grin broke the skin on his face as he stumbled backward. "No! You leave him alone—"

I choked. Blood soaked my throat and coughs rumbled in my chest. My power dissolved, the rage still buzzed in my veins with no power to back it up. "Leave him!"

Leo Ashwood broke into a run across the pen as I stumbled forward. No! Panic ate my muscles as I forced my body to move. My magic failed me. I was useless! No! Frankie! My body crumpled into a million pieces as Leo scooped Frankie up from the fence line and shoved him head first into the ground. I knelt in the grass frozen in place as he ripped Frankie's left leg from his body like a cooked chicken and stuffed it in his oozing, shredded mouth.

There is nothing that can describe the hollow feeling that devoured me as I knelt there in wet grass, unable to stop the monster who killed my baby brother before my eyes.

And then something sharp broke through my skin, and I blinked. An illusion! My heart leaped in my chest. I lay sprawled on the ground, my head forced into the hay by the meaty hand of Leo Ashwood, his face inches from mine. He opened his mouth wide, his rotten insides exposed to me, teeth soiled and half dissolved, his tongue sliced down the middle. I screamed.

Leo forcibly wrenched himself from my body as I lurched to my side. Vomit built up in my mouth faster than the speed of light and spilled all over the burn pile in my yard. Blood trickled from a small cut along my arm, a sharp rock lodged in my arm. I pulled the rock from my bicep with trembling fingers, my body in cold shock. My eyes searched the yard and found two pairs of sneakers that I knew very well and a pair of bare feet I didn't have to even guess. "There's only one witch I know that doesn't wear shoes."

"Good thing we got here when we did!" Quinn dropped to the hay and hoisted me up off the hot ground. Her face glowed a pale light as she poked at a small wound in my arm. I hissed in pain but smiled. "Best way to wake someone up from an illusion, physical pain, apologies."

"Don't, that was the worst nightmare I've ever had," I croaked as I spat the last remains of my vomit onto the ground.

"Don't thank me just yet," she whimpered.

My heart sank. "No..."

"Maggie, I'm—"

I shot up from the ground onto my feet with enough momentum that my eyes spun. Not that it distracted me from the reality that surrounded me. Frankie lay in pieces in the driveway, surrounded by my mother's torso. My father existed only as part of a skull halfway across the yard. Cecelia's soft voice broke the dead silence in my head. "Maggie..."

"No," I whispered. "I woke up..."

"Maggie, breathe," Jess choked on her words as Leo Ashwood lumbered across the splintered yard. Pens were shattered, glass spread across every blade of grass, half shattered corpses of chickens and animals painted my farm in blood. Numbness turned to tingles along my skin as my mouth fell open. How? When did he have the time?

Was this whole day an illusion? When did it start? Panic swirled in my brain as my eyes darted between the bodies. My family's bodies! My family!

"No..." I muttered as my legs stumbled forward. "It's an illusion, it's gotta be..."

"Maggie—"

"No!" I screeched. The ground rumbled as everything shook. Leo Ashwood shook, his body let loose pieces of flesh that fell to the ground. He grabbed onto posts of my front porch, his head flung backward. "No!"

My screams doubled as I broke at my knees, and my hands clutched my chest. Blood filled my vision, and my throat sliced itself open and dribbled down the sides. Rage pumped fresh through my veins. My magic coursed through me in shots of lava. Red tinted my vision once more.

Leo Ashwood swung at himself, his hands clawed at chunks of his body. His arm severed but hung on by the mere bone, I shattered it. I watched his fist collapse inwards. His howls of pain were nothing compared to mine as I knelt halfway across the yard from him. First, he swung at his left leg, then his right, he broke down into little pieces.

The ground rumbled. Goats screamed as they flew through the air and out of the pen. Chickens escaped and the world trembled. The earth rumbled beneath my feet, and the driveway cracked. A large gouge ran across the yard, like a crack in ice as it spread. Fury and pain filling my stomach, I turned up my volume. Leo Ashwood attacked himself, a shark in a feeding frenzy of himself. Physical pain fought against emotional pain and my hands clawed at myself. I lost control.

A hand came across my face and clamped down over my mouth. I fought against the palm as the world stilled. My vision wavered as my magic tumbled to the wayside and coughs bubbled up in my chest. Pain erupted in my core and ran along my throat. I blinked away tears as a stranger pulled me close against their chest. Words soft like pillows after a long day filled my ears, my body wrapped in soft silk. I watched helplessly as Quinn launched across the yard, joined by three women and a book that flew on its own. Cecelia and a woman in leather stepped in front of me.

"Raphael, take care of her," the purple haired woman whispered.

My eyelids turned into cement as I lulled my head in the crook of an arm. I peered up into the face of an angel. He smiled down at me with warmth that welled fresh tears and pain in my chest. He had black skin the color of night and eyes of soft lilac with speckles of pink. His white eyebrows were the only hair on his head.

He pulled his hand from my mouth and cupped my cheeks. "You're safe," he cooed.

"That means nothing when they're dead." I choked up as my head fell to the side, my eyes on the yard. Emptiness filled my insides as I descended into an abyss. It devoured me whole.

Chapter Twenty-Two

Quinn Chases a Ghost

Frozen air lingered under a setting sun; even the tree line descended into a glistening orange light. The farm settled into a tense silence as all eyes landed on the undead monster. Leo Ashwood hovered in front of the shattered porch of Maggie Walton's home, his face pinched on the left side, muscles twitched and his eyes glistened. His corpse progressed in decomposition while his magic refused to let him fall apart. Blood coated his face.

A wave of frenzied magic washed over my system and left my skin a stripped wire, sparks of madness flashed around me. A porch seat flew through the air and landed in a cloud of dust beside me. The wires in my brain snapped. Magic flooded my system and I launched across the farm.

"Quinn!" My aunt's shouts fell on deaf ears. Light blinded me, magic whizzed by my face. Objects flung themselves at my monster, the wind picked up around me. Actual bullets shot through the air around my head and embedded into his skin. "Quinn! Get away from it!"

Rage engulfed me. I had him! My fingers wrapped around a chunk of his flesh. He exploded beneath my bloody nails. Blood soaked my vision, everything colored a dirty red. My senses fractured, unable to bring me back to reality. Electricity filled my body as I sank him to the ground. No illusions this time, no tricks, just blood and my magic. I grinned from ear to ear as a scream filled the air. I grabbed at him, over and over as pieces of him burst like pus filled pimples. Blood splattered my face, rotten flesh ripped aside as my magic tore him piece by piece.

Leo Ashwood was in my grasp until he wasn't. I had him! He was mine! Then he disappeared and I never felt fury like that before. He punched me with his brick wall hands and threw me from him. And then he disintegrated in a puff of smoke. For the fourth time, he escaped! His body decomposed, Maggie shattered his bones and ripped skin off his corpse. But with the fresh kill of Maggie's family, he rebounded like a toddler hyped up on sugary drinks. Then he left. Darlin held me back from running around the farm a third time. His blood disappeared, the scent slipped from my nose. I snarled like a rabid animal as I lurched back and forth. He escaped again! "How! How does he continue to evade me!"

"We need to go," Darlin whispered in my ears.

"I have to kill him!" I snapped as I whipped from her grip. The words tumbled out of my mouth in fast succession. "He has destroyed too many lives! I won't let him get away again! He has to pay for what he's done!"

Darlin straightened her back, hands clenched, she eyed me with fear. Anger refused to digest the look on her face. "You can't destroy this monster behind bars," Darlin growled darkly as she snatched up my bicep.

I thrashed in her grasp until a slap cleared me of madness. Sharp pain ran through my face and clarity filled my brain. With a blink, I calmed my body and took a deep breath inward. "Sorry..." I muttered. "I... I... don't know... what took over me."

"You're upset, and rightly so, but the police are coming and we must leave now." Darlin tugged me away from the driveway of the Walton's farm. Maggie laid limp in Raphael's arms, her head curled up against his chest. Cecelia lingered inches behind him, her eyes on Maggie. Tears trickled down her face, her hands clutched at her armpits as if to hide the shake of her limbs. Jess stared over her shoulder at me, a sharpness in her soft features.

Darlin pushed me forward into the collection of people and put the spool of thread in my hand. Her voice fell into the background noise as she pulled the thread around all of us and connected the thread around my back and into my hand. Enclosed in the thread, my stomach lurched as we moved as a full unit.

"I didn't know you could adjust the spell to move more than one person." I choked on my ignorance. The warmth of the swamp after the sun baked the leaves all day filled my bones. I dropped the spool and watched it zoom around all of us like a bee does a flower. It landed back in my hand, wound tight and hot with magic.

"You, of all people, should be the least surprised." Darlin cocked a brow. She cupped my cheek with one hand as the other took up the spool with the other. "You have lived with my spell experimentation for your whole life."

With a sigh, Darlin trudged right past me. Raphael put Maggie into the arms of Amendir as she followed after

Darlin. Cecelia rushed after Maggie, Jess hot on her heels. Serias spared a moment at my side, a soft hand to my shoulder. She brushed past me with a soft word whispered in my ear. "Gwenevieve…"

My heart stopped in my chest at the mere mention of my mother's first name. I spun to watch Serias clamber up through the soggy dirt onto the porch. It left Winestra to my left and Raphael to my right. Poisoned blood pumped through my body. Detective Smith's lifeforce, the blood of the monster, the lawyer, Maggie's tainted blood, it all pooled in my insides. I swallowed down a lump made from all of them. If I killed him… If I never brought him back… Maggie would still have a family. Fury tickled at my insides as I stared at the house. Built around the swamp, meant to protect, meant to heal and soothe. It was supposed to be full of good food and lots of books. It was supposed to be a home. Yet, I saw it as a prison for the last few years, now transformed into a paradise I wish I never left.

"What was all of that, Quinn?" Winestra stepped out in front of my face.

"What was what—"

"Don't give me that! You became a feral monster out there. You've never shown aggression like that!" Winestra growled as she slid out in front of me.

"You clearly don't know me as well as you thought," I spat as I brushed past her. My words tainted with disgust, but not for her. My venom dripped inwardly, disgusted with myself. I was poisoned, tainted and full of rage. A thick hand grasped my wrist and whirled me to face Raphael and Winestra. I wrenched my hand back. "Don't touch me."

"You launched across a farm of bodies and grabbed that monster." Raphael cocked a white brow halfway up his forehead.

"Someone needed to kill him before he used another illusion. Not that I need to answer to you, Raff. You can't even swing a stick." The venom poured out of my mouth without a filter. Hate filled my front lobe and words formed on my tongue without my permission. "Why don't you be useful for once and go heal Maggie? You know, the witch who did something today! Or are you going to brag to my face about all the good you're doing in the world, but not in the one place it matters!"

"Hey!" Winestra barked.

"For your information, I am doing good in the world. Unlike someone who can seem to do nothing but get herself in trouble!" Raphael sneered as he stepped toward me.

My face scrunched up as I met him step for step. "Oh! Wow, why don't you tell us all about the orphans you've healed of malaria or any other good things you done! That's all you're good at, isn't it, bragging?" I spat as I shoved him on the chest. "Go on, rub it in my face."

"No need! You've got the mud all over your face—"

"It's blood! The blood of a monster you did nothing to stop!" I screeched.

"My bad, I didn't know I was needed when overlord Quinn, ruler of dark magic had everything under control!" He shoved me back.

"It's not dark magic, you spineless, judgmental, self-obsessed—"

"Whoa! That's enough." Winestra bust between the two of us.

"Oh yeah, take his side, like always. Must be nice to have an older sister to protect you always, Raff," I scoffed, a sharp glare thrown at him. Then I cocked a brow to Winestra. "Maybe Darlin is right—she ought to take over my training from here on out. I'm too advanced for the likes of you."

Winestra slapped me, a blunt, sharp connection. Her force knocked me back a foot back in the water. "Go on, then, hot stuff, swing."

I blinked slowly, and my hand moved to my cheek. Despite the physical force behind it, I felt no pain. Unlike when Darlin slapped me to clear my fury, this slap did nothing. The poison built up behind my teeth, my blood boiled from my waist down. No pain. My sensibility and logic sucked out of my skull by the power that filled my veins again.

"Whoa, Win—" Raphael faltered with his words, his eyes shifted to me in worry. A smile crawled across my face as I stared at the swamp beneath my feet.

"No! She wants to puff up like a big witch, she ought to be able to back it up," Winestra snapped. Her cheeks were covered in soil and dried blood where she hit the ground in a sharp roll. Leo Ashwood swung at everything, he sent many porch items in the air across the lawn. Her braids were covered in wood shards, hay, and corn stuck out in small chunks. Raphael looked absolutely spotless as always in a soft cotton V-neck over a simple pair of jeans, never a wrinkle or stitch out of place. How I wanted to rough him up, a smidgen, enough to deflate that ego. She took his side, never made him answer for anything.

Sweet nothings whispered in my ear, and my power lured me into a dark abyss.

"You wanted to know what was all of that, back there... I'll show you."

Sharp tingles ran the length of my arms as my fingers flexed out before me. Magic filled the air, thick and electric. I buzzed from every bone, all my nerves tingling within me.

Winestra cocked a brow, her lips curled up in a smirk... until her right leg jerked down to the right. A pair of jaws clamped down on her leg and yanked her across the ground. I swung my left arm sharply to my side. Raphael yelped as another pair of jaws took hold of his legs. His face hit the ground first, and his fingers dug into the soggy soil as my beast dragged him across the ground.

Harsh winds billowed around me and threw me back to the ground. My nails dug into the earth as magic pulsed around me. Curdled blood filled my nose as the water shook vigorously around. All the stagnant moss and water erupted with beasts from below—half-eaten corpses, vessels bent to my will, climbing to the surface and rolling into one another. Bones cracked and smacked into one another. A whole new set of beasts born from rage snarled in Winestra's direction.

"What the hell, Quinn!" Winestra sent the pair of jaws across the swamp with a harsh flare shot from her hand. A second flare shot at me from her fingertips and barely missed me. It sizzled as it skidded across the soil behind me.

"I've learned a few new tricks!" I barked as I clapped my hands together. My newest creation, sprung to life, better than the last, made of mashed pieces of flesh and bound with magic and bones. The body a Frankenstein collection of pairs in a vaguely humanoid fashion—eyes of a bass, mouth of a gator,. It stood on two feet of seven toes, clawed hands, death and poisonous blood wafted from rotten flesh.

Winestra's face twisted up as I ripped my hands apart. The beast flung across the ground at her. Suddenly, it flung up into the air and spun by its mangled ankles. It twisted and snarled with no sound but the way its teeth clinked together. I whirled to see Amendir appeared a foot from me, her eyes narrowed in on me specifically. "What *exactly* is the meaning of this?"

"She picked a fight with me!" I tossed my hands out. My beast flung out of Amendir's grip and flung to the swamp moss. It scrambled onto all fours, and its claws dug into the water and flew over the top. Winestra yelped as she pedaled over the ground toward me. Once more, Amendir yanked my beast up by its toes into the air. I jerked my fist down and my beast plummeted to the ground.

"She's lost it!" Winestra raised her hand.

I let out a cackle. "You're about to lose it!" I howled as my beast launched at Winestra at full force. It tossed her with the flick of its mangled head, she flew into the soil inches from my feet. Something within me clicked. Lights shot through the air and chained my monster to the air above me. My hands caught Winestra by the throat. Sweet blood filled my nostrils as I clamped my palm closed around her windpipe. Panic filled her eyes as I pressed my teacher into the mud. Festering flesh popped open around my palms.

"Quinn?"

I stopped dead in my tracks as lilac slithered into my nose. Fury cleared out from the front of my forehead. Sheer panic and disgust devoured my insides as I wrenched my hands back from Winestra's throat. She wheezed for air, her cheeks less plump than before, the life sucked directly out of her pores.

My reflection in Winestra's eyes stabbed into my heart—a girl covered in blood, ready to kill someone she truly loved. My beast stilled, the beastly face calmed and bones fell slack in the magic hold as I glanced up at the porch.

Cecelia lingered on a step, her hands clamped around her. Her brows knitted down as she digested the scene before her. The cogs turned physically on her face as she stepped down onto the soil. My mouth opened, my words wavered. "Cecelia, go inside."

"Quinn...Maybe you should *come* inside." She emphasized the word with a shaky whisper of a voice. My throat dried up as she stared at me. "Maggie needs us—both of us."

"I..."

And the fury left, my hands fell to my side as she walked three steps out toward me. Her hands pried off her sides and opened toward me. Guilt took hold of me like a hook to a fish's mouth. I stumbled forward across the ground till my magic sank into my toes. My beast crawled to a stop before it toppled apart behind me. Cecelia held still as she opened her arms to me without hesitation. Lilac covered up the death, it cleansed the blood and it devoured my anger. Tears clouded my vision as I scooped up both her hands. Air filled my lungs as she closed her palms around my hands and squeezed.

My eyes trailed up her arms to her eyes, red and puffy from tears trickling down her face. Her fingers squeezed my hands affectionately before she edged toward the stairs. I followed without a word, eyes glued to her face. She led me up the stairs toward the porch.

I stopped at the top step to spare a look to Winestra and Raphael. "I'm... I'm so sorry."

"Uh, no worries, girlie. Just practicing. Right, Raphael?" Winestra laughed nervously as she shot a glance at Raphael.

He clambered out of the mud with a stumble and a whine. "My shirt."

"Yeah, just getting it out of our system. It's been a day." Winestra sighed.

"It's been a week..." I murmured.

"Or two." Cecelia added at an arm's length away. She tugged with her hand and I followed without another word. Her blood cleared the mania in my senses, her aura cleansed me. My brows knitted down on my face as I stepped through the doorway. Maggie lay sprawled on pillows and blankets in the living room. Darlin knelt beside her, book open to her side, her fingers hovered over her. Cecelia never let go of my hand.

I stared back through the doorway to find Winestra and Raphael appeared inches behind me. Raphael broke away from me and Cecelia, his eyes focused on Maggie. White lines crawled along his fingers as he knelt down beside her, hands placed on her hands.

"Her disease has progressed aggressively; she should be dead," Darlin whispered hoarsely.

"Human medicine is rather ineffective," Raphael muttered.

"Well, that's all she's got," Jess huffed from the doorway to the kitchen. Tears trickled down the sides of her scrunched face. Orange hair stuck to the sides of her face as she marched across the floor toward me. I saw the fury in her face before I smelt the sharpness of her blood. Her fingers were balled up tight. "Cecelia, move aside."

"Jess, no—" Cecelia barely had time to interject before Jess snatched me up by the front of my shirt.

"Whoa, whoa!" Serias emerged from the kitchen with a bewildered look upon her face. "Trust me, Jessica Harris, that does not end well for you."

"Jess!" Cecelia dropped my hand to wheel Jess back by the arm.

"You keep babying her emotions! What does it matter? She's the reason all of this happened!" Jess announced and my blood ran cold. She could punch me all she wanted, she could curse my name all she wanted... I took up the front of her T-shirt without hesitation and flung her backward.

"Quinn!" Cecelia squeaked.

Frenzy filled my lungs and panic nibbled at my toes. I was out of control. If Jess spoke another word, they would know. If I looked like an emotional mess, I could get away with my outburst. They could never know. The three elders in my home, all eyes on me. The dominos trembled as the top layers of my control toppled over.

"Your friend needs to bite her tongue!" I shot Cecelia a sharp look.

"What is she talking about?" Raphael wheeled around from Maggie. Muscles tightened around my ribcage like fingers ready to crack my bones. I struggled to breath.

"Don't worry about it, Raff. Just heal Maggie!" I barked. My teeth snapped shut hard enough to shatter my jaw. My eyes darted from Cecelia to Raphael. Maggie's skin returned to a healthy glow under his touch. If Raphael stopped, she might descend into a worse condition. If Jess stood up and opened her mouth, the whole room would descend into chaos. Vomit rose up in my throat.

"Quinn! Enough is enough! I know you're upset, but this is out of line." Darlin broke away from Maggie. "You are out of line."

"Why are you taking her side?" I scoffed.

"Because you made Leo Ashwood, didn't you?" Amendir's voice ran down the length of my spine like a sharp needle.

All the air squeezed out of my lungs. Raphael gripped Maggie's hands tightly. Winestra whipped to look at me. Jess wobbled as she stood up, Serias' hands under her arms to hoist her back up. Every ounce of control in my body trickled out of my body onto the floor beneath me. My confession lingered on my lips as they quivered. "Yes."

"We thought him the creation of a witch angry with this community. Maybe a mistake, a dark, troubled mixed-up spell. But he can cast magic, he can speak, he thinks, he has slaughtered forty people in the night, forty-three now with your friend's family. What. Have. You. Done?"

My aunt's face fell to the floor, her heart visibly shattered as I stumbled back away from them all. I trembled from my toes to my lips. "I didn't mean to..."

Amendir launched across the floor with a swiftness that shocked my system. I gasped as she grabbed up my arms. The anger in her face was smooth, almost untraceable as she dragged me through the doorway toward the hallway. Fear woke me up as she snapped her free fingers and flames lit up her nail tips.

"No! Please! Amendir, stop! I can explain!"

"What's going on?" Cecelia cried out as I thrashed in Amendir's grip. She dug her sharp claws into my skin as she yanked me harder toward the room. I felt the candle wax on my skin already, the pain that surged through my body. Panic caused a new frenzy in my system. My hands slapped at her and I screamed out in anticipation of pain as she pinned me to the opposite kitchen doorway.

"Amendir! Ple—"

"Shut up!" she snarled, her nails to my face.

"Wait! Stop!" Cecelia barked.

"Stay out of this!" Amendir whirled to face Cecelia as I jerked back and forth in her grip. Darlin burst into the kitchen, her eyes locked with Amendir. "Don't try to stop me Darlin!"

"Please! Amendir, think about this—"

"Did you not hear your niece? She made the monster! She confessed!" Amendir growled as her hands left my arm and snatched me up by the neck. She turned back to me and closed the space between us. Inches from my nose, she zeroed in on my eyes with sharp fury in her golden irises.

"I didn't mean to!" I whimpered, my knees weak.

Amendir dropped me against the doorframe as everyone trickled into the kitchen in slow, hushed steps. I sank against the frame and nearly toppled to the floor. The reality of my actions tugged me further to the ground. Leo Ashwood, my accident, murdered people and I did not stop him.

What had I become?

"Quinn... you lied to me?" Darlin whispered, her nose scrunched up at the bridge. "To my face!"

"I didn't mean to!" I cried out. "I tried to bring Berry back, not him! I didn't know! I swear! I panicked!"

"How did you do it? How did you create him?" Amendir drilled into me with disgust that dribbled out of her pores.

I let out a soft whine. "I don't know! I didn't create him; he was dead. He killed Berry, and so I lost control. I killed him and tried to bring her back... but then he came back instead." I gasped for air.

"Impossible," Serias scoffed.

"It's not! I didn't make him. Leo Ashwood was a real person who I brought back."

"Quinn?" Winestra gasped as my eyes darted between all of them. My insides turned into a hive of wasps; my organs torn to shreds at the range of disgust upon all their faces. All except Cecelia, who only sighed. Winestra's sharp eyes sliced through Cecelia. "You, did you know?"

"What?" Cecelia squeaked.

"Leave her out of this—" I gasped.

"This ends now," Amendir snapped, I flinched away from her as she turned toward me. Her hands flew out toward me as I lurched away from her. "I am tired of the lies and the secrets, Quinn."

"I'm not lying! I don't know how I did it! I just I knew that if- I didn't mean... You've got to believe me. Don't do that spell again! Please! Don't throw me out of the family, please! I tried to fix it, but I don't know how! I don't want anyone else to get hurt." My words jumbled up in my mouth as panic bit into my kneecaps. I toppled to the ground, knelt in the corner I backed myself into. How could they believe me? I lied so much. I did this! I did this to me. Panic created fat tears in my eyes.

"Darlin, I am done. You promised she would never be like Gwenevieve." Amendir stormed across the room after me.

"Amendir, don't," Darlin blurted out. Tears broke over my eyelids and flooded my cheeks as Amendir hovered over me. I held still as I looked between the two. My mother? Why would I never be like my mother? I trembled as I stared at my aunt.

"What do you mean, like what happened to my mom?" The words sunk to the bottom of the swamp, like the last breaths of air in my lungs squeezed out between two hands.

"Darlin." Amendir ripped around, her back to me. "Are you serious?"

"I was going to tell her!" Darlin confessed with a wounded gasp for air. Her hands clutched around her.

"Please, she's young, she doesn't know what her magic can do. I was just trying to keep her safe."

"I thought she knew the whole time! Darlin, you made me promise not to bring her up!" Amendir snarled.

"Tell me about my mother!" I cried out.

"Amendir, please!" Darlin begged.

"What is going on?" Cecelia stepped forward, her eyes darted between me and Amendir.

Amendir snatched me by the ear and hoisted me up to my feet. I jerked away from her but her grip tightened. She tossed me across the floor. My face collided with the floorboards. The air ripped from my lungs aggressively, I gagged on my breathlessness. Numbness confused all the wires in my brain as I clawed at the flooring. No pain spread through my body. I blinked. My body clambered back to my feet with no hesitation. Magic ripped me off my feet and flung me to the floor again. I couldn't breathe. Pain refused to filter through my senses, and I shuffled back up to my feet.

Cecelia and Jess jolted forward but were yanked backward by their shirts by Serias. Amendir cast again. Magic pulled my hair by the ends up into the air. My body thrashed as she flung me to the ground with a harder force. I weaseled out of the grip and scrambled away from Amendir's invisible grip.

"She doesn't know how to use her magic, huh? She's already taken the life of someone. She feels no pain!" Amendir accused me. "Gwenevieve didn't learn that till she was an adult."

"Please—" I gasped for air.

"Silence!" Amendir boomed. "You have been babied for far too long. You want to know about your mother, Quinn?"

"Amendir, stop!" Darlin barked. Her hand wrapped around my bicep and jerked me toward her. I struggled to free myself from her embrace. "She's not like her."

"She's just like her!" Amendir snarled.

"You don't know what you're talking about!" Darlin hissed.

"Out of everyone, I know exactly what I'm talking about, Darlin. I was there!"

"Auntie, please, what are you hiding from me?" I shoved her at the torso.

"Your mother is dead because Darlin killed her."

Every hair stood up on edge. Serias shifted into my vision as my heart stopped mid-beat. She let go of Cecelia and Jess. My shoulders sank. My hands fell limp to my side. The floor filled my vision—the floor I waddled on as a lonely toddler. The floor crafted for our family out of love, that I drew on with crayon imagining who I would fall in love with. Dark oak floorboards that I lay on crying, broken hearted, confused and alone in the world... with my aunt who held me, and swore to make it all better. Two sets of hands reached out to me, neither of them were my aunt. I peered up to see Jess took hold of one of my arms, Cecelia held onto the other. "Why?"

"Quinn, lovely, my hands were forced," Darlin whimpered.

"Why would you kill her?" My lips quivered.

"She tried to kill you..." Darlin's mouth hung open as silence filled the air.

I stared into her eyes, the one physical trait I shared with her, a trait I would have shared with my mother. Betrayal seeped into my system and turned my insides to mush. She killed her. She refused to speak of her. She took my mother out of my life and acted like it was a horrible accident. She lied to my face!

I suddenly knew how she felt, but yet, I felt less guilty over my lie.

"After she killed countless others." Amendir's voice broke through the silence. I turned my head swiftly, my eyes glued to Amendir. Her long hair loose around her tan face, a golden ring protruded from her right nostril, a single ruby dangled from it.

"I would never..." I muttered. Liar, I was a dirty liar. I've already killed multiple people, without Leo Ashwood's help.

"You follow in her footsteps," Amendir whispered.

Monster. I am a monster, made from a murderer. "I told you, I didn't mean to. I don't know how I did it," I confessed, panic rattled my vocal chords.

"And what's to say you won't learn to do it again, this time, less childish panic and more malicious intent?" Amendir snarled.

"Amendir, that's enough," Serias sighed.

"Amendir, what did my mother do?" I gasped for air.

Amendir straightened her spine and her face cooled to marble stone. Her eyes iced over as she stared at me. "She lost control. She grew into a frenzy. She murdered humans and used their blood to attack witches. Then she got a taste for witch blood, the stronger the better. She used them to build an army of thralls, zombies made out of parts of other bodies. It was a game for her. We tried to stop her, to find a way to clear out the insanity. Your aunt made the gloves, I made a cleansing spell just for her, the one I used on you but stronger. Then she came up with the wild idea that if she used your blood, she would have the strength of two of her."

A dagger buried deep in my chest as I sank into the arms of Jess and Cecelia. Lilac filled my nose and tears welled up in my eyes again. My cheeks stung, actually stung, from the salt in my tears as they let me down onto the floor gently.

"Lovely, Quinn, I was forced to choose." My aunt's voice floated around my head. "To save you, I had to ..."

Silence settled over the whole room as my body went limp in Jess and Cecelia's arms. Then I inhaled in through my nose and let it out slower through my mouth. I looked up from the floor to Amendir. "Cast the spell on me again."

Amendir's eyebrows furrowed as I pulled my arms from Cecelia and Jess's grasp softly. "You are volunteering?"

"I don't want to become a monster," I whispered as I struggled to my feet. "I'll wear the gloves, I'll let you cast the spell on me, if it means that I can make it right."

Amendir's face softened, and her lips fell into a soft frown as she stepped forward. She put out her hand and I took it without question.

Cecelia snatched my shoulder. "Hey, wait, what is going to happen?"

"Don't worry. It's going to be fine. Just look after Maggie, and when I wake up tomorrow, we'll go after Leo

Ashwood again. Okay?" I smiled weakly as Amendir tugged me away from her. "I promised, didn't I? That I would stop him, whatever it takes. And I'm sworn to my promise. I won't let anything happen to you."

Cecelia's face fell, her hand still out toward me as I walked backward after Amendir. "Quinn, how do I know you're not lying?" her voice cracked as I shrugged, a weak smile glued to my lips. Her lilac was the last thing I tasted as Amendir wheeled me into the small library and shut the door behind us.

Chapter Twenty-Three

Cecelia and Jess Talk About the Abyss

"I want to join. I want you to teach me," I confessed to Serias at the kitchen table. After an hour in the room, Amendir emerged, silent and alone. I tried to peer into the room, but she shut the door and Darlin locked it up with hands that glowed red.

Jess sat by my side the whole time, silent. It put me on edge to know she felt just as out of place as I did. Then Serias sat down beside me and offered us both frosty root beer in glass bottles. Between slow sips, Jess loosened up to my left and slouched back in the chair, the day finally processed. That's when I glanced at Serias. "And I want to make it clear that I am still going to go to school."

"That is completely your choice, but I will not ease up your lessons because you want both," she replied with a soft smile. "But I am beyond happy to hear that you want this too. I will have Amendir and Darlin sit down with you later. Maybe not today, and you can sign your acceptance."

I nodded silently, but Jess spoke up. "So it'll be like an after school tutoring lesson?"

"Kind of, we can figure out time and place on a later date. Today's been long, best to just digest today first." Serias put her glass down. "But, this means Jessica, you will sign with us too."

"What?" I choked on soda, a cough rattling my cage.

"You brought her into this, and I doubt you will allow us to erase her memories of magic. Amendir and Darlin and I agree, you will have to be brought into the coven as a human ambassador, of sorts. You will be sworn to uphold the same rules and laws, and to the secrecy just like everyone else." Serias looked to Jess. My best friend, the strongest woman second to my mother, took a long swig of root beer before she nodded.

"I'm all right with this," she stated before she put her bottle down on the table. "On one condition."

"You're not really in the position to ask for any conditions." Serias cocked a brow.

"I'm kind of cheeky like that," Jess let out a small snort. "I want Cecelia and I to have access to information on Quinn's mother. I wanna know what happened, all the books and data that Darlin made of her. It doesn't have to be today, but later, I wanna know everything about blood witches."

I furrowed my brows as I snapped my eyes to Jess. Her poker face stayed strong as she stared down Serias. My eyes darted to Serias who nodded slowly with a sigh. "That can be arranged, but I will let you know... it's not much."

"What?" I whispered.

"Gwenevieve was the first blood witch to be born in a long line of Spellslingers and enchanters. It was a rather unusual genetic anomaly. Then for Quinn to be born, let alone born a blood witch, was even stranger, as we have no information on her father. We know very little, because the last blood witch before Gwenevieve was over two hundred years ago, that we know of. They are rare..." Serias confessed as she tossed back the last of her soda. "And very dangerous."

"Because their magic is hard to control." I added with my head cocked.

Serias put her pointer finger to her nose, then she settled her eyes on my face and hands on my shoulders. "The closer you are to the sun, the more likely you are to be burned," she whispered with a pat to my shoulder. Then she slid up to her feet and walked away from the table.

I sat in complete silence before I shot a look to Jess. "Dude," I blurted out.

"What?" she huffed.

"What was that?"

"Seemed like a good time to ask for the down low on what the flying heck is going on here. We've been flying blind, Ce, it's time we finally know what's going on. Plus, the more we know about *what* Quinn is, the better you can keep her from going Elisabeth Bathory on more people."

Jess shrugged. She took both our empty glasses and stood up to toss them. I straightened up. Jess nodded before she nodded again toward the doorway. We moved from the kitchen toward the living room. Maggie lay on just a silk blanket now, embroidered and colored with a design much like the floor they put below her before. Except now, it was covered with her and crystal globes that floated around her and Raphael.

I stopped to speak but Jess tugged my arms and pulled me toward the door. Raphael chanted under his breath in a tongue that felt familiar and off, like I'd heard some words but not all of them. His dark skin lit up with pure white veins that glowed in the dark of the room. Eyes open and glossed over like a snake in a shed, he held his hands to the sides of her throat, fingers glowing brighter than an iPhone flashlight in the dark of night. Winestra sat in the corner of the room, head on her knees and hands on the back of her neck. Jess tugged me out of the room.

We ended up sitting on the porch, legs dangling off the side and arms poking through the railing. Torches lit up the swamp, and lightning bugs speckled the air around us. It took everything in me not to scream out in the silence. I stared out into the abyss and a chill of wind ran down my spine. Jess leaned her forehead against the railing, her eyes closed softly.

All of it blew up in our faces. Quinn's secrets, Maggie's emotions, my ineffectiveness, the only person who couldn't be faulted for the way things turned out was Jess.

Jess perked up from the railing as she stretched out her hands and cracked her back. "So... you wanna talk about the eye collector part, the chasing thin air part, or the fact you asked about your real parents part?"

A sigh passed through my lips. "All of it and none of it."

"I'm just saying, cause, you blindsided the snot out of me," Jess snorted as she scanned the horizon. "Askin' about your parents... Ce, you've never cared before."

"Well, I didn't need to before. To be honest, up until this point, you and Gretchen were the only people who mattered. My genetics never changed anything until my visions became nightmares." I hugged myself around a post that pierced the handrail of the porch. My eyes followed Jess as she slid up to the edge beside me and hugged her own pole. Then our eyes met, and I tried my hardest not to cry. The tears welled up in my eyes and the world blurred around her. "I know I'm weird, but like... did I have to be *this* weird?"

The whine in my throat almost made me laugh. Jess, misty eyed and pouty lipped as she nodded back at me. Her weak smile was the catalyst for a pathetic chuckle that trickled off my lips. She let out a broken laugh, her face crinkled in a bigger, truer smile. "Yes, because if you weren't an absolute *Twilight Zone* episode hidden under a trench coat of a person, then we couldn't be friends."

"Hey!" I coughed on my own saliva as Jess sputtered into a bigger laugh. We sat there, sad laughter bubbled out of our lips and tears that trickled one by one down our cheeks. I reached out and took her hand. Jess grinned softly as she squeezed my hand and placed our fingers against the warm wood. "Am I really that bad?"

"Are you really that odd and unexplainable and full of questions that never get answered? Yes. Bad? Absolutely not," Jess whispered as she rubbed her thumb against the back of mine.

"Thanks," I whispered hoarsely. She nodded silently. My eyes fluttered shut as the crickets filled my ears. Tears stained my cheeks warmth radiated through the wood and leaves of the swamp. Musty water filtered through thick foliage and filled my nostrils.

"So... the collector of eyes part?" she quipped.

I let out a low groan. "I don't know how to explain it. Like I hit this complete moment of sheer panic and terror and I was ripped into a vision while I was wide awake. It's never happened that way. And I was in the pool of souls, like in Hercules but *way* more creepy. There was just nothing; it was just dark, and it ate everything. And this thing, I dunno if it was anything but a thing, just kept asking me to ask it something, so I asked it how to find Quinn."

"And it told you where to find her?" Jess cocked a brow.

"No! It went all shady answer in a riddle wizard nonsense," I whined.

"Like use your inner eye to see the way forward?" Jess laughed.

"Exactly, except it said to use my sight!" I rolled my eyes as Jess doubled over in more laughter.

We giggled for a long moment then died into silence. Jess squeezed my hand again, and lay her head back against the post. The croaks of frogs and chirps of insects filled the silence. It felt oddly like home, surrounded by magic and nature. I melted into my post and closed my eyes again, until Jess squeezed my hand again and I opened my eyes.

"So why now? Why do the parents matter now?" Jess interrupted my moment of peace to anchor me back to earth.

"Because now I'm a collector of eyes, or so says the void. Because I spasmed, which my back still hurts, thanks, and I was in a lake of souls. I spoke to something that knew my real name," I confessed as the words poured out of my mouth.

"Whoa, whoa, whoa, hold the phone, what are you talking about—real name?" Jess scoffed.

"Cecelia's not my name. Or well, not my birth name." I shrugged. "I'm adopted—"

"I know you're adopted, Ce, Gretchen Montreal is the color of whipped cream even when tan and is a ginger! You're telling me you know the name your birth mom named you?" Jess eyed me as I shrugged. The realization sent a rock the size of my fist into my stomach, I'd never told Jess.

"My birth name is Feng Mian Su..."

A rumble ran through me and into the swamp. Sparks lit up behind my eyes and my head pounded. I gripped the rail of the house as everything tumbled down on top of me. Pressure built behind my skull and I couldn't see. Left blind in complete darkness as a foreboding feeling gnawed on my stomach lining. Jess cried out to me, but the voice wafted in and out, further away than before. My mind whisked me away from the porch and deposited onto the cold tile floor of a kitchen floor. Like that of a trailer, the tile wasn't even real, the walls were dirty, and the counters covered in Walmart bags.

I clambered to my feet to see Gretchen at a tiny table, a baby in a carrier before her. Tears covered her face as she rocked that baby back and forth. A woman loomed over her, face pinched as she took back the blanket I was found in.

"I will pay for everything—"

"I don't want your money." Gretchen snarled as she looked up sharply.

"Let me put you in a house, a real house. I can't keep you safe if you don't let me." The woman looked at Gretchen and stepped into the kitchen light. I finally saw her face, and my heart stopped. She looked exactly like my mother, like me—round face, soft brown eyes, a freckle over her left eyebrow. Taller than the trailer, she hunched over till she sat down into one of the rickety wooden chairs. Dressed in black robes of silk, her hair like a curtain around her, this woman put a soft hand to Gretchen's forearm.

"I don't need anyone to keep me safe." Gretchen scowled hard.

"I know, that's exactly why my sister chose you. Please, I want to help! They can't ever find her! If they get even one finger around her, people will die. They will destroy whole cities to get at her gift. I beg of you, Gretchen Montreal, just let me take care of you both," she whispered softly, like rose petals against my ears.

Gretchen leaned back in the seat and eyed her. "What do you want in return?" Gretchen cocked a brow.

"Raise her as human as possible. Raise her to know no life other than a very normal, human one. Give her a new name. Send her to a normal and unspectacular school, cement her in a human life. My sister chose you, out of everyone, she sees in you the only life, the only chance that my niece has at survival. You are my niece's savior. All I ask is you keep her safe. And never speak her real name."

My body lurched and ripped me from the vision. My heart in my mouth, it pounded against my teeth. Jess hugged me close to her, hands clamped around my body with whispers to my hair. "Please, oh god, Ce, don't do this again."

"Jess," I croaked. Jess jerked back and pulled me away from her to stare at my face. Horror etched into both our faces as my stomach dropped through the floor and sank into the swamp. "I've done something..."

"Oh, oh no, what do you mean something?" she squeaked, her eyes searching my face. Silence filled the air. No frogs, no insects, no crackles of torches, the sound died as my eyes looked all around.

"I don't know, but I think, maybe, I broke a protection on me," I muttered as I looked around the swamp, from the lights around me to the circular house. Nothing moved, not even lightening bugs. Paranoia pumped through my system like spikey lava. "I don't think Leo Ashwood is our biggest problem anymore."

About Lizzie Strong

Lizzie Strong was born a marine brat and spent many years bouncing from state to state. This gave her a love of reading where she could escape to far off places and explore magic. Her father a high fantasy buff and her mother was a horror enthusiast, she combined her love of both to create notebooks full of paranormal fantasy with a splash of spooky for good measure. It's important to her to represent her Pansexuality and write books she wished her younger self had access too. Currently a Florida resident, Lizzie writes books full of magic and monsters, devours new horror books, and collects anything vaguely bunny shaped.

Email
Lizziestrongauthor@gmail.com

Facebook
www.facebook.com/Lizziestrongauthor

Twitter
@myregardslizzie

Also from NineStar Press

Power Surge by Sara Codair

Erin has just realized that for the entirety of their life, their family has lied to them. Their Sight has been masked for years, so Erin thought the Pixies and Mermaids were hallucinations. Not only are the supernatural creatures they see daily real, but their grandmother is an Elf, meaning Erin isn't fully human. On top of that, the dreams Erin thought were nightmares are actually prophecies.

While dealing with the anger they have over all of the lies, they are getting used to their new boyfriend, their boyfriend's bullying ex, and the fact that they come from a family of Demon Hunters. As Erin struggles through everything weighing on them, they uncover a Demon plot to take over the world.

Erin just wants some time to work through it all on their own terms, but that's going to have to wait until after they help save the world.

The Harbinger by Mary Eicher

In a picturesque California town, the deafening sound of bells brings dozens of people to their knees. Three days later a horrific accident claims their lives. Among the dead is the twin brother of Artemis Andronikos, a beautiful attorney, who abandons the ill-fated vacation and returns home to grieve.

Her mourning is interrupted by Lucy Breem a reporter who suspects a connection between the strange bell sound and subsequent deaths. Disturbed by the possibility that the phenomenon had presaged her brother's death, Artemis agrees to join forces with Lucy to investigate the mysterious premonitions. Utilizing her considerable physical and deductive talents, Artemis battles nefarious forces and seeks information from friends in high places. Their research takes them to various global venues. But the solution to the mystery proves illusive and the couple discovers that neither science nor religion can provide an explanation for what has become known as the Harbinger.

The Grimm Assistant by Jodi Hutchins

Postal carrier and amateur surfer, Samantha Diaz, lives an uncomplicated life. Well, other than helping her sister with childcare, crushing on her unavailable customer, Lauren Brennan, and catching as many waves as possible before hurricane season begins. Suffice to say, she isn't looking for much more, but when Lauren invites her to a monthly game night at her house, Sam happily agrees.

When Sam sets out on an early morning surf, the last thing she expects to do is die, but a sudden thunderstorm thrashes offshore, creating a riptide that steals Sam's life. She awakens to a snarky woman named Margo speaking cryptic nonsense. Not only does she claim to be one of the many Grim Reapers, or Grims, in the world, Margo makes Sam an offer: she'll bring Sam back from the dead, as long as she becomes Margo's temporary assistant. Sam accepts but soon realizes the deal was too good to be true, and the consequences she faces may be worse than the death she dodged.

Connect with NineStar Press

www.ninestarpress.com

www.facebook.com/ninestarpress

www.facebook.com/groups/NineStarNiche

www.twitter.com/ninestarpress

www.instagram.com/ninestarpress

www.ingramcontent.com/pod-product-compliance
Lightning Source LLC
Chambersburg PA
CBHW021456110726
47899CB00001BA/173